DOWN
THE HIGH TOMB

Thank you so much!

Enjoy!!!

by

JUD WIDING

HINDSIGHT

Lives shift in silence. Listen.

This one had been a fragile thing, a globe of clouded crystal that could still catch the light, if held at the right angle. Such an angle as could be found at the slack end of thirty years' fast grip, for example. As the prize slipped from her fingers.

Never would her ball of brittle dotage appear as beautiful to her as when it was falling to the floor. That was the nature of things, she supposed.

Shh.

Before that she had been happy, which was to say she'd found ways to keep a half-step's lead on her disposition. This would become apparent to her later, too late, with the other horrors. Until then, Jenmarie Bell ground on, not greeting each new day but squaring up with it. Fight the sunlight to a draw, and retire. The nature of things. What rest she could pry from the dark would have to suffice for the coming day's battle. This, she had convinced herself, was just life in the city. It was normal to feel this way, in the city.

The city, then. It was too tall, too loud, too dirty, too angry. New York, in other words. This was not a place for people to live, she would realize. It was a playground that construction equipment had built for itself. Humans were not inhabitants — they were an infestation.

That was the noise talking. Jenmarie had never had thoughts like that before moving here. Such bargain basement nihilism wasn't her. It was beneath her. Had been.

Of the five years she and Eddie had been together, and of the two years they had been (and would be) married, only the last of them had been spent here. This second anniversary was a far less joyous affair than had been their first, which they'd celebrated back in Atlanta, but Jenmarie considered this a natural enough consequence of time's passing. Days chip away at the gleeful peaks, piece by piece. Yet this was not without consolation; as the heights sloughed down to ground level, their runoff lifted the valleys. Time as an equalizer. What a novel thought.

That was the sort of thought Jenmarie would once have cared enough to voice to her then-husband. Eddie Mark had been a philosophy major at Emory. In Jenmarie's defense, she hadn't known that until their third date. She'd just assumed he was a fellow medical student, having met him at a purported medical resident's getaway that her best-friend-since-third-grade Mavis' brother Lucky had organized in Athens. Georgia, not Greece, though she'd first met Eddie in quite the Socratic mood; absolutely blasted on cheap wine, and full of questions. On that score, he was well-met; Jenmarie had gotten a Zyp car to the first-night party after pregaming in some soggy dive on Edgewood. As she'd been drinking, she'd quite naturally been dancing, and vice versa, quite naturally. Had she expected to be going as hard as she had (turned out it was Earth Wind & Fire night, and she was only human), she wouldn't have worn her three-inch heels. But she hadn't and had, respectively, which made for a pair of unhappy feet delivering their burden into the Zyp car. So of course Jenmarie kicked those little terrors off during the ride, and of course again, she failed to reclaim her discomfort at the ride's end. It was only as she stepped shoeless onto the driveway of the faux-Colonial house Lucky had rented for the week – rented not off AirBnb but instead from VRBO, a detail Jenmarie was inexplicably annoyed that she knew – that she realized she had lost her sole mates. It was hard to miss; the driveway was gravel, and her feet were marshmallow. Too bad; the Zyp car was already vanishing into the night, and what chase the fully turnt Jenmarie could give was indistinguishable from her doing a line dance in a hurricane. Not that she didn't try.

"You forget something?" a voice from the porch called.

Jenmarie stumbled to a halt and looked to the house. The porch lights were off, but the voice sounded like it was coming from the vaguely unsettling silhouette on the moon-kissed bench swing which no doubt creaked every time the wind blew. The house itself wasn't old enough to be haunted, but the swing seemed like it had been installed to give the impression that it was. "Yeah," she replied to the night, gesturing to her feet.

"You can call them," the porchvoice suggested, which was rich given that quite a lot of the heartbreak five years in Jenmarie's future would come via fucking text message. "That's an option on the…" The voice did a poor job of stifling a sneeze.

"…the app."

Indeed it was: Jenmarie said "gesundheit" and then called the driver and told him about the shoes. The driver asked her what kind of shoes they were, as though there were countless pairs rolling around the well of his back seat. Three-inches, she informed him. Black. Strappy. Mhm, the driver averred, before calling out the description to somebody else. He had another ride already, it emerged – he would swing back with the shoes. When? Once he was done with his latest fare. Which would be? Later.

She hung up, and the porchvoice asked her "you gonna get your shoes back?"

"He'll be back with them after a while," she told him. A *h-while*. That Tennessee drawl had a way of creeping up on her, and fully pounced whenever she let slip that stupid folkism. *After a h-while*. She'd caught that young, like a disease.

"Well," wondered the voice, "you mind if I keep you company while you wait?"

Jenmarie didn't. In fact, she welcomed it.

She scaled the six-or-so steps up to the porch, clinging to the fat wooden handrail of the steps, jerking and slamming her way up as though crossing the deck of a storm-tossed schooner. When she finally completed the ascent – the most challenging climb any human had ever attempted – she saluted the silhouette on the swing.

The silhouette laughed and returned the honor.

"I'm Jenmarie," she told him, as she staggered over to the swing. "Move over."

The porchvoice – now a porchperson – did as bidden. "Is that hyphenated?"

"What?"

"Is Jen-Marie hyphenated, or is it two separ-"

8

"It's not two names. It's not one name. It's…it *is* one name." She lifted her arms and swept her hands through the space before her, a gesture suggestive of a name in lights. "Jenmarie. I'm not Jen, and I'm not Marie. I'm both at the same t-" She made to plant her elbow on her knee, but missed, nearly rolling forward off the bench. "Shoot," she mumbled as she straightened herself back up. "I'm both at the same time." She blinked. "That was really embarrassing."

"You're throwing yourself off balance. You talk with your hands so much."

"Hm." Jenmarie tried to think of a flirtatious response to that, but came up short. So she said "hm" again, and followed it up with "what's your name?"

"I'm Eddie."

"Hi, Eddie."

He smiled. It was only as he smiled that Jenmarie realized she could make out features on the silhouette. *Make out,* what a versatile little pair of words that was. "Hi, Jenmarie."

She suddenly felt very, very sober, and also very much the opposite. Not sober, not drunk, but both at the same time. Like her name. Like a callback. Her first inside joke with Eddie. She couldn't wait to tell him.

But she did wait. And then she forgot, because Eddie proved an able conversationalist. The time positively flew by, time enough for Jenmarie to well and truly sober up, yet in the end the Zyp driver still returned with her footwear far too soon for her liking. So she and Eddie turned the end into just another middle bit, remaining on the porch even after the shoes were back on, or rather under, her feet. In hindsight, knowing his peccadillos as she would come to, it was probably the sight of the strappy black heels that really got Eddie's engine revving. His questions became less Socratic and more Machiavellian. Steering the conversation, with a rather charming lack of finesse, towards a carnal conclusion. At this distance, she couldn't remember any of those piercing interrogatives save the last, for which she had been waiting patiently, and to which her answer had been 'yes.'

They ended up not having sex that night; Eddie couldn't get it up. He would briefly try to spin this as his having been moved by a chaste and chivalrous spirit to leave off the blotto maiden, and Jenmarie would take great pleasure in disabusing him of this notion. So the night wasn't a wash after all.

That was how it began, not that Jenmarie imagined there was any 'it' to, well, it. They didn't have much interaction for the rest of the getaway. Back at Emory, though, they bumped into one another at the DUC-ling. That led to a proper (read: successful) hookup, which led to another, which led to a proper date (Italian at some local joint neither had been to, but which had four stars on Yelp), which led to their first sexual encounter that could be considered something more than just a hookup, which led to a second date (drinks at a local bar called Checkers that had all kinds of board games, though they spent more time talking than playing), which led to a third (at which they discussed all of the things they liked more in theory than in practice, like hiking and stand-up comedy, a conversation which helped narrow the focus on what they *would* do for date number four). Given Jenmarie's grueling residency schedule, the outings were far apart and often at slightly awkward hours. That Eddie bent over backwards to make these work, she took to be a good sign. This had the potential to become something to which there was an 'it.'

Eddie graduated with no particular academic distinctions (i.e. a doctorate in philosophy). His focus was in political philosophy, and so his dissertation, which he insisted he'd done "a hell of a job" articulating and defending, had been called "Radical Metan-thropontological-Scientism: A New Study Of The Politics Of Thought As Occurs In The Body, As Contrasted With Those Thoughts As Occur In The Mind, And Let's Not Forget Heideg-ger." Something like that, anyway. He'd once read some of it to Jenmarie, during which recitation there were *three* instances of him needing to take a breath in the middle of a word. When called upon to summarize what the fuck he was trying to say with all of those twelve-syllable words, Eddie had flashed his pulse-quickening grin and told her "I'm trying to say, 'somebody give me a faculty position, please.'" He was uncommonly virile that night.

Yes, Eddie was after a faculty position, which could come from any quarter of the country. Yet he consulted Jenmarie each step of the way – should I be looking on the East Coast or West Coast, what do you think about Minneapolis – which led her to suspect the very thing she put to him one quiet Friday night in line for a food truck specializing in 'savory ice cream.'

"I feel like we're going to be together," she mused, arms crossed and shoulders slightly hunched, casual as if she'd been remarking on an unexpected cold snap.

Eddie visibly wrestled with a witty riposte, then smiled, wrap-ped his arm around her, and held her closer to him. "I hope so." He leaned his head against hers. "I love you, Jenmarie."

Jenmarie, despite herself, gasped quietly. No one she'd dated had ever said that to her. At least, not in such a way as made her believe it. She pulled her head back and boggled at him, not car-ing how idiotic the grin she shined up at him was. "What?"

He met her eyes and repeated himself.

Gasping a few more times, Jenmarie couldn't manage a reply before the hipster dockhand running the food truck pointed at

them and shouted "you two, what do you want?" A bit of awkward chuckling and shuffling ensued as they disengaged from each
other and went to place their order. So it wasn't until Jenmarie
had a cone of savory, overpriced ice cream in her hand that she
managed to reply "I love you, Eddie."

It turned out that the savory ice cream was basically just
mashed potatoes, but that wasn't terribly important.

Eight months later, they moved in together, into a cramped
studio in Home Park with a wall-mounted A/C unit that sounded like two jumbo jets making love. Eddie didn't have any great
affection for Atlanta, so he'd done a bit of harrumphing about
signing the lease, but Jenmarie still needed to finish her grueling
radiation oncology residency, and Eddie hadn't wanted to move
in to her old place. Thus: the new place, with the kitchenette that
was just a tile countertop set opposite the windows, and the dusty
ethernet hookup dangling off the street-facing wall from a few
technicolor wires. Not a great place, this new place. But Jenmarie
and Eddie were in love, and destined for better things. So it was
cute. It was fine.

In the final months of said residency (and after nearly a year
of generally blissful cohabitation, except for...well, all couples
fight, don't they, so yes, call it *generally* blissful), an apocalyptically
exhausted Jenmarie lucked into a week off of her professional
duties, during which she hoped to take a trip with Eddie. Ideally
something active; yeah, she was wiped from the brain-liquifying
hours and emotional extremity in which she spent most of her
day, but she also had an atomic fuck-ton of nervous energy to
burn. Classic Jenmarie. Hiking (yes, hiking, she really *was* anxious) an approachable middle bit of the Rockies was her first
choice, but she was open to just about anything. Which was more
than could be said for Eddie; every idea she proposed, he shot

down with a shrug. Rafting in Asheville? Eh. Dancing in New Orleans? Maybe some other time. Skydiving at…actually no, she didn't want to skydive, but, uh, camping in Big Sur? Not this year.

"Alright," Jenmarie demanded. "What do *you* want to do?"

"Jem," Eddie replied, his pet portmanteau for her, which obligingly sidestepped her distaste for hearing her name split in two, "we just don't have the money this year."

This was flatly untrue. Eddie's parents had paid for his degree, so he was free of student debt. Jenmarie was not, but she had folded the payments into her monthly budget, which budget also appropriated a modest sum for her savings account, which account she intended to tap for a trip. *This year,* by god! She told him as much.

"You're right," Eddie replied at once. "I should have said *I* don't have enough."

That was a new one. Eddie, who was so fond of splashing out on just about any concert or art show that caught his eye, suddenly turning his pockets inside-out? Oh, but those frivolous expenses were most often going towards experiences that *he* wanted to have, that had been *his* idea.

"I'll pay for the whole thing," she offered, knowing it would be in vain.

Eddie proved her right by shaking his head.

"Please. I need to let off some steam. I really want this," she added.

Her boyfriend looked at her as though she were a dog he were putting down, wishing *desperately* that he could just make her understand.

"Eddie. We have the money."

"…no we don't."

"I mean, unless you've been sneaking out to the horsie races, we absolutely do."

"Maybe, but we can't spare it."

"…and why is that?"

Jenmarie could practically hear the Wheel of Excuses clicking along in his mind, with force enough to snap its mount and go rolling off into the ocean. "We just can't!"

"What's your problem? If you don't want to go, just tell me!"

"That has nothing to do with it. I *want* to go, bu-"

"Since when do you not have the money for fucking *anything* that *you* want to do?!"

"Since I'm trying to save up and buy you a fucking ring, Jem!"

"…" was Jenmarie's reply. She added, "…"

Eddie looked at his lap and smiled.

Jenmarie did the same. Looking at her own lap, that was. Not his.

"You're gonna have to give me a proper proposal, you know," she finally said. "That doesn't count."

They both laughed, because at that point it was funny. It would remain funny right up until the divorce, at which point it would retroactively become an omen. Jenmarie would come to wonder if Eddie truly had been saving to buy her a ring, or if he'd used that as a dramatic deflection from the simple truth upon which she'd struck, that he simply didn't want to go on a vacation that hadn't been his idea. Eddie, after all, loved being right. He loved *winning*. The revelation about the ring had been, if nothing else, a way to do just that, to shut Jenmarie down, cast himself as a martyr, and even make her feel a little bit bad about having pressed him into spilling the beans. The man had more than a bit of Machiavelli in him; she'd learned that, and *recognized* that, on the night they'd met. Had he been exercising that manipulative muscle on the day of the not-so-proposal? This was a question that would only occur to her once she was certain of the answer.

The proposal itself, which came a few months later, wasn't much better. It was classic Eddie, post-divorce Jenmarie would note. Flawless optics; he'd rented out Cobbler's Wife (the obscenely sophisticated, would-you-like-some-meal-with-your-garnish-type restaurant which crowned the towering De Dernberg hotel), and curated a four-course dining experience with all of her favorites, impossibly juicy salmon and a semi-sweet pinot gris being the main event, with the *actual* main event being some heavenly cinnamon-sprinkled riff on bread pudding, all consumed to the sweet sounds of a string quartet that had learned just about every song by The Dear Hunter, Jenmarie's favorite band at the time. The Buckhead neighborhood of Atlanta glittered outside the windows; indeed, this may well have been the first time Jenmarie had ever associated the words "Atlanta" and "glitter" without making the connection via the word "bomb." But glitter or sparkle or shimmer or shine, whatever you wanted to call it, the city was gorgeous, stretching through clarity to the horizon, and over the far side. It was a perfect proposal, right up until Eddie got down on one knee and actually proposed.

"Jenmarie Bell," he said, proposingly, "would you marry me?"

Would. Like it was a hypothetical. Like he wasn't kneeling in front of her, brandishing a stone that could stand shoulder-to-shoulder with a Ring Pop (which – worth mentioning – was about as far from Jenmarie's self-consciously unpretentious shirt-and-jeans aesthetic as one could get).

"I would," she replied, with an acidity that paired poorly with the meal, "if you asked me properly."

"Will," was all he offered by way of correction.

Even at the time, that had seemed a pretty ominous way to

start things off. But she'd said yes, and so felt that a portion of the blame for the forthcoming pain was hers.

Until then, they were happy, remaining in their studio and saving up their pennies for the next step after Jenmarie graduated. She exhausted herself at residency, and was refreshed by her time at home with Eddie. They dreamt dreams about where they'd go next (Jenmarie having to constantly remind Eddie that she was limited to "wherever I can get a fellowship," a caveat that never quite seemed to penetrate his limitless ideals) as they made an art of the night in, laughing away the hours with nothing but a bottle of wine and a deck of cards. Here was another omen-in-hindsight; Eddie, tired of losing hand after hand to Jenmarie, had taken up trash-talking from behind. If the object of the game was to get rid of one's cards, as in Speed, he would ironically taunt Jenmarie with variations on the theme of "gosh, it must be hard to shuffle with so few cards." Then he'd riffle his stack of cards – nearly the entire deck – and make relieved noises. Or if they were giving the cards a break and playing Jenga, and Eddie pulled out the block that toppled the tower, he would leap up and dance around the room as though that had been his plan all along. At first it was funny in a cute way, which was to say it wasn't actually funny, just endearing enough to pass. But then he kept doing it, continuing to revel in failure in a way that denied Jenmarie her victories. The mock-celebrations became indistinguishable from real ones; Jenmarie couldn't help but wonder if Eddie had perhaps convinced himself that for him and him alone, participation and triumph were joined at the hip. An inverse relationship developed between Jenmarie's patience for the ostensibly harmless behavior, and the degree to which the behavior seemed emblematic of larger trends in the relationship.

But they were just games, she reminded herself. It was ridiculous to fret over things like that. Over games. She was being ridiculous.

They got married in New Orleans, a city that both of them had visited and fallen in love with independently, to which they had never been together. Both had suggested Preservation Hall, the legendary jazz venue in the French Quarter, as a wedding venue, neither quite believing they would be able to get it. Surprise surprise, the Hall was available, and within their means. And so, utilizing the limited capacity of the space as an excuse to keep the guest list small – sorry, *exclusive* – Jenmarie and Eddie were wed by a so-called Humanist Chaplain named Sean, who spoke movingly of the institution (though from the depths of her newly-single despair, Jenmarie would hate-Google "quotes about marriage" and discover that Sean had cadged most of his material from the top result, a page called "30 Adorable Quotes That Best Sum Up Marriage"). Even better, he kept his comments brief. Jenmarie and Eddie exchanged vows, both opting for a balance between humor and sincerity, Jenmarie favoring the latter, Eddie the former. Then they smooched by Sean's command, and hey presto, they were wed. Eddie Mark remained Eddie Mark, and Jenmarie Bell remained Jenmarie Bell. "The last thing I need," she averred in a tone that would brook no further discussion, "is another first name." Eddie never pushed the point.

The happy couple deferred their honeymoon until after Jenmarie's graduation; there was no sense jetsetting to parts unknown (or at least, as-yet-to-be-determined) with a beeper that didn't know the meaning of the words "out of network." Hindsight again: Jenmarie couldn't believe that, deep down, she hadn't recognized the honeymoon would need to be postponed once more, until she could complete her fellowship interviews and have some sense of direction, some concept of where she and

Eddie had to choose from for their much-discussed next step. Within a few months she had completed the interviews and received offers from: NYU Langone in New York, Brigham and Women's in Boston, and UW in Seattle. Naturally, she could have gotten one at Emory, but not for a single second did she consider staying in Atlanta. Life was starting to feel a bit…stale, that was a way to put it. Not the *right* way, but *a* way. And a change of venue was just the shake-up she needed. Plus, Eddie was chomping at the bit to move on, having stuck around for her to finish her residency. And so, she looked elsewhere. She'd really been hoping for an offer from LSU in New Orleans, but none was forthcoming. Eddie pitched this as a positive: "visiting's cool, but why would you want to *live* in a city that's perpetually about to be wiped off the map?" Jenmarie, from her privileged position of 'not underwater,' found something romantic about living, metaphorically speaking, on the precipice of a great height. As is always the case, amongst those who cannot conceive of taking a great fall.

Her heart drove her towards Boston, a city in which she had a great many friends – well…she had *some* friends, *a great many* was relative, and honestly, who needs *a great many friends*, quality over quantity, you know? – and for which she had a boundless adoration. It was such a *quaint* little city, wasn't it? Hardly any buildings over three or four stories tall. Granted, last she'd checked it had been largely overrun by chain restaurants, and there was that not-so-undercurrent of racism (though, she hated herself for noting with mixed feelings, her skin was light enough that she would be spared the worst of it)…but the rest of it was positively storybook. So, on second thought, called it *boundful* adoration. Some friends, and boundful adoration. Cool.

The moment she pitched this to Eddie, she knew they weren't

going to Boston.

It was his face, the way it wrinkled and narrowed, that gave him away. Even as he said "that's definitely an option," which wasn't much more than a factual statement *a la* "that's definitely a city," Jenmarie knew that he was lying. It wasn't an option. Eddie didn't want to go to Boston, but he would never admit this to her, sure as he would never back down. He had to be right. He had to *win*.

He would. He did. Eddie, it emerged, wanted to give the Big Apple a try. He'd been a few times, and loved what he'd seen. And what he'd seen, Jenmarie discovered, was Times Square. That he'd loved it was a fact that fell upon Jenmarie as heavily as if she'd discovered he was having an affair. In some ways, she might have preferred that. He had *loved* Times Square? Her Eddie, who owned no tweed jackets but acted as though he was always wearing one, who sipped wine and smacked his smiling lips as though he were joking (when in fact Jenmarie knew he was using irony to shield his pretensions to having a palate), who had long insisted to anybody who would listen that he only had a Hulu subscription because they owned the full Criterion Collection, but hadn't cancelled said membership even after the Criterion titles fucked off to their own streaming channel? *He* had walked into the endless noon of Times Square and thought *what a terrific place for a human to be?!*

He had. He would again.

The argument wasn't much of an argument. It wasn't even persuasion. It was seduction. Eddie made a quality pitch for New York – the music, the food, the dancing, the *life* – and, to his credit, never pushed or cajoled. He may not have had space in his heart for Boston, but even in the bitter After, Jenmarie was convinced that his openness to Seattle had been genuine, at least

19

at the beginning. It wasn't so much that Eddie had pressured Jenmarie into New York — not *entirely*, anyway — it was more that she had convinced herself she could make it work.

"As long as you know," she would remind him endlessly, "*if* we end up going to New York, I'm not gonna know anybody there. I'll have to lean on you for a while." *A h-while.* She hated that word.

"Absolutely," Eddie would reply with mounting enthusiasm, as he recognized that Jenmarie was slowly coming around to his first choice. "Always!"

Jenmarie would wonder what might have happened if she'd chosen her fellowship based not on what was best for her marriage, but what was best for her. That wasn't any way for a married person to be thinking, of course, but the other sort of thinking would, in short order, render her a no-longer-married person, so it was worth considering. She had effectively followed Eddie's heart to New York. Would he have followed hers to Boston?

No. He wouldn't have. This she knew for certain; she would later discover that, by the time she'd said yes, he'd already secured himself a faculty spot at Columbia's Philosophy department.

Regardless, the die were cast: New York City it would be, a city to which Jenmarie had never once imagined herself moving, for which she had no particular affinity. No matter. She would grow to love it, she told herself. It would be hard for a year or so, and then she would get in the New York Groove. She would make it there, and, consequently, be able to make it anywhere. And in those moments she faltered or lost her way, her beloved would be by her side to help her up.

The honeymoon was postponed, yet again. They had to save up for the move, after all.

It was easy, now, to think herself a fool. How had she let Eddie cut her off from her dreams, her friends, her *life?* That was the hindsight talking, of course; it could distort just as easily as it could clarify. There was no reliable way to recall her frame of mind at any given point in the relationship. Her *current* frame of mind, quite a dismal frame indeed, would always bleed into the image, poison it. For if she was being honest with herself (something she avoided, lest it become a habit), she had experienced moments of genuine happiness in this period. Which surely meant that she had been genuinely happy, in this period. Didn't it? It must. Surely.

There was a time when she'd have been able to convince herself of that.

S
E
T
T
L
E

That year of matrimony spent in New York was tough. Jenmarie's fellowship started at $45,000, but she had insisted she and Eddie live in one of the quieter areas of Brooklyn (she'd only have considered living on Manhattan if they could be *way* above the mayhem of midtown, somewhere in Washington Heights or even Harlem), and Eddie had eagerly consented. She'd sensed he'd had his heart set on somewhere nearer Greenwich or Chelsea, but she'd put her foot down. And when that hadn't worked, she'd run down the financials with him. One of those two approaches had dissuaded him from pressing the issue. She liked to imagine it had been her foot.

In fact, it wasn't hard to imagine, because the cost of living in a gentrified area like Williamsburg or Dumbo was only marginally more manageable than a room in an old Manhattan walkup would have been. Even factoring in Eddie's salary, just shy of $60,000, the not-so-newlyweds had less than $100,000 to play with, after taxes. Where Jenmarie had grown up in Chuckey, Tennessee, a hundred grand was enough to declare oneself King of the County for life. In a tony part of Brooklyn, that would get you a pretty good one bedroom on the third floor of a brownstone, and *maybe* a parking spot. Eddie balked slightly at sinking so much of their money into their living space, to which Jenmarie reminded him that it was their *living* space, where they *lived*. And besides, it was non-negotiable that she needed a proper hermitage, somewhere with thick walls that would keep out the chaos of New York. Alas, the tissue-walled building in which they wound up barely rose to that challenge. The baby crying next door would serve as the pedal tone to the next year's affective fugue, each up and down returning to that stark reminder of what their next *next step* could well have in store for them. Jenmarie wasted no time investing in a soundbar with a subwoofer, to reclaim control over the score of her waking hours. The baby, alas, wept well into the night. Every night.

Within a month or so, they were pretty well settled, neighbor babies notwithstanding. The living room was a loveseat (even for the amount they were paying, they didn't have enough space for the sectional of Jenmarie's dreams) with its back to the double-wide window, facing a titanic combination bookcase/TV console they'd created through the painstaking work of assembling various separate IKEA pieces and, here was the trick, putting them next to each other. They went for the black ones, which Jenmarie had always thought looked cheap, but perhaps cheap was better than dumb, which was how the white ones looked on the faux-hardwood floor. Besides, once Jenmarie and Eddie's books had stocked the shelves (their two collections combined numbering nearly fifteen hundred volumes), it took real effort to give the shelves themselves any notice at all.

It had been Jenmarie's idea to keep the books separated; hers on the left side of the unit, his on the right. Eddie had clearly been hurt by that. But her books were her babies, she reminded him. Perhaps a poor choice of metaphor, given Eddie's desire to have children with Jenmarie one day. Not that she could have known; he'd yet to articulate that wish to her. Would do, just hadn't yet. Still, it must have chilled him to hear her considering 'babies' to be *hers*.

They could both agree, at least, that after the bookcase, the rest was gravy. The rest, then: a halfway decent rug they'd found on sale via Wayfare set beneath a glasstop coffee table, itself set between the loveseat and the bookcase behemoth, with standing lamps on either side of the loveseat. They'd each selected their own lamps, each with a little task light attached, Eddie's a fake bronze with glass lamp shades, Jenmarie's a more honest shade of silver (though with equally ostentatious shades). Each used their lamp to stake a claim to 'their' side of the couch, never once articulating the conquest, never once doubting it.

The lamps and the books would be just about the only things they didn't have to bicker over, as they divvied up their joint purchases in less than a year's time.

Jenmarie settled into her fellowship, ever-so-slightly less intensive than the demands of residency, but no less exhausting. So, in point of fact, there wasn't all that much *settling* – it was more about hammering herself into whatever form would best meet the exigencies of the day. And, of course, creating a social life in this unfriendly new city rarely suggested itself with the urgency of her proper responsibilities. So she left it, time and again, as it was something she could do *later*. Who had the time or energy to meet new people? So much easier to convince herself that the people met in the hospital – all just as busy, each with their own divergent schedules that kept them from ever seeing one another in their, ha, free time – were enough. Such was the extent of her isolation that the Eddie-less social encounters of her last wedded year can be rather swiftly summarized: four times she went out for drinks with other fellows from the hospital, three of those times being, at her behest, to a bar in Williamsburg called Lucky-dog that not only allowed but encouraged patrons to bring their pups with them. As it happened, though, Jenmarie had always been the sort to hang out with the dog at each and every house party she went to, which habit she made no effort to break now. Knowing history, she nonetheless repeated it. Her would-be friends became close acquaintances, and her Instagram feed filled with dogs whose owners unfailingly handed her business cards on the pooch's behalf.

There were also, in that year, seven Facetime conversations with Mavis, her lifelong best friend from Atlanta (and before that, Chuckey, Tennessee) whose brother had organized the resident's getaway at which (or outside of which) Jenmarie and Eddie had first met. Mavis had remained in Georgia (she was quite fond of the ATL), but the bond she and Jenmarie had was of the unbreakable sort, one stress-tested against drunken spats and prolonged absences. Their first two Facetimes were of the catching-up variety; the next two were for *just checking in;* the remainder were dedicated to Mavis trying to console Jenmarie. By this point, her isolation, which Jenmarie would reluctantly concede was self-imposed – but only *partially* – was eating her alive. Mavis could see it, even through the shitty Macbook camera that somehow made pixels look wet, even across hundreds and hundreds of miles. But Jenmarie couldn't. Even if she could understand, and articulate to Mavis, how dissatisfying her current situation was, Jenmarie flatly refused to see herself as in any way ensnared by that dissatisfaction. She was happy, she insisted, because she was happily married, which was to say married. Love conquered all. So long as she was with Eddie, with her husband, she would be happy, because she was love and married conquered all. Right. What? Close enough. Mavis, for whom candor was a load-bearing column in any friendship, only bothered to tread lightly the first time she suggested Jenmarie take a harder look at her circumstances.

"I love Eddie," Jenmarie insisted.

Mavis replied through drawn lips. "I'm not saying you don't, or shouldn't."

But Jenmarie had retreated into her conch, and Mavis let her. Until the next time. At which point, she adopted the demeanor of an inspirational guidance counselor who was herself in desperate need of all three of those things.

"You can't change anything if you don't admit the thing needs changing," she told Jenmarie with a shake of her head.

"I just have to make some friends here," Jenmarie replied a bit too quickly. "I just have to get out more."

"Is that what you want, though? You don't *like* it there."

"I don't have to like it here, because I have *love* here."

Mavis would roll her eyes at things like that, to which Jenmarie would invariably fire back something to the effect of "you don't understand, you're not married," which she had the decency to recognize as disingenuous even as she said it. She couldn't help it, though; her inability to ever *win* with Eddie, to ever *be right*, had driven her to seek satisfaction in other theaters of battle. This, too, was something she recognized, but was quick to justify as one of the many normal (*perfectly* normal) side effects of *Getting Settled In A New City*.

Getting Settled In A New City was a glorious catchall, an affliction which lasted precisely one year to the date, the symptoms of which were any and every unhappy thought or feeling one might have during that year. Drinking a bit more than you used to? Perhaps enough to send you to the internet, asking every search engine in town "is it bad if I drink a bottle of wine by myself every night" and scrolling through the results until you find one that says "no"? Not a problem – you're just *Getting Settled In A New City*. Not eating as well as you used to, which is to say, eating far *more* than you used to? Mostly snacks with colorful labels that only manage to list fewer than seven hundred calories per serving by setting said serving size at an eighth of a cup? Fear not; you can lose that weight once you're done *Getting Settled In A New City*. Having more and more arguments with your spouse about decreasingly important things (which, of course, makes the arguments easier to write off), even when the fact of those arguments belie a fault line through the very foundations of your relationship? All together now: *Getting Settled In A New City!*

"I'm just getting settled in a new city," Jenmarie would patiently explain to Mavis.

"I'm worried about you," her friend would reply.

"Well, don't be. I'm getting settled. I'll get used to it."

There was only one other sort of social interaction Jenmarie had during that year, the kind she had more often than any other: those with Eddie. Make no mistake, the two still had fun together. Most nights, in fact, were quite happy ones. They made each other laugh, they made love, and they made it work.

Yet after about eight months or so, the deep well in Jenmarie's mind, the one into which she tossed all of her prickly thoughts, was near to full up. The truth could still be denied, but this was increasingly done by an act of will rather than passive indifference. She and Eddie were *making it work*. Which was another way of saying it wasn't working.

But this was fine, right? By this point they'd been together for over four years. The so-called "honeymoon phase" was over. A good job, then, that they'd postponed their actual honeymoon – what better way to rekindle that magic than with its namesake getaway? Until then, though, a functioning relationship was an act of creation. Ok. That was fine. This was normal. She was also, she decided, *Getting Settled In A New Living Situation*.

Normality, creation, comfort; playthings for swift silence. She would come to know this, as she would all unpleasant truths.

You know when.

B
R
E
A
K

It was a Tuesday. Off to a good start. Safe. Since when had dramatic, terrible things happened on Tuesdays? Besides the Black Tuesday financial crash in 1929. Or the first day of the Tet Offensive in 1968. Or Elvis' death in 1977. Or the *Challenger* exploding in 1986. Or 9/11 in 2001. Ok, so maybe Tuesday wasn't a great day to have a momentous event. But since when had Tuesdays been dramatic and terrible for your average, no-account, non-Elvis private citizen, huh?

Well, since Jenmarie was sitting at home, reading a book. She liked to read in her downtime; TV would ostensibly have been more relaxing, but she found it too amenable to a mind looking to wander. TV was the substitute teacher who let you go to the

31

bathroom and couldn't care less whether or not you came back. A book gave you a hall pass, sure, but if your mind hadn't returned by the time your eyes reached the bottom of the page, then you could hike them right back up and start it all over again, missy.

And thus she was reading, curled up on her side of the loveseat with her feet tucked beneath her right hip. It was January, so she had bundled herself up with her favorite throw blanket, a royal blue microplush. Not as glamorous or sophisticated as a woolen throw, no, but as with most unsophisticated things, it was more comfortable than the pricier alternative. Which had gotten her thinking about Cobbler's Wife. Which got her thinking about Adam Sandler. He'd done a movie about a cobbler once, wife? Sorry, *right?* Which got her thinking about Canadians, and their reputation for apologizing. She'd wondered if they always *meant* it, those contrite hockeymongers up there, or if they simply said sorry because it was an easy way to smooth out a sticky situation, as Americans tended to. Which got…oh, but she'd lost her place in the book. So she hiked her eyes right back up and took the page from the top.

What had she been reading? Hard to say. Her memory of that day was still sharp enough to draw blood where it counted, but for the most part it had gone all runny. Come to think of it, she wasn't sure she'd ever even finished the book. By the time she felt coherent enough to read again, she'd forgotten where she'd left off in the story. Where was that book now, anyway? Had she kept it? Or had…

Ugh. Enough stalling. Time to face the music. Oh, some music would have been nice. Something moody, sinister, low strings. Anticipating a slow, grisly bit with a buzzsaw.

There had been no music. Just silence. Silence and the sound of Eddie on the phone in the bedroom, talking to his parents.

Jenmarie had always found hearing just one half of a phone conversation far more disruptive and distracting than being within earshot of a normal, in-person conversation. It was a distaste that had redoubled as it was vindicated; she had once stumbled upon a study demonstrating the near-universality of this reaction. It was science, then.

Rational creature that she was, she considered putting on her headphones, plugging in to RainyMood (her preferred source of white noise, which endlessly cycled through a half-hour loop of rain sounds, an eternal recurrence she could really get behind) and continuing with her book. It was an idle sort of consideration she offered the matter, as her headphones were on the table, all the way over *there,* and she was oh so comfortable all the way over *here,* under her microplush blanket, with a book she couldn't remember. So she didn't bother with the headphones.

Had she bothered, she might still be married. Probably not. But maybe. Because had she bothered, she might not have heard Eddie tell his parents, through the tissue-thin wall separating the bedroom from the living room, that "we" had looked at some housing options down there, and he didn't want to put "them" (Jenmarie thought *them* was different from *we, them* probably being Eddie's parents) out so "we" were looking at AirBnB options. The mysterious *we* thought they had the flights pretty well locked down, though.

Jenmarie was *acutely* aware of her eyes sliding down the page this time. Only this time, it was the words themselves which had gone runny, oozing off the paper as the corners held fast, each edge a patient little razor, just waiting to catch a moving finger at the right angle, to cut it to the bone.

Suffice it to say, she lost her place.

Was…was Eddie planning on taking a trip? Who was he going with? Why hadn't he told her? And he was already looking at housing options? When was he *planning* on telling her, when he'd bought his fucking tickets? When it was *fait accompli*, and she would have no choice but to wish him happy trails? Jenmarie gripped her book so tight she nearly ripped it in half.

She paused and took a deep breath, recalling the clumsiness of his proposal. Eddie loved to surprise Jenmarie; he just wasn't very good at it. Perhaps this was another would-be surprise, a romantic getaw…

But then who the fuck was *we?* She sure as hell wasn't a part of it. She had looked at neither housing nor flights; she didn't even know where *we*, which almost certainly did not include *her*, were heading.

Given Eddie's penchant for casual manipulation, it occurred to her (many months later, once the most aggressive self-recriminations had worked themselves out) that her husband may well have anticipated Jenmarie's reaction to this phone call. Maybe he'd wanted a divorce, but hadn't the balls to just say so. He had seen her sans headphones, after all; he knew the walls were thin; he knew his voice carried. It would have been an uncharacteristically sinister bit of table-setting, sure, but considering what followed, Jenmarie was forced to concede that she'd not been as fully acquainted with her husband's character as she'd imagined.

He stepped out of the bedroom with an atypically big grin, the kind unique to those with red hands, and Jenmarie put her book down next to her. Not open-faced, to keep her place, but closed. That external indicator was, curiously enough, the first thing to clue her in to just how well and truly angry she was – it was rare enough for her to put down a book before reaching some kind of section break. To not mark her place at all was *unprecedented*.

34

DOWN THE HIGH TOMB

But, well, desperate times and all that.

"You're going on a trip?" she asked him, with as level a voice as she could manage.

He looked at her with overcranked confusion, as though she'd asked if he was planning on going to work tomorrow with *both* of his eyebrows. "...yeah?"

"Where?"

"North Carolina." Where his parents lived. She ought to have guessed that one from context clues.

Jenmarie gave Eddie a moment to elaborate.

Eddie did not elaborate.

So Jenmarie asked "with who?" as delicately as she felt herself capable.

Eddie shrugged defensively. "Some of my old college buddies."

"When were you going to tell me?"

"I was going to tell you today."

She glared at him.

He averted his gaze and shrugged. "It's not a big deal."

"Then why wouldn't you tell me sooner?"

"Because we were just...it was just, not set in stone. It was just...vague talk."

"You're looking at places to stay!"

"Don't make this a big thing. It was just vague talk!"

"I don't think it's unreasonable for me to ask why you didn't bother mentioning to me that you were planning on leav-"

Eddie met Jenmarie's glare in kind now. "Why are you grilling me about this?"

Jenmarie blinked, feeling her lips tighten like a fist. "Oh, sorry, what should my response be, to hearing you've made travel plans without me?"

Eddie rolled his eyes. "I should have invited you, that's the problem?"

Yes, she nearly replied, but that'd be giving him an opportunity to pivot into making this about her. Which opening he absolutely would have exploited. "You should have told me! *That's* the problem!"

"I'm telling you now!"

Jenmarie couldn't help it: she laughed. "No, you told your parents, and I overheard you!"

"You shouldn't have been eavesdropping, then."

Jenmarie knocked on the wall. "I didn't have much choice, did I?"

"Where are your headphones?"

"They're on the ta-" Jenmarie interrupted herself with a vigorous shaking of the head. "Eddie. Seriously. Were you planning on telling me when you bought the tickets, or were you just gonna leave a note after you'd gone?"

"That's exactly it, though. I haven't bought the tickets. We haven't *made* the plans yet. I w-"

Here, Jenmarie realized, was where she gave him the ammunition to *win*. The only thing worse than the realization itself was that she had it at the very moment of the question's articulation. "And who's *we*, anyway?"

Eddie narrowed his eyes slightly. "I just told you. They're just buddies from college."

"Specifically."

"You don't know them."

Jenmarie dug the hole deeper, knowing she was, unable to stop: "Do they have names?"

Eddie's face darkened, the way it did when his 'that's just your opinion' shrugging had been gainsaid one too many times.

"What's this about? You think I'm cheating on you?"

Recognizing his shift in tone as the argumentative gloves coming off, Jenmarie floated like a butterfly back into a more mutedly defensive corner. "I think it's reasonable to wonder who my husband is planning a trip with behind my back."

"It's not *behind your back*, Jesus! It's not my fault you're at work when this stuff happens! If it was *behind your back*, I wouldn't have called them while you were here, would I?"

"Who's *they*? Your parents, right, that's not what I meant. I meant who's *we?*"

"Are you even listening to me? You don't know any of them!"

Jenmarie shook her head. She was on the verge of replying when Eddie closed the distance between them, sat on one of the wooden chairs at the kitchen table (*not* on the loveseat next to her) and leaned his elbows on his knees.

This was, for lack of a better term, the fulcrum.

"Do you think we should take a break?" he mumbled at the floor. "Is that what you're saying?"

Jenmarie may not have known her husband as well as she thought she did, but she knew this game well enough. Eddie, never wanting to be the bad guy, never wanting to be in the *wrong*, only ever formulated big decisions as questions, or else positioned them as having been her idea. Sometimes she let him get away with it; it wasn't always worth a fight.

This, on the other hand...

"What?" was all she could think so say. Followed by, "no! Of course not!"

"I just think...maybe it would give you time to meet new people, don't you?"

"No! I don't want to meet new people!"

"Isn't that the problem, though?"

NO! she wanted to scream. *The problem is you making plans without me!* But, of course, that opened her up to the obvious riposte, one she feared had more validity than she wanted to grant: she was upset about his making plans without her *because* he was her only point of contact in the city. That, of course, was far from the only reason for her hurt at being so sidelined by the love of her life, her best friend in the world… but she couldn't honestly deny that it was *one* of them, could she?

"Do *you* want to take a break?" she asked him.

"No," he replied, "but I just think, maybe, you know, it would gi-"

"Stop making this about me. *You* want to take a break. Right?"

"It's about *us*, Jenmarie." When she heard her full name – not Jem but *Jenmarie* – pass from his lips to her ears for the first time since the day of their wedding, she knew the break was going to be more than a break. That was different from *believing* it, of course; it would be a solid week or two before the knowledge that one conversation, hardly even an argument, was all it took to shatter a lovely little thing five years in the making, that there needn't be any protracted fumbling or bumbling, no couples therapists or marriage counselors need be recruited, no, the thing could simply fall, be *knocked,* and so fall, and so shatter, if that was the will of one person, it took only one person to knock the thing, while the other could only watch, watch the fall, and what came next. It would be a week or two before the fact of this fully wriggled its way into Jenmarie's prefrontal cortex and made a bed for itself. By which point, its much larger and more unpleasant bedfellow was nearly on its way.

Still, denial is a powerful thing. Convinced that it was a matter of space by Eddie's announcement that he would go couchsurf with buddies for a while, Jenmarie matched him her own departure; she rang up Lenny, the only fellow, uh, fellow with whom she had anything resembling a genuine friendship, and subjected herself to the humiliation of inviting herself over indefinitely. A married man himself, he and his husband bent over backwards to accommodate Jenmarie, going so far as to obtain an extra key from their landlord (said keys being the big square kind with NO COPIES ALLOWED stamped on them), which was no small ask in this city, in a city such as this. She stayed with them for two weeks, doing her best to give Eddie the space she'd never realized (which was to say, he'd never told her) he'd needed. Just as she had never before imagined her phone humming against her thigh so frequently, the operative term being *imagined;* the phantom vibrations became so distracting she took to putting her ringer on (a rarity amongst her generation) and putting the damned device on tables or chairs or her lap, wherever she would be able to clearly see the screen light up with Eddie's name and face (his was the only contact to which she'd added a picture) whenever he called to apologize, and take her back. Day after day, she waited and watched, regularly poking at the home button just to make sure she hadn't somehow missed the telltale *BING BING* that would call her home. Unfortunately, by this point the grapevine had come alive, and so her phone took to *BING BING*ing around the clock, heralding the concern of her and Eddie's mutual acquaintances. Heard you were having some issues, a bit of a rough spot, going through an icy patch, these things happen, couples argue, no need to worry, I'm here for you if you need anything, just text, just drop me a line, I'm here for whatever you need. She had only one text she ever wanted to send back, one question she wanted to pose them; what exactly had Eddie said to them, or what had been whispered to them from up the lane? What, as they understood it, as her husband had *framed* it, was the precise nature of the 'issues' they were having? Had they heard that Eddie and Jenmarie were taking a break? Or something a bit more permanent? She never asked this of them; not for a single moment did she expect a straight answer. Nor did she want one.

Eddie, for his part, could offer no clarity. After two weeks he emerged from whatever trench he'd crawled into and launched an assault of contradictory information. Via text message. Not a call. Not a well-penned letter. He sent her a fucking *text*, and then another, and another. They were taking a break, he insisted in one fucking text. He'd read that taking a break can be healthy for a relationship, he clarified in another fucking text. Jenmarie had, of course, read those same articles by now, all of which made clear that setting boundaries, not the least of which being a concrete duration, was essential to keeping the break from becoming a more irrevocable fracture. So, she asked him, what was the timeline? He balked, insisting he needed space without restriction. Not with his voice, though. Not with his fucking voice.

Here emerged the pattern: he would push her away. She would try to give him space. Then he would pull her back in, dangling hope and knowing full well she'd throw herself at it with abandon. In this first instance, the pull was a specific anecdote, about two sweethearts from his high school who'd taken two months off their marriage, thereby saving it. Ok, Jenmarie thought. Two months is doable. She texted as much to Eddie, and so, was pushed: two months was what had worked for *those* people's marriage, it wasn't a universal prescription for success. Stumbling backwards, Jenmarie wondered (via text) how long, then. It could be a day (pull), Eddie insisted, or a year (push). Pulled and pushed and pushed and pulled, what followed was a dizzy week for Jenmarie; to be fair, her positively literary intake

40

of whiskey probably had something to do with that. Lenny voiced his concern to Jenmarie, blah blah worried about you blah blah self-destructive behavior blah blah throwing up on the fridge. This was just a part of the phase she was going through, she knew. That was all. Nothing to be worried about. She tried to tell them this from the floor of their bathroom, laying in her own vomit, as Lenny's husband explained to the 911 dispatcher that he'd gotten up to pee and found her like that, no he didn't know how long she'd been there, yes she was conscious but her eyes were moving strangely, separately. Jenmarie tried to assure him that she was fine, a hospital bill was the last thing she needed right now. She'd sleep it off. Only she couldn't manage to mold her gurgles into words. So she slept it off in the hospital. Nobody had remembered to grab her glasses, which had fallen off as she'd crashed to the tile floor, so the world remained a shapeless blur for the next several hours, until Lenny managed to get her back to his place. He told her to take the day, but that tomorrow she would need to pack up and move on. By giving her a place to stay, he said, he feared he was enabling her. He didn't need to say how; they both knew.

That night, Jenmarie called Eddie. Called, not texted. A clear escalation. She told him that they needed to meet, *needed* to put some shape on this…whatever it was. Not knowing what was happening, whether it was a break or a longer-term separation or even something *more*, was driving her mad. Literally, she feared. She didn't tell him about her trip to the hospital, because she wanted to so very badly. She wanted to parade it in front of him. Look what you've done to me, look at how I suffer on your account, and so on, and so forth. But no, she knew herself well enough to distrust any desire as intense as this one, which was why she wouldn't tell him. Though she failed to apply a similar line of logic, as pertained to desire and the eyebrow-raising intensity thereof, to the purchase of a handle of Wild Turkey. She would wait a night to start drinking again, yes she would – but just one night.

Make that two, because the following evening she cajoled Eddie into meeting with her, talking this out. They met at their place, which she mortified herself by describing as "*your* place" (a miserable slip of the tongue that Eddie had ample time to correct, an opportunity at which he did not jump), and had a uniquely unilluminating discussion. She cried – scratch that, she *wept, bawled, howled* – and Eddie watched. He cooed reassurances, insisted that he was also very upset, he'd just done all of his crying earlier, you see, *off-camera* as it were. Which allowed him to be both the cause of, and the consolation for, Jenmarie's grief. This was yet another horrible little victory Jenmarie couldn't bear to let him have. But all the same, his hand felt steadying on her shoulder. So she let it stay there, for a time.

Going to the AirBnB she'd rented (there'd be no Lennys to judge her *there*…nor would they be there to call an ambulance, she noted with mixed feelings), Jenmarie had scarcely walked back in the door when she got a text from Eddie.

She read it once. Read it again. Squinted at it like a gunslinger with her hand on her holster. Tried to find another way to interpret it, a way that wasn't suggesting, in such a way as made it sound like maybe it had actually been *her* idea, that they ought to get a divorce. Over another fucking goddamned shitkicking *text*. Right after they'd had a face to face conversation.

"Can I call you?" she fucking texted him.

"Sure," was apparently all he could think to fucking text back. Asshole.

The phone call, which consisted primarily of Jenmarie blubbering and gasping (again) as Eddie listened (again), was quick. Eddie didn't want to try couples therapy – he reminded her, not inaccurately, that he'd been pressing for her to get some kind of professional help for her depression. This was no hypocrisy; Eddie attended therapy twice a week. He didn't need to remind her that it was Jenmarie herself who had pushed *him* into going. A part of her entertained the idea that the therapist was somehow responsible for this, that she'd whispered venomous little promises into Eddie's ears about the blank slate that awaited him on the far side of a separation…but she didn't have the opportunity to press the issue. No therapy, no break, no discussion. Eddie wanted a divorce, and he wanted it done quickly and cleanly. He also, as it happened, wanted them to stay friends. They could start being just regular best friends right away, as far as Eddie was concerned.

Here, at least and last, was an opportunity for Jenmarie to exercise some agency in how the single most important relationship in her life imploded. A great many words could describe the divorce. Quick and clean were not among them.

L
U
C
K
Y

After all of that (*that* having slugged on for another seven months), Jenmarie thought what well and truly fucked her up was finally relaxing enough to see where Eddie was coming from. Never would she understand the *way* he had gone about the separation, of course. That herky-jerky, push-pull manipulation was borne of Eddie's inability to make a firm decision; he probably hadn't even known what he'd wanted until he'd texted (*texted!*) her his wish to split for good. She'd read ill-intent into his actions, but a more charitable assessment was probably the more accurate one. Eddie had been confused and scared, and she'd mistaken the emotional remove at which he'd held himself, for his own protection, for indifference. That didn't excuse it, absofuckinglutely not, but it drew him back from the realm of comic book villainy into something more approachably, comprehensibly human.

What's more, this clarity borne of distance helped her see her own culpability in the dissolution anew. She recognized how miserable she'd been, how deeply unhappy this city made her (though still, in these Technicolor daydreams that saw Eddie on her doorstep tearfully repenting for all he'd ever done wrong, she was *still* prepared to absolve him, embrace him, and most astonishingly, extend her sentence in New York by another year, even as here, in the greyscale real, the divorce proceedings were just getting started), and how that had slowly but surely twisted her out of true, into a version of herself that deserved to live under a bridge and riddle at passersby. Self-destructive was the word that Lenny had used, and it was a word Jenmarie shamefully accepted. She found a therapist and went twice weekly (until she dialed it back to once weekly). She stopped drinking (except socially, when the shame of being seen ordering *another* knock would keep in her line). She started eating better (though she treated herself to Popeyes every now and again, because she fucking deserved it). She made every effort, in other words, to be self-*con*structive. At first she believed she was doing it for herself. It wasn't until she was on the phone with her baby brother Tomjohn – the only member of her family with whom she still had any kind of relationship, even if it was conducted primarily through speakers and screens – for one of their semi-regular *let's disapprove of each other's choices* check-ins that she admitted, to herself as much as her brother, that she was doing all of this because, *still*, she wanted to get in shape so that, somehow, word would get back to Eddie about how she'd turned her life around, and then he'd take her back.

"Don't do that," Tomjohn counseled.

"Yeah," Jenmarie sighed, glancing around the aggressively furnished month-to-month sublet she'd landed in while she looked for somewhere proper to finish out her fellowship here in New York, "I know it's not healthy in terms of, psychologically, er, motivation. But if I'm being healthy for unhealthy reasons, that's st-"

"Dude, fuck Eddie."

"Yeah, I know."

"Just let him go."

"I know. It's not that easy, though."

Jenmarie could *hear* Tomjohn shrug over the phone. "It was for him."

"Oh, *wow.*" She could only hope Tomjohn could, in turn, hear her hackles snapping to attention. "What's the longest you've ever dated anybody?"

"…that's not relevant."

"You cried for like, *three weeks* when Emily broke up wi-"

"That was really complicated, and not relevant!"

"Oh, was it, Tomjohn? Was it *really complicated?*"

"Yeah, actually, it was! And not relevant!"

From there, Jenmarie successfully diverted attention from her own affairs, a terrain she always regretted visiting with Tomjohn. Which wasn't to say those calls weren't productive; there was a reason she subjected herself to them on a semi-regular basis, after all. For this one, as all the others, granted clarity, less for what Tomjohn offered than the mere fact of Jenmarie's articulating her problems. It took speaking her dilemma aloud to accept that these two competing impulses – the desire to improve herself and the desire to somehow win back Eddie – would simply have to coexist until the former could smother the latter.

And what better way to nudge that process along, she mused

47

to herself, than getting back out, as it were, *there?* She downloaded Snifter, one of the many gimmicky dating apps that had sprung up after a slew of thinkpieces declared Tinder to be dead. Part of Snifter's appeal, one the company trumpeted with unbecoming aplomb, was that its premise was strange enough to cull the "normies" (their words) from its user base. New registrants to Snifter would be sent a plain white T-shirt, with instructions to wear it while undertaking some form of vigorous exercise. Once it was fully soaked through with sweat, the T-shirt was to be removed, placed into the special airtight bag provided, and mailed back to Snifter HQ in the prepaid box. The white coats at Snifter would then put the T-shirt in a big box and press a button that said *bleep bloop* (Jenmarie wasn't entirely clear on this part) and hey presto, a 'pheromone profile' is added to your dating profile. The primary swipe-right-for-yes-and-left-for-no selection engine remained identical to that of any other dating app, though the match percentages were based not on questionnaires but on chemicals. Pheromone First, that was one of Snifter's many, many slogans.

So Jenmarie got the shirt, went for a long run in it, sent it back, and within a week she'd swiped right on a guy who had an 86.7% pheromone match. That struck her as a very specific number to be derived from an odor, but one of the downsides of being as scientifically specialized as Jenmarie was that she respected both the boundaries of her understanding, as well as the explanatory power of large words (or, put more pithily: she felt out-scienced enough by the algorithm to take its output at face value). Her match's name was K.J. Hanifan; she'd swiped right on him largely because of a picture on his profile that showed him cradling a bulldog puppy in his arms. Puppies and kittens were cheap dating app pandering, of course, but Jenmarie would never have claimed to be immune. Besides, it was more than the dog itself; it was the way K.J. smiled at it. It wasn't a big, toothy, quick-take-my-picture grin. It was softer, smaller, acknowledging the delicacy of the creature he held to his not-especially-defined chest. K.J. wasn't pudgy, but the angle at which he tilted his head had bunched a roll of fat up beneath his chin. Most people screened photos like this out on these sorts of apps. That K.J. hadn't got her attention. Also attention-getting: he liked The Dear Hunter. That was at least two topics of conversation queued up right there! And if they should exhaust those, perhaps they could just smell each other for the remainder of the date and be 86.7% pleased with the whole affair.

So she swiped, they matched, and the very next night they were scheduled to meet at a cramped (which was to say, trendy) bar in SoHo. K.J. had recommended the place, of which Jenmarie was glad.

With the help of Mavis, live via Facetime, Jenmarie dressed herself for her first first-date in well over half a decade. It was an arduous process, but after a few hours and a dozen-odd costume changes (*none* of which were little black dresses – too obvious), a final decision was reached. The top was a slim-fit Portofino shirt, black with a floral print that looked a bit like some ghastly wallpaper from the 70's but was, by the strange alchemy of fashion, currently quite hip, the key word there being *currently*. Jenmarie fretted, only half-facetiously, about the shirt going out of style halfway through the night. Mavis pointed out that if the night went well, 'halfway through' was precisely when the shirt would no longer be a part of the equation. The skirt (quiet, Mavis) was a matching black, billowing to right about knee-height, terminating in a subtle lace valance. That gave her some options, in terms of how much of her bare legs she was going to show. Her shoes were the very same three-inch heels she'd forgotten in a Zyp car all those years ago – Mavis was against them, ostensibly because they didn't match the outfit, in point of fact due to the memories of Eddie they were bound to stir up. That, of course, was precisely why Jenmarie wanted to wear them. The way to move forward wasn't by ignoring the Eddie-shaped holes in her life; it was by reclaiming those objects and histories freighted with painful memory, and jamming them into those horrible little heart-holes. Her next steps needed to be taken in those shoes, Jenmarie averred, and being nothing but a face on a screen in this situation, Mavis had no choice but to accept that and move on to the accessories. Choker, clutch, rings (though none for the naked third finger), bracelets. Hair. Makeup. Ready.

Jenmarie arrived at the bar early and was pleased to see that K.J. had as well. He was about the same height as her, which she hadn't been expecting (she generally preferred her fellas taller), but the rest was just what had been promised on the tin, so to speak: close-cropped hair save the swoop up top, a round face atop a body with soft edges but impeccable posture, and a kind, open smile. His shirt was of the button-up variety, which he'd fully fastened save the top three buttons, hanging loose over his waistline. She would have bet anything it was one of those needlessly expensive ones that had been "specially designed" to fit well when untucked. He wore jeans, but nice jeans. Tight, but not so tight that his balls looked like Han Solo frozen in carbonite. The shoes were the only dissonant note, New Balance sneakers of a color scheme more befitting Skittles, but he wore them with the confidence of someone who could call himself a "sneakerhead" with a straight face. He was handsome, in other words, less for his appearance than his bearing. But hey, handsome is handsome.

The first round was all small talk. K.J. was fun to chat with, though it took ever-so-slightly longer than necessary; he had a curious habit of pausing before he spoke, for juuuuust a second or two beyond what could be considered "comfortable," like he was coming to her live on location and there was a signal delay between them. As was her wont, she peppered silly questions in with her real ones, the thinking being that if a guy couldn't roll with her goofy side, she didn't want to have a goofy roll with him. And so, "would you rather your eyes and nipples trade places, or your fingers and your toes?"

K.J. took a big long pause before answering that one, which she appreciated. "…fingers and toes, I'd say."

Jenmarie cocked her head to one side. "Really?"

"I just feel like nipples on my face would be…" he lifted a loose palm towards his smile. "Well, I'd lose my glasses every time it got cold."

Jenmarie laughed. "Why are you wearing nipple glasses?"

"To cover up. These are sunglasses, they're not prescription."

"Oh, that's good. But," she pointed to her own eyes, "you could wear them further down your nose, to cover your face nipples, then just wear really thin cotton or something so you can see out of your tit-eyes."

"That's true," K.J. granted. "That's a good point."

"Because, if you've got stubby little toe-fingers, and long finger-toes…gonna have a hard time at the ATM, for one."

"But if you've got eyes on your, um, your breasts, you're go-"

"You can say *tits.*"

Tape delay. "I think I might save that for the second date."

"Oh, look at you, being confident."

K.J. averted his gaze and shrugged, which rather cut that assessment off at the knees. But there was something charming in the man's timidity, too.

They weren't even on to the second round before the topic of conversation turned to the nasal basis of their match. The transition was a subtle one; Jenmarie couldn't be sure if it was she who'd steered talk in that direction, or K.J. At any rate, broaching the subject, and discussing it openly, quickly became tantamount to discussing the logistics of where and how they would conduct further experiments as to their compatible stenches. By round three, K.J. had recaptured enough confidence to start a volley with some of Jenmarie's more suggestive serves, until they both knew, and *knew* they both knew, that they were going to be getting lucky that night. In which case, it wasn't really luck, was it? If one *knew* one had luck coming one's way, that was just pleasant certainty. And luck precluded certainty, didn't it? And wasn't the inverse also, necessarily, true?

Ah, but this was veering dangerously close to Eddie's kingdom of the gazéd navel. Far more pleasurable to dwell in less rarified realms. To wit: K.J. did a pretty good job. A bit quick on the draw, as she'd found some fellas were the first time (either that or, depending on the amount of liquor consumed, geologically slow), but he made a few compelling cases for keeping his fingers just where they were, and with a lingual crescendo that delivered her to climax well before him, an act of full-tilt generosity that she couldn't help but find slightly unnerving for a maiden voyage (not to mention, it somewhat diminished the pleasure of the penetrative act itself). Still, good intentions and all that. K.J. was far sweeter and more attentive than she'd expected of a man whose pattern of speech could best be described as *suspicious of itself.*

That weekend she and K.J. had their second date – on which he did not say the word *tits* – at the House of YES, one of the best places to cut a rug in Brooklyn. This seemed a safe setting, which was to say, it was one at which she was unlikely to see Eddie. The man had, as of the last year or so, needed to be *cajoled* into dancing (presumably so he could make a great big entrance onto the floor), which should have been a red flag in itself. K.J., thank heavens, did dance, and happily. His style was self-conscious, and Jenmarie couldn't help but smile as she watched him try and fail to launch into moves he'd clearly watched YouTube tutorials for in preparation for this evening. K.J. was a few rungs below enlightenment on Jenmarie's Hierarchy of Groove; he was still dancing for other people, which was to say, he was dancing *as though* he was dancing like nobody was watching. One step up was dancing like nobody was watching, an improvement that nonetheless still defined itself by optics (the implication being that one would be restrained were others to be watching). The pinnacle, upon which Jenmarie did her wrecking ball pirouettes, was dancing as one was compelled to dance according to the music and the mood. She straight up bodied the light fantastic with a fury that had sought release, for so, so long, and often found the avenues wanting. The only dancing people back in Tennessee did was line dancing, fingers tucked into belts, going through motions ordered by the man with the microphone. That wasn't dancing, by god, it was a military revue! Jenmarie had only ever longed to bust her own moves, cut rugs according to her specifications, get down with whichever self, bad or otherwise, caught her fancy at the moment. None of this was to say she was a *good* dancer, but nor was it to say she couldn't draw a crowd when the spirit moved her. So, House of YES, then: essentially a big converted ice warehouse, filled to bursting with sex-positive party people of every imaginable stripe and shade, all gathering for something that lived between a rave and a cabaret performance. With extra emphasis on the word *lived.*

See Jenmarie tearing shit up, like a ballerina who's just been told there's a spider on her shoulder, to a KNOWER song – she couldn't recognize the specific track, but the band's sound was unmistakable. Next thing she KNEW, K.J. reached a hand through her personal whirlwind, grinning the idiotic grin of a man for whom dancing was not an end unto itself but a means to half-mast, and plopped it on her shoulder. The hand, that was. She took this ploppage as the beginning of some sort of partners dance move, and while she detested any kind of so-called "sexy" (i.e. self-conscious) dancing, spinning and twirling were well within her purview. K.J. seemed confused by her taking his hand and lifting it, but Jenmarie knew how to lead as well as follow. Preferred to do neither, if it came to that – even when dancing "with" someone, she preferred to be the master of her own dom-ain, for the first commandment of dance, "freeth thine mind, and thine ass shalt follow," seemed to demand a bit of elbow room – but she could do both. So she reached out her other hand and started spinning the man. Laughing, K.J. allowed himself to be spun, then lifted his own hand and let Jenmarie whirl herself around. As she spun, she gainsaid gravity. As she spun, she disc-overed that some things work from both ends: she freed her ass, and her mind followed. As she spun, K.J.'s face sometimes swept through her vision looking like Eddie's. So she spun faster, until K.J.'s face didn't look like anything at all.

S
Y
N
C
O
P
E

The last thing she remembered, prior to peeling her cheek off of the cold (wet?) tiling of the bathroom floor, was padding across the kitchenette and telling her relentlessly beeping microwave to *relax*.

Then she blinked into a cloud of truck exhaust, ash-grey, thick, suffocating.

Another blink brought her face-to-base with the porcelain stem of the toilet. The side of her head that wasn't cold and wet was warm and wet. She wasn't sure which side was which yet. Had she thrown up again? How? The last thing she'd had to drink was that night at House of YES, gosh, a week ago now? Or two weeks? How did time work?

Wait. Her face. Which half was cold? The one on the floor.

Why was it cold? Well, the floor was cold. Why was the floor on her face? Something had gone wrong, and the microwave knew it. That was why it kept beeping.

Something in her mouth. She spat the something out of her mouth and onto the floor in front of her, outside the web of wet and onto the dry.

The something was small, no bigger than one of those little pellets they used to fill Beanie Babies, the Beanie Babies she'd collected when she was a kid and that her cousin had bought from her, convinced they would be worth something someday. Had she eaten a Beanie Baby? Was that why she was on the floor?

No. The white thing was not a Beanie Baby bit, or a BB, or anything else that started with a B. Running her tongue around her upper teeth cracked the case: it was a chunk of her left canine. She'd just spat out a piece of her smile.

Did she croak the word "help" into an empty house? She might have done that. Hard to say, through the melting fog.

A minute and a half later she was back on unsteady feet, teetering drunkenly (though not actually *drunk*, that would have been preferable) to the rhythm of the eternally-eager microwave, one hand clamped firmly on the wet white of the washy-bin. *Sink*.

Shit.

Her hand slipped off the *sink,* nearly sending her back to the ground, smearing a long red palm across that wet white as she caught herself.

It would amuse her, when she'd put some space between herself and this evening, that she chose to investigate the floor before the mirror.

In fairness, there was a puddle of blood on the floor, about the diameter of a Frisbee. Just the sort of thing to draw the eye.

Beep beep beep, the microwave shrieked.

Now, finally, at long last, the mirror. She knew what she expected to see, and was not disappointed: her face split clean in two, the flesh from the left side having been torn off for nefarious purposes. No. Scratch that. More than a scratch, actually.

She blinked as hard as she could, and something that resembled, but was not, sense weighed in.

The left half of her face was glazed with her own blood, in which she'd been laying for an indeterminate amount of time as the microwave screeched, not wondering if she was alright, just deeply concerned that whatever she had put in there might overcook in the latent heat. What had she put in there? Her chin. No. Cheese. Mac and cheese. A frozen meal for one. Title of her memoir. Ha, ha.

Having the presence of mind to not dab at herself with one of the fabric handtowels she had in here (because they weren't *her* towels, it wasn't *her* place, this was just a sublet, the month-to-month sublet from which she'd watched her divorce chunder onwards), she cupped her hand beneath her chin to catch the blood drip drip dripping onto the floor, and staggered into the kitchenette. She opened and closed the door of the microwave, at long last silencing the infernal *beep*, then ripped a handful of paper towels off the countertop spindle and struggled her way back to the bathroom. The first towel she put up dry, dabbing as much of the blood from her face as possible. Through all of this, she marveled at her own calm. If she wasn't thinking entirely clearly, it wasn't on account of any panic or hysteria. She *wasn't* thinking entirely clearly. She knew why she *wasn't* wasn't thinking entirely clearly. So why *was* she wasn't thinking entirely clearly? Clear? She'd hit her head. She'd hit her *chin*, she realized as she pulled the towel from the offending area. The offend*ed* area. 'Twas the tiling gave the offense.

A gash had split her chin, perhaps two inches across, right at the part where the jaw swoops back to shape the neck. She wasn't a whaddyacallit, a face doctor, a schlomologist, what? No. She didn't know about that, but she *did* know that the face got a lot of blood. Pump-through. Fuck, *circulation*. That was it. That was why she'd bled so much from such a small wound. Bunching up another paper towel and applying pressure to her chin, she look-ed back down at the floor, at the puddle, at her blood. How long had she been down there?

Regret. No, sorry. *Time*. She would have regret to work this... *time*, not regret. She would have time to regret this out. Ah, fuck it.

She needed stitches, that much was obvious. But she wasn't about to pay for *another* ride in an ambulance (the bill from her last one was still a point of contention between herself and her insurance provider), so she called up K.J., explained the situa-tion, and then asked "why not?"

"...I get woozy around blood," he confessed. "...I wouldn't feel safe behind the wheel, knowing you were bleeding next to me."

Jenmarie struggled through a tape delay of her own. "...I need to get to the hospital."

"...I mean, I rea-"

"Dude. Please."

So on the strength of either the 'dude' or the 'please', K.J. agr-eed to drive Jenmarie to the hospital. While she waited for him, she sopped up her vitality as best she could with one hand clamp-ed to her chin, regretting (her newest hobby, it seemed) that she'd gone with the cheaper, store-brand paper towels rather than the Bounty ones with the dubious mathematics on them. "2 = 4!" the thicker ply towels insisted, confident that their powers of absorption were mighty enough to slurp up the laws of the universe and leave a blank slate upon which a new order could be written, an order in which 12 rolls was equivalent to 16, in which 18 was equivalent to 34, in which 3 was equivalent to 51.

She'd cleaned up just about all the blood when she got dizzy again. That nearly sent her right back down, but she threw her back against the wall and slid to her ass before things got too topsy-turvy.

That jogged her memory a little, but it wasn't until she was in the car with K.J., explaining what had happened, that the full chronology of it returned to her. She was, in effect, learning about her loss of consciousness right along with K.J.

She had put her dinner in the beep box and pressed *beep beep*. The beep box began its five-minute sigh, never eager to pick up a new gig, yet never happier than when it finished one. Then she'd started walking back over to the TV, probably to pull up some show or other she'd wanted to watch (best as she could recall – not that she'd made a study of the living room on her way out the door – the TV had been tuned to some streaming menu), when her vision had begun to close in on itself, her ears had begun to ring, her sight had telescoped and then *melted*, colors and shapes doubling and flattening and streaking as the ringing grew louder, louder, *LOUDER* and the lights expanded and slurped up the colorshapes and the aperture closed but what lay beyond it wasn't darkness it wasn't just black but nor was it color it was just *beyond* it was something she couldn't describe and then she knew she was going to throw up so she'd hustled for the bathroom but she hadn't made it well apparently she *had* made it and she hadn't thrown up so it was probably worth celebrating the little victories, no sense dwelling on the fact that she'd fallen flat on her face and split it open, and would probably have a scar right there on her chin for the rest of her life, so now every date she ever went on she'd know that the guy was wondering about the scar but wouldn't ask about it until right after they'd had sex or some other time when such questions were for some reason more acceptable, not that it was ever acceptable for a woman to have a scar on her face.

K.J. listened to all of this calmly (even the bit in which Jenmarie rather cavalierly kvetched over forthcoming dates with people who were not K.J.), radiating a focus and presence he'd never quite managed in more casual settings. She wondered which was his default, this or the stuporous daze, and which was a product of circumstance. Either way, bless his little heart, he didn't try to reassure her. He didn't offer platitudes. He just nodded, hands at ten and two, eyes on the road.

"Thank you," she told him, far more mawkishly than she'd meant to.

He smiled, but didn't take his eyes off the road. Which was to say, he was a good driver. The smile split into a grin (with a shiver, Jenmarie imagined the split in her chin becoming its own little grin, growing tiny little teeth) as K.J. replied, "you just better have something really wrong with you. I gave up a phenomenal parking space for this."

Jenmarie laughed, and so did her chin. "Ow!" she giggled.

"Ow's not enough. I'm talking super fucked up."

"Well, I'll probably need some stitches."

K.J. smiled through a grimace and shook his head. His pre-speech pauses had returned. "...not enough."

"I'll just ask them to replace the whole chin, shall I?"

Eyes still on the road, K.J. pursed his lips in mock-awe and drew his head back like a confused chicken. "*Shall* you?"

She giggled again, wincing as she did. "I think I'm getting a big head, having my own personal chauffeur."

"Well, maybe they can just replace the whole head."

"I wouldn't be opposed," Jenmarie replied, her chin smiling far more deeply than her mouth.

The laughs flagged ever so slightly during the *eight fucking hours* they were at the hospital. K.J. stayed almost the entire time, despite Jenmarie's repeated insistence that he go home and get some rest, she could get a Zyp or Lyft or some other orthographically dubious rideshare service to take her home. It was only the prod of an early shift at a construction gig (for K.J. was a working man, so he was) that finally sent him off at four in the morning, but in the intervening hours the two had a conversation as effortless and freewheeling as any Jenmarie had ever had. Things got off to a rocky start when she discovered that he was, like her, from the South (Kentucky instead of Tennessee, but near enough the border that that was a distinction without a difference), and *unlike* her, he was quite proud of his provenance. Why then, she asked him, did he speak with such a perfectly flat newscaster accent?

In an instant, K.J. vanished, and in his stead came KUY-JUY. Such was the depth and punch of his drawl (or *draw-all*). "Ain't never far from me," he chuckled, as much at the change in his voice as the concomitant change on Jenmarie's face. "I only fetch it for parties now."

"Is that why you pause before you speak, uh..."

K.J. chuckled. "Normally?"

"Yeah."

"Probably. I..." K.J. hung his head sheepishly. "I didn't think it was that noticeable."

"Why do you do it?" Jenmarie pressed. "If you like Kentucky so much?"

K.J. shrugged. "I guess it's like when somebody who isn't

white but looks it just pretends they're white because it's easier."

Jenmarie narrowed her eyes at this; it was a sensitive subject, particularly when broached by a clueless white guy. She was fairer of skin than any of her siblings; her brothers – both the living Tomjohn and the late Harmon – and one sister Melody were all nearer to their father's darker skin tone, while Jenmarie found herself on what she couldn't help but think of as the *wrong side* of her mother's lighter hue. No shame in looking like her, of course, but all the same…well, it was a sensitive subject. "You're comparing changing your accent to white passing?"

"Well, why not? Why do *you* hide your accent, then?" He darted his eyes to the far wall, then back. "It's all *code switching*, right?"

Jenmarie laughed. "Those are normal words!"

K.J. blinked. "What?"

"You're pronouncing them like they're a Harry Potter spell or something." She mimicked his enunciation: "*Co-duh swit-ching.*"

"Well didn't I use it right?"

"What podcast did you hear about code switching on? No way you didn't hear about it on a podcast."

K.J. grinned like he had an egg hidden in his mouth.

"You hear about it on a podcast?"

"Yeah. And you're gonna love this, the podcast's called *Code Switch.*"

Jenmarie got partway into a hearty guffaw, then winced and cupped her hand around her chin. "Ow, fuck."

K.J.'s smile didn't exactly vanish; it just did a poor job of covering his concern. "Hurts?"

"Why else would we be here?" she snapped. She sniffed and averted her eyes.

K.J. stared at her for a moment, his expression soft, then scratched his eyebrow and said "well, you didn't answer my question. Why the accent change?"

Ah, hell. *H-why else h-would h-we be here.* More than one reason to regret having said that, then. "Ah. Yeah. I just…I don't know. The south is backwards, man."

From there, they launched into a surprisingly spirited discussion about the relative virtues and not-so-virtues of the part of the country they had no choice but to call home. That spun into a broader political discussion, undertaken with all the throat-clearing timidity of two people who thought they probably had a lot in common as far as the Big Issues went, but were equally worried about discovering that perhaps they didn't. Lucky for Jenmarie, they turned out to be kindred spirits in more ways than their both having moved from south of the Mason-Dixon to New York City (and, of course, having compatible smells, according to an app. The world of tomorrow, indeed). Just as importantly, their disagreements were mercifully minor. K.J. was a bit more sympathetic to gun ownership than Jenmarie was (long story how that came up), that was the hairiest one, but they managed to have a civil enough back-and-forth about it, after which he wound up telling an anecdote about a summer job he had welding pipe at a mysterious military installation at an undisclosed location.

Jenmarie only noticed her mouth flopping open once her chin let her know. "Excuse me?" she tittered nervously.

"It was this big bunker under a mountain," he explained, in a twang that Jenmarie suspected K.J. preferred – in the same way that she *preferred* sweatpants but recognized their, ah, *presentational disutility* in most situations – with an expansive hand gesture to convey just how big, "where they put all the C4. Well, a lot of it anyway." His hands collapsed, one falling away into his lap, the other hovering in front of his face, first finger and thumb held apart like he was imagining squishing Jenmarie's head between them. "I got to see them detonate a blob about this big. They did it twice. Once it went down," he punched his hand towards the floor and made a loud *BOOSH* noise, "the other time it blew *up.*" He reversed and repeated the motion. "Up like upwards. It was the loudest damn thing I ever heard in my life."

"So you were welding pipes next to explosives?"

"Not right next to them. But sure as hell on top of 'em. Boy, that bunker was *deep!*"

Jenmarie smiled, despite the ever-increasing grief her chin was giving her. In the short time she'd spent with him, she knew K.J. to be an intelligent, thoughtful man. Yet the southern accent into which he kept slipping sounded so…well, *stupid.* She was ashamed to admit that it fundamentally, albeit temporarily, altered her perception of him. Just as surely, she knew that were he saying precisely the same things in a more "normal" – which was to say "Northern" – accent, she'd never have thought twice about him. The blue-collar content of the story wasn't the hang-up, but the delivery. What did that say about her?

K.J. continued, regaling her with a surprisingly gripping account of his daily commute to work; driving to his contractor's office, being picked up by a bus which ferried him to the undisclosed location (he still had no idea where the factory was, and had been sufficiently unnerved by the experience to not go looking for it), the bus being stopped outside one of the nearly half-dozen chainlink fences, the heavily armed guards who ran dogs around the bus and mirrors underneath, the one time a very-soon-to-be-ex-coworker had mistakenly forgotten to put his gun, for which he had a permit, in his truck before getting on the bus, and nobody had seen the guy after he'd been pulled off by the guards, not that K.J. thought he'd been sent to Guantanamo or anything, but, still, it was pretty fucking creepy. There were two intermissions in this story, one brief one in the person of a friendly nurse with earrings so big Jenmarie was rather shocked the woman was allowed to wear them on her rounds, the second, longer pause coming when a less-chipper nurse wheeled Jenmarie to the other end of the hospital for a CAT scan (her mounting headache and lingering nausea raised the specter of a concussion). As the machine spun and buzzed and hummed around her head, which Jenmarie couldn't help but hear as disapproving puzzlement over what it was seeing sloshing around her skull, she could only think of K.J. waiting patiently in her room (which was to say in the curtained-off section of the hallway in which they'd stuffed her, her wheely-bed, and all manner of machines that *beep beep beeped* but would never heat your mac and cheese), and how she hardly knew this guy, how he hardly knew her, yet how far out of his way he was going for her, how profoundly he was inconveniencing himself (it was already two in the morning by this point).

The machine wound itself down, the frowny-faced nurse wheeled Jenmarie back to K.J., and the story of the mysterious C4 factory resumed. It was fascinating to hear a first-hand account of someone who'd gone to work in the sort of off-the-grid, top-secret government facility that had become such an staple of airport paperbacks. But the mechanical banality of what actually occurred there somehow chilled Jenmarie far nearer the bone than tales of inexplicable noises from subbasement Z, or Stargate experiments gone awry. They were stockpiling war ordinances – K.J. couldn't even be sure if they were producing new C4 or just collecting up what had already been produced and tucking it away for not-so-safekeeping. Either way, there was a mountain in or around Kentucky that was full of plastic explosives, and somewhere within that mountain there were pipes that K.J. had welded for purposes unknown, and on one of those pipes he had scratched a picture of a blue Jay with its wings stretched out in a K shape, because he thought carving his own initials would have been too risky, but the ornithological, homonymic hieroglyph seemed a suitably cryptic substitute.

Regretfully for both of them (albeit after some nudging from Jenmarie), K.J. took his leave at four AM. Jenmarie thanked him profusely. He grinned, told her to "keep her chin up" (a dad joke at which she laughed hard enough for it to count as *enabling*), then placed a hand on her blanketed shin and squeezed gently.

"Hey," she said to him as he turned to leave, and that was all she had to say.

It was only after seeing three separate nurses and undergoing as many diagnostic procedures that her chin was finally stitched up. The worst part of the entire affair, worse even than waking up in a pool of her own blood (ok, *pool* was perhaps a bit dramatic, but waking up in any amount of one's own blood authorized more than a little license, she felt), was the process of numbing her face just prior to the stitchy bit. Nurse number four took a needle, poked it into the fleshy bottom of her jaw…and drove it deeper and deeper and deeper, to just about the hilt, until Jenmarie was certain she would feel it come out the other side and stick the bottom of her tongue. The pain was unspeakable (and not only because, with her jaw on a skewer and her hands white-knuckling fistfuls of blanket, language generation was rather emphatically off the table), and even after the numbing agent was injected and the needle removed, the Cronenberg-esque horror of being so deeply violated by a syringe lingered. Then deepened. Some more. And more. Then, at long last, she made good on her nausea and had a grand old upchuck. She clapped one hand over her mouth and gestured frantically to the nurse, a high-stakes round of charades this woman had very clearly played before; she was whipcrack-quick on the draw with a profoundly strange sort of long, slender barf bag. More a barf *sleeve,* really. Jenmarie filled it near to the top.

The second anaesthetizing needle and the insertion of the stitches were convenient excuses for not talking to the nurses, who were awfully fucking chatty given the time (and less receptive to Jenmarie's nonverbal cues than that last nurse, most of Jenmarie's current signals driving towards the concept of *shut up and go away, or if you won't shut up, then go* very far *away*). When the doctor came whirling into the room, Jenmarie was in no more of a conversational mood, even if this was just the woman she'd been waiting to see.

The proper whitecoat, a woman called Thirlby, had an effortless charisma that, likeable though it was, couldn't be anything but slightly annoying at such an unreasonable hour. Her bedside manner was impeccable: she had the presence of mind to recognize that the barrage of good news she had for Jenmarie was, in fact, kind of bad news. CAT scans came back normal, indicating perhaps a minor, *minor* concussion. Rest would take care of that. Blood work was great, a slight deficiency in Vitamin D, which basically everybody had and could be easily addressed with a once-daily over-the-counter supplement. EKG readings were aces, blood pressure was 120/80 (as always, Jenmarie had to ask if those were good numbers – thus far, the answer had always been 'yes'), all systems were go. There was, in other words, nothing wrong with her.

"Um," Jenmarie explained to the doctor.

Dr. Thirlby nodded knowingly. "Right, I know, that's not helpful. *Something* made you pass out."

"Yeah."

"Well," Dr. Thirlby continued as she lowered herself gently onto the side of Jenmarie's bed, which was a pretty damn presumptuous thing for anyone other than a parent to do (at their *own* child's bedside, critically). And yet, Dr. Thirlby met the mattress so effortlessly, with such authority, that Jenmarie felt safe under her aegis. Jenmarie hoped that one day *she* could be the sort of doctor who had an aegis to take patients under. She knew herself well enough to know she wasn't the aegis type, though.

"In terms of a proper diagnosis," Dr. Thirlby sighed, "I can't offer much. I will tell you, though, that it sounds to me as though you suffered a vasovagal syncope."

Jenmarie tried and sort-of-managed to repeat the words. "Sounds like something I'd hear from my gynecologist."

Dr. Thirlby smiled tolerantly, as though she'd heard that one a million times, and handed Jenmarie a thin packet of 8.5 x 11 pages secured by a staple that was a little too close to the top-left corner. "There's some information in here. A lot, actually, not phrased for ease of understanding. Basically, though, vasovagal syncope is about blood flow to your brain. Not enough, specifically. This is the first time you've had this problem, yes?"

"That's right."

Dr. Thirlby nodded. "Good. If it keeps happening, and I mean on a pretty regular basis, you should see a cardiologist. Otherwise, though, the most likely trigger for this kind of episode is stress. Have you been under a lot of stress lately?"

"I'm, uh…" Jenmarie nearly succumbed to the good doctor's confessional air, nearly unburdened herself fully, from the top, about Eddie and K.J. and her fellowship that she was hardly able to focus on and her not even wanting to be in this fucking shithole city anymore (but she had to finish that fucking unfocusable fellowship, not to mention all the fucking divorce paperwork) and the cold macaroni and cheese in her microwave and the missing chunk of tooth in her mouth and the bugbite on her right elbow and how her eyes got dry this time of year and all of it. Fortunately for her, she realized in advance that she simply didn't have the energy for that right now. So she shrugged and answered in the affirmative.

"Then I might simplify things and tell you, Ms. Bell, that you've probably just had a panic attack. Basically."

Jenmarie started crying a little bit. Not a lot, nothing weepy or dramatic. Just some little droplets in the corners of the eyes. The doctor must have assumed this was, what, a reaction to being told she'd had a panic attack? No. To have a label for what had happened to her was a relief.

What had prompted the tears was hearing herself referred to, for the first time since the divorce had gotten underway, as *Miss* Bell. She'd somehow made it months without the formal address. And the tears, well, they weren't of an entirely unpleasant sort. It was with a divided mind that she thought about how this was not a consequence of the divorce that Eddie would, or could, experience.

B
R
E
A
T
H
E

Turns out, everybody on the fucking planet was an expert on anxiety and depression.

Oh, yes, it was anxiety *and* depression. Jenmarie went to her GP, who recommended she see a psychologist…at least, Jenmarie *thought* she'd said psychologist, only to discover that in point of fact the GP had recommended she see a *psychiatrist*, the difference between a psychologist and a psychiatrist being of no concern to Jenmarie until her psychologist made clear that based on what Jenmarie was looking for she really ought to see a psychiatrist, which she finally did, on, as it happened, the day she got her stitches out. The psychiatrist then referred her to a therapist, whose name was Arlene, a name that Jenmarie took to be an appropriate name for a therapist. Arlene worked on the sliding scale, which suited Jenmarie down to the ground, as visits to a mental health professional weren't covered by her insurance. Hospital visits due to falls caused by her mental health issues *were*, of course, which probably said something about Big Insurance or something, whatever, she should probably have cared more about it, but post-residency she rarely interfaced directly with the insurance apparatus, and the ACA had caused her enough head-aches to last a lifetime, so now she was just happy to be sitting on the side of the curtain where the sausage *wasn't* made.

Better still, of course, was forgoing the curtain entirely. Which was to say, Jenmarie wasn't going to therapy. Been there, done that. Even if none of her previous therapists had been called Arlene, which was an appropriate name.

She was firm in that decision for all of a week and a half, until her next call with Tomjohn, during which he told her "you have to go to therapy."

"Why?" Jenmarie fired back. "I already talk about my prob-lems. With you."

The Tomjohn-shaped pixels on her screen took a pull of pils-ner and nodded. "Yeah, that's why you have to go. I'm not gonna be your fucking therapist. Unless you want to pay me. Do you wanna pay me?"

"Jesus, you're punchy tonight."

"I'm making a point."

"You're being a punchy dumbass."

Tomjohn gestured between himself and his laptop camera. "This is what I'm trying to preserve. This love we have for each other."

"I don't have any love for you, Tomjohn."

Jenmarie had meant that as a joke, and in the end, Tomjohn played it off as one. But there was an instant between the meaning and the playing, just a blink, when she could see that her words had perhaps landed incorrectly. It certainly occurred to her to apologize, but by then her brother had played the comment off. At which point, it seemed worse to circle back. Nothing good could come of that. Leave it to the past. Yes, that was best.

"And I'm hoping to keep it that way," Tomjohn replied.

That incident was one of the many, many things Jenmarie neglected to mention to Arlene when she went to see her. Because, yes, Jenmarie went to see her. She went back to therapy. For the meds. Her psychiatrist was loath to prescribe them unless Jenmarie was seeing a therapist. Which seemed pretty dang invasive, but what're ya gonna do, right? See a therapist. Right.

Arlene wrote something in her little booklet.

"What was the question?" Jenmarie asked.

"Um," Arlene the trained therapist hemmed, "I asked about your parents."

"Right. Seems like a pretty weedy subject for the first session, doesn't it?"

"Oh. I was just asking if they were, uh, still alive."

"Right. They are."

"Is anyone in your immediate family passed?"

"My older brother was killed by a drunk driver."

Arlene considered this new fact. "Hm. That doesn't seem useful." She cleared her throat and shuffled papers that had been minding their own business on the table next to her.

"Funny you should say that," Jenmarie drawled, "that was the consensus amongst my family as well." She couldn't help but notice Arlene didn't have any diplomas mounted on her wall.

Arlene was short. Probably not short enough to qualify as a dwarf, but certainly short enough that there were rides at the carnival she wouldn't be allowed on. Her legs dangled off the side of her big leather chair, and when Arlene felt she was on the scent of some particularly potent trauma truffle she had a habit of kicking them up and down ever-so-slightly. Over the weeks and then months of their sessions together, Jenmarie would develop a Pavlovian response to these tootsie tremors, a glass of water rumbling at the approach of a Tyrannosaurus-sized personal revelation. Unnervingly adolescent though Arlene could seem at first glance, and untried a psychonaut though she was (the only recently-certified Arlene participated in the aforementioned sliding fee scale largely to build up a client list), she was quite good at confronting Jenmarie with observations the latter would deny vociferously, and then the following week recognize had actually been, on the whole, fair points. Curiously enough, these were rarely hard truths about her psyche, *a la* 'you didn't hold the door for the guy at Panera because want to fuck your father and kill your mother, with any luck at the same time', none of the Freudian flimflam. They were more often challenges to her conception of her own past. Had Eddie taken her for granted? Had he not actually been as good a partner as she'd thought, as she'd built him up to be? Had her depression, which was no less real for having gone undiagnosed, driven her to erect a scaffolding of happiness on Eddie's back, knowing that she hadn't the wherewithal to support it herself in this city? Each of these, she conceded the week after being confronted with them, were fair points, and if not entirely accurate, they were at least instructive approximations of a truth. What disappointed her, as she racked up the sessions, was that none of these realizations landed with the force of a true-blue eureka. She thought the therapy was making her feel a little bit better, but it wasn't quite *changing her life* the way TV had led her to believe it would. This, after a time, led to a sort of emotional backslide. Denied any grand leaps into enlightenment, Jenmarie grew restive, and then downright depressed, by the weekly elucidation of her unhappiness. She became frustrated by Arlene's single-minded fixation upon her familial history; Jenmarie felt pretty goddamned clear on where and how she'd been fucked up by that particular passage of her life. The areas she wanted help parsing began with the Eddie years and stretched through to now, into the K.J. rebound (which, even months after the visit to the ER, had yet to feel like anything *but* a rebound). This wasn't how therapy worked, Arlene would gently explain whenever Jenmarie voiced her frustrations. Then her legs would start bouncing again, and Jenmarie would buckle up.

Of course, what would a relationship with a therapist be without the meds? Arlene (and, more to the point, the psychiatrist hookup) tried Jenmarie on a whole battery over the course of several months, which in hindsight Jenmarie would be almost *positive* was far too short a period of time to be learning anything useful about her reactions to these drugs, and that was putting the health considerations firmly to the side. At any rate, the next few months were an unending bellyflop into brain chemistry, mostly via SSRIs (citalopram and paroxetine and escitalopram) with a few SNRIs thrown in (venlaxafine and duloxetine), until finally, *finally* they found a pill that *didn't* reduce her to a pile of side effects in a skin suit. It was an SSRI called Sertraline, and a hundred milligrams a day evened her out pretty well. The only side effect was, admittedly, a doozy – she found it nearly impossible to get to sleep. A secondary prescription of trazodone (seventy-five milligrams) took care of that, and further tilted her mood towards, if not quite into, equilibrium. Lenny, the friend and fellow who had taken Jenmarie in back when she'd thought the problem with her marriage was as simple as 'space,' made some disapproving noises about Jenmarie's taking antidepression medication, which nearly earned him a pop on the nose. "Would you say that to a diabetic about *their* medication?" Jenmarie asked more acidly than she'd wanted to. Lenny shrugged that off, but Jenmarie's frustration lingered. It was, ultimately, frustration at herself as much as Lenny, frustration at her own perceived weakness. This was a point she was self-aware enough to recognize and communicate to Arlene herself, as opposed to waiting for the squat little brainiac to pull it out of her. "I just hate that I'm dependent on these pills now," Jenmarie confessed. "It's such a vulnerable feeling. I accidentally ran out of Sertraline a week back, and my face went *numb* after, like, two hours. It was crazy. I mean, I bet it was psychosomatic as much as anything, but I've just got withdrawal hanging over my head now." At this, Arlene's legs starting bouncing, and Jenmarie quickly realized that the legs were bouncing for *her* point, rather than one Arlene wanted to make. Jenmarie felt inordinately proud of herself for that.

Lenny, of course, was just the vanguard in what would become a Shermanesque march of unsolicited advice. Everybody, as mentioned, was an expert on these sorts of things, because to most people being depressed was just being sad but, you know, *big time*. "Cheer up," that was the number one piece of advice. Other hits included: Listen to happy music! Listen to sad music! Don't dwell on it! Don't run away from it! Take a vacation! Confront your ex! Fire your therapist! Do a wilderness retreat! Go vegan! Take this health supplement! Visit a reiki healer! Try acupuncture! Pray about it! Start a blog! Start a journal! Stop eating gluten! Learn an instrument! The advice rushed over Jenmarie as a flood that wouldn't be satisfied until it had drowned her, and failing that then by god it would see her dashed upon the rocks. In this crashing din, the voices that spoke from experience were vanishingly few, and those few she heard were so quiet as to be inaudible. Those who had actually been touched by the noonday demon, be it their own struggle or that of a loved one, these people had far less frantic suggestions: Identify your anxiety triggers. Recognize your strengths and limitations with the same clarity. Don't stop taking your medication, even if you feel like you can. Call me, if you need to talk, about anything at all.

This last offer came from exactly three people in Jenmarie's life: best friend Mavis, brother Tomjohn, and...K.J. Hanifan. The night after she received the text containing said offer from the latter, Jenmarie had her second panic attack, this time recognizing it as it began, which gave her the opportunity to say "oh goddamnit" and lower herself to the ground before her consciousness fled her. This was a sub-optimal solution, being smack in the center of a Barnes & Noble when it happened, but it was certainly preferable to tilting forward and splitting her face open on the buy-two-get-one paperback table.

The reason for the attack was as immediately apparent as the trigger: she knew, in that moment, that she would never be able to see K.J. as anything other than a rebound. This wasn't strictly a function of their relationship's timing – there remained some Eddie-shaped baggage of which Jenmarie had yet to divest herself. It felt unlikely she would ever be able to, but the only halfway decent chance she had of doing so required a more even keel than a new romance could afford.

"It's just a question of *when* I'm going to hurt him," she recalled monologuing to her brother on another one of their bare-knuckle, definitely-not-therapy calls the night prior, the words coming back to her even as she took the final few inches to the floor of the Barnes and Noble in a limp fish flop. "I have to end it."

"Your problem's not K.J.," Tomjohn had suggested with a

sigh.

"I know."

"Your problem is you're not over Eddie yet."

"Yeah, I fucking know that, Tomjohn."

"Okay, but, do you? Because y-"

"*Yes. I do.*"

"Then why dump K.J.?"

"I don't…" Jenmarie had sighed. "I just don't feel like there's a future in…I don't know. It just doesn't feel right. I'm just not in a place to give him what he needs."

"Ew."

"*Emotionally.*"

"I know what you meant. It's gross that you're making this a martyr thing. That's what the *ew* was."

"I'm being objective right now."

"If you wanna break up with him, break up with him. But don't pretend it's heroic. *Especially* don't say that to him."

The way her brother's voice had quivered then led Jenmarie to suspect he'd been speaking from some kind of experience. So, knowing him as she did (and being eager to change the subject as she had been), she said "I didn't realize you'd been going out with anybody." And then they were talking about his problems, which Jenmarie was *more* than happy to do.

That had been then. This was now. Nothing had changed in the interim. Which was the problem.

She had to end things with K.J. She had to be the one to do it. She had to *do it*. Which she did, right after she picked herself up off the floor of the Barnes & Noble, and made a quick stop to the self-help section to buy a few books with titles like *The Boost: What Science Tells Us 17 Ways How To Confidence Brains And Better*, the purchase of which ultimately diminished her confidence.

Too bad, because K.J. really didn't make the ending of things easy. It was abundantly clear that he really *really* liked her – clear from the way he lit up each time he saw her, clear from the way he texted her goofy shit throughout the day just to make her laugh, and clearest of all from his endless sensitivity to her raw posttherapy moods. Yes, K.J. was clearly the stuff of which committed partners were made; he had done even more research into each and every prescription she had cycled through than she herself had (sometimes, Jenmarie wondered if K.J.'s Google-gained knowledgability on each drug didn't outstrip even Arlene's). Which, given how fresh their ill-fated relationship was, ultimately worried Jenmarie. She wondered how K.J. could possibly see her as anything more than the chemical compounds she ingested – he'd hardly known her without them, had he? This wasn't to say he was a doormat of a man; he would from time to time challenge her on the topic – even as he proved so supportive and *there* in so many other ways – which only served to underline just how much he cared about her, how much he respected her. Reflecting on this did little to dim her enthusiasm for him, little to make the ripping of the Band-Aid any easier. So she tried not to reflect on it. Guess how well that went.

Okay, here was an irksome little assertion that certainly hardened the heart: "You went right to medication," K.J. had mewled on multiple occasions, "but you never tried medi*ta*tion." Jenmarie would invariably roll her eyes at this, scarcely able to imagine how pleased with himself K.J. must have been when he'd figured that one out. She would shrug and inform him that she felt good, and that was what mattered. To that, K.J. couldn't reasonably object, though Jenmarie suspected he fostered reservations that would remain unspoken.

Jenmarie *did* feel good, all things considered. Certainly better than she had since the divorce. Which had finally concluded, acrimoniously delivering Jenmarie to more or less where she would have been, financially speaking, had she never been snared by matrimony to begin with. More to the point, she'd gotten her books and that honestly-silver floor lamp with the little task arm out of the deal. All of which were standing unused in the corner of the studio apartment she'd moved into. A lonely, dusty studio apartment down in Prospect-Lefferts, from which she would complete her goddamned fellowship, which was slowly but surely sucking the life from her, keeping her lonely, keeping her apartment dusty…

Ok, so maybe Jenmarie didn't feel *great*. Except for when K.J. made her feel good. Which made it impossible for her to call it quits with him. Why mess a good thing? If her personal life was still confusing, albeit in a different way than before (and this time the mess was, by and large, one of her own making), and if her professional life was as draining and chaotic as it had ever been, she felt she had developed a firmer foundation from which to address these challenges. She could self-advocate herself to such a mindset, in her more bullish moods. Which were fewer and further between than was once the case; the medication probably cut some of the affective highs from her life, she conceded this. It was true that, since starting them, she had yet to achieve any buzzing euphoria of the sort she'd once been capable. Even dancing, in those rare instances when she forced herself back out onto one of the city's many floors, had lost its jubilance, coming to feel instead like retracing her steps in an effort to remember where she'd left her keys, when she was already running late, so late. But this was a cost to be entered into a more complicated calculation, because the meds lifted her emotional floor up out of the crisis zone, in which ideation made its own plans. Those leaps into the giddy vaults had been inertial, she was sure, made possible by the running start they could get from what she only now recognized to have been benthic valleys in her mood. So if the cost of saving herself from the depths was to limit herself to dancing *amongst* the clouds, as opposed to *above* them…that was a price well worth paying.

It wasn't as simple as that, of course. But, as with all of her greatest revelations, Jenmarie wouldn't realize this until it was too late for the knowledge to be useful. That was just the rut in which she was forever twisting her metaphysical ankle. Three guesses as to when she would realize *that*.

So instead of dumping K.J., Jenmarie pulled him closer by taking him up on his calls to meditate…with him as her guide, naturally. Sure, there were plenty of apps out there, but, uh, well, yeah. There were plenty of apps out there. But she was going to meditate with K.J. Deal with it, better judgment!

Upon further consideration, it was surely her hesitance to give meditation a real shot, a hesitance she couldn't really account for (though perhaps it had something to do with its most passionate adherents positioning it as mutually exclusive to medication; maybe the syllabic switcheroo didn't sound as cool if it were phrased in a more open-ended way), that made it actually quite a wise and good idea to keep K.J. around. Accountability, if nothing else. He'd keep her coming back to *the cushion,* as meditators were apparently so fond of saying. Or, indeed, he would get her onto *the cushion* for the first time, which was turning out to be a bigger ask than she'd expected. Why the reticence, she wondered? What could a few minutes on *the cushion* (in her case, the removable seat pillow of a chair from her kitchen table, the chairs at the table being the only proper seating in the whole apartment) hurt, after all? Best as she could tell, it was just napping with better posture. She loved naps. Either it would be boring, and she'd stop, or she'd fall asleep. Or, she tacked on as an afterthought, it might work. Whatever that meant.

So, making clear to him that she was still taking her medications, and if he had a problem with that she had a dose of medicine for *him* that all the sugar spoonfuls in the world couldn't help down, Jenmarie asked K.J. what, precisely, was the deal with meditation. His answer was mercifully devoid of any spiritual claptrap or mystical mummery. It was, in fact, a single word preceded by a patented pause: …mindfulness. Being aware, there were two more words with nary a hesitation. Aware of *what*, Jenmarie wondered, which was three words. *Everything*, K.J. replied, in another single word. That's *way too much*, Jenmarie insisted, to which K.J. agreed, explaining that this was why it was so common to begin focusing on the breathing, or on some other regular, automatic stimulus that required no thought in and of itself. Jenmarie had lost count of the words at this point.

K.J. sat her down and guided her through her first-ever meditation session, from which she learned exactly three things. Thing one: this was a lot fucking harder than it looked. The goal, he continued to insist, was not to clear the mind but to focus upon, and rest in, its own boundless expanse. When a new thought wanders in, you don't try to shoot it down with mental anti-aircraft ordinance. You simply recognize it for what it is until it inevitably unravels, and then rest in/as the space in which it had appeared. Which still seemed *terrifically* esoteric to Jenmarie's ears, so K.J. offered a simpler object of focus: the breath.

Jenmarie, an asthmatic in her youth who had somehow just sort of outgrown it after escaping the sinister, pollen-spewing south, had no especial affinity for her breath. It was something she tolerated because it was necessary. Focusing on it only accentuated its ragged edges, the pretensions to depth that escaped its capacity. Her breath, in short, was dumb and stupid. Also lame and weak. It was to the mental thesaurus that her attention seemed determined to wander during this first meditation, mindful that there should be no repetition in the ten-minute roast of her respiration. Doltish and embarrassing. Clumsy and unworthy. Say, that last one was almost self-aggrandizing, in a weird way! Progress of a kind, that!

Lesson the second: For brief, very brief, the briefest of brief moments, so brief she hadn't even time to consult the well-thumbed thesaurus of her thoughts…in those briefy brief briefs, she found herself of the be-rief that this was working. There would be snatches of stillness – not enlightenment, no grand explosions of self-knowledge, just the silence in which something like that might be nurtured into being. The resultant thrill would invariably knock her off-balance, allowing the usual mayhem that was the inside of her head to clobber her on its dash back to the cockpit. These glimpses of something quieter, something almost diametrically opposed to the world as she had known it over the past few years, both inside and outside her head, prompted one of the quickest about-faces of her life; before her first session was…maybe halfway done…how long had she been doing this? Anyway, eyes still shut, mind still doing its best to put the breath in a half nelson, Jenmarie realized that she really wanted to give this mindfulness racket a shot. Throw herself at it bodily, or whatever the appropriately dignified, yogic phrasing would be. She only recognized the earnestness of this thought by the fact that her spending more time with K.J. in pursuit of that awakening proved a secondary consideration.

This, unfortunately, led directly to her third revelation, and in the grand tradition of history's top ten revelations, this one was all the more forceful for being tendered without the least shred of evidence: down this path lay a platonic relationship with K.J. She didn't know how she knew it, she had no reason to even suspect it, yet she found herself incapable of imagining a scenario in which she stitched K.J. into her mental health self-care toolbelt, and simultaneously retained him as a romantic partner. Which was...good, right? It was what she wanted. Right? To lose him as a romantic entanglement but keep him as a friend struck her as being the best of all possible conclusions to the K.J. coupling dilemma. But all the same, Jenmarie was mortified by the prospect. Why?

Say...these were all thoughts. She'd gotten swept up in her thoughts.

Son of a bitch, meditation really *did* work, didn't it? Just not in the way she'd hoped. All of these epiphanies made it quite difficult to focus on her breath. Her screwball and dipshit breath.

Jenmarie cracked an eye open and whispered "how long have I been meditating?" out the side of her mouth.

K.J. interrupted his own instruction, all the while maintaining that low, deep vocal affectation he'd led the session with, the one that sounded like Michael Barbaro trying to convince a bank robber to *drop...the gun.* "If you feel your mind wandering, simply bring it b-"

"K.J."

"About four minutes."

Jenmarie opened her eyes. "Seriously?"

K.J. sighed, in a way that didn't sound as though he was focusing on that particular breath all that closely. "Seriously as in you thought it would have been more or less time?"

"Ah..." she took as deep a breath as her cowardly, churlish

lungs would allow. "Plead the fifth. Though I really am enjoying this."

"Enjoyment…is just another emotional state. Notice that."

"Fuck yourself."

K.J. smiled and closed his eyes. "Let's return to the breath, shall we?" He took a deep breath in through his nose, on which he was presumably quite focused. His concentration flagged noticeably when Jenmarie lunged forward and planted her lips on his. He opened his eyes for that; it was anybody's guess as to who looked more surprised.

There followed a great deal of husky breathing, though precious little focus was placed upon it.

V
I
N
E

Video calls were a bad invention. Jenmarie had never been a fan of them, and now, confronted with Mavis' drawn, disapproving face splattered across the screen of her MacBook, she found them to be nothing less than a technological step backwards into the dark ages. What was the line from *Jurassic Park?* Something something see if they can, never stopped to ask if they *should*. Something. Oh, great, now she was thinking about the glass of water just before the T-rex arrived, which sent her mind straight back to Arlene. Oh, how that lady's little legs would get to pumping when Jenmarie told her about *this* mess! If only she could get her therapist on one of those pedal-powered generators, she'd cut her energy bill in half.

With the newfound sense of self-possession granted her by

one two count 'em *three* yoga sessions, and twice as many post-*yes I absolutely must break up with K.J.* lovemaking sessions with a very much not-broken-up-with K.J., she…wait, go back. *Meditation*, she'd done three *meditation* sessions, not yoga, though the lovemaking certainly had involved deep stretching and adventurous spinal contortions. Anyway, Jenmarie was really smart at brain thinky focusizing now, and it was with these newfound powers that she recognized the wandering of her mind from the point at hand. Which was actually a face. Mavis' face. Not a happy face, at this moment. Never one to mince words, Mavis was in the middle of reminding Jenmarie of her recent panic attacks, and suggesting that maybe thrusting herself deeper into the stressful situation of a confusing relationship might have triggered them, and so gifted her the scar on her chin that was still red and tender. Maybe, Mavis further suggested, that wasn't a great strategy for long-term happiness. Jenmarie considered saying that, *au contraire mon frère*, it was the stressful situation that had thrust himself deeper into *her*, but at the last second decided that actually she *would* say that, and so did. Mavis did chuckle at it, but quickly regained her scowl and reminded Jenmarie that *frère* meant *brother*.

"So what's sister?"

"*Sœur*."

"*Au contraire mon sœur* doesn't sound as good."

"Don't try to change the subject."

"I'm not. What were we talking about? Literally *anything* other than my personal life, right?"

Not so much. After a great deal of prodding, Mavis finally convinced Jenmarie to take some kind of a step towards clarity, even if it was just asking K.J. if they could take a *break*, but not break *up*. Jenmarie chuckled at the concept, as she might have at a child discussing Santa's favorite kind of cookie, when she herself had only just discovered the truth about Mr. Kringle.

Goddamnitall, why had she done this to herself? Why hadn't she just savored her newfound (well, newconsigned was probably more apt) singlehood? Why had she rushed right into a rebound – rebounding back to the rebound, really – and why did it disturb her so much that said rebound made her happy?

Arlene had quite a few things to say about that, and Jenmarie couldn't well dispute any of them. She *was* falling in to old patterns, failing to trust in her own ability to hold herself up, and so using others as crutches. Her codependency (a character flaw Arlene attributed to her far more offhandedly than a more experienced therapist probably would have, Jenmarie grumbled to herself) was a byproduct of a deficiency in self-confidence. Which wasn't exactly a confidence booster, she pointed out to Arlene, who simply bounced her legs and smiled, perhaps thinking this a joke, more likely knowing that it was anything but. Jenmarie, for her part, knew that Arlene was right. Self-confidence had always been just out of reach for her. What self-possession she did, well, possess, was self-consciously adopted. She'd watched TED talks on how confident people stood, sat, spoke, and stepped. They were all performances, refusals to humor her natural impulses towards making herself small. Perhaps this was why she'd taken such an immediate shine to meditation, then: it promised a respite from the self, however brief. Yes, detachment from one's own identity was a hallmark of all confident people, she decided. Self-confidence could only be achieved by not truly knowing oneself; how else to ignore one's manifold faults? This was a satisfying explanation to one lacking in the quality being explained.

Events in rapid succession: Jenmarie made the self-conscious decision to improve her self-confidence by presenting herself as more self-possessed. Then she meditated to try to flush all of the *self* out of hers-…uh, her. Then she went to sleep. Then she had a dream about a mighty ash tree atop a soft, sloping rise, its verdure reaching up and out and up and out, boughs creaking as they grew faster and faster, now this was a tree who had seen the TED talk on power poses, this sucker's policy was shoot first, ash questions later. Wanting for any sense of scale (the field, flat save its gentle roll, vanished over the horizon in all directions), it was impossible to suss out the size of the ever-expanding timber – until one pressed in for a closer look. The leaves gave it away, as did the scaling of the bark. The tree was too big. No tree should reach such a size as this. It was impossible to take in, crane your neck all you like, even in a dream the human eye, the *mind's* eye, was incapable of beholding the entire topiary at once. Up beyond the clouds, over to chase the knolls off the far side of the earth, the tree grew and consumed and yet hungered even still. So whence the vine? It was impossible to say much beyond what was seen: with that herky-jerky rapidity unique to only the oldest sorts of footage (those old-timey handcrank cameras, back when no cinema was complete without a live pianist) and some of the newest (timelapse photography), a vine as thick as a four-door sedan slithered up from the ever-turning folds of soil churning in the tree's seeking roots, snaking its way up around up around up up up around the ash's trunk, snapping out tendrils to ensnare each branch, then tightening squeezing crushing, its deathgrip on the tree splitting the bark, sucking color from the foliage, pulping whatever dreadful heart it may once have had. The vine had no heart no hunger, the vine was yellow and the tree was brown and the vine was green and the tree was grey and the earth was black and the sky was hidden behind the leaves of the tree which were grey because the vine was green and its heart simply wasn't and the vine simply was and was and was until the tree was no more. Yet still it stood. The tree did not fall because the vine was strong, the vine would not let it. Fall. The tree had given the vine life, and now gave it shape. The vine no longer needed the tree, yet it could not dispense with it, so tightly had it wound itself to the ash's form. Over the years the tree rotted, peeling into ribbons, crumbling into dust, carried off by a breeze that brought ill tidings from colder places, places that had once been like this one, had once been but were no longer, not for long, not at all. The tree rotted and the vine was, the winds came and snapped the dry leaves from the branches and the vine was, the rains came and stripped the bark from the trunk and the vine was, the storms came and smote the tree from on high and the vine was, the fire swept down and swallowed what remained and the vine was, the winds returned to finish what they'd started and the vine was, the ashes from the tree blew across the black of the field and so fertilized it, that another ash might one day take root, fodder for the vine, or perhaps not, it hardy mattered because the leaves were gone but the sky was still grey and the field was still black and the vine was, would be.

Jenmarie awoke and immediately resented herself for having such an obviously SYMBOLIC dream, so much so that she very nearly refrained from communicating it to Arlene, and so giving her subconscious the satisfaction and attention for which it was, frankly, too thirsty. But she ultimately caved, recounting the atypically vivid dream about the tree and the vine, concluding by demanding Arlene explain to her which she was, and why.

"Which what?" Arlene asked in her I-already-know-the-answer voice.

"Am I the tree," Jenmarie explained in her actually-you-do-

not-know-the-answer-because-I-am-really-unique-and-complic-
ated voice that she would, as always, come to regret having used
by the following week, "or the vine? I figure I'm one and my
depression is the other, right? Or my co-dependency? Or something?"

"Couldn't you also be the field?"

"..."

"Or the sky?"

"..."

"How do you feel about my proposing those alternatives? Are
you feeling defensive?"

"Yes."

"Why?"

"I don't know."

So Arlene was a bust, then. Jenmarie tried the dream out on
Mavis, who somehow managed to supply an even less satisfactory answer than Arlene. "Isn't an ash tree, like, mythologically
important?"

"Norse mythology," Jenmarie informed her, having once dated a guy who was really into Norse mythology, which was to say
he'd been trying out affectations, one of the *Thor* movies had just
come out, and so he'd bought a book called *Norse Myths* in the
hope it might serve as an adequate substitute for a personality. It
hadn't. "Yggdrasil was an ash tree."

"You what?"

"Yggdrasil."

"Sounds like one of those pills your doctor had you taking."

Jenmarie laughed and adopted a soft, soothing commercial
voice. *"Yggdrasil should not be taken if you are, or may become, pregnant."*

Mavis got very very quiet. The kind of quiet that, to a very
dear friend, couldn't shut up. The kind of quiet that told Jenmarie

that Mavis was pregnant, and therefore was about to be a far less accessible shoulder to cry on. As she worked all of this out, Jenmarie herself fell silent, and her silence communicated to Mavis just how much Jenmarie had intuited. And despite all of these realizations having gone unspoken, despite the enigma code being crackable only between near and dear friends, Jenmarie fully accepted that somehow, the NSA had probably listened in and worked all of that out too, because the internet and websites. This thought made her smile, which helped her pretend she was more happy about the pregnancy than she was terrified of losing Mavis. "I didn't realize you were trying."

"I wasn't," Mavis chuckled. "It just sort of happened. I'd love for you to be the little shit's godmother."

"Little shit, huh?"

"It's kicking like you wouldn't believe. I don't know how, it's not even supposed to have feet yet!"

As they talked about Mavis' baby, how her husband Stephen had reacted upon being told ("he literally *jumped* for joy," Mavis laughed, which prompted Jenmarie to once more dredge up the memory of sneering "you don't understand, you're not married" to Mavis not so long ago, oh how the tables had turned), names they'd batted around, how they'd decided they wouldn't learn the gender ahead of time, how they were doing their best not to code their child's room, and so on, Jenmarie focused on her breathing, even as her best friend spoke. Tried to obliterate the self for just a moment. Because, she had no choice but to admit, it somewhat mortified her that she hadn't known any of this about Mavis. She'd really only been using their video calls to talk about herself lately, about her own problems, about her own depression. She'd not left a great deal of room for Mavis to return fire. It took effort to not let justifications pile up in her brain like Stooges in a doorway. *I'm just going through a lot right now and Mavis is in a pretty steady relationship which granted a baby will probably change that but I didn't know about the baby and anyway she probably didn't either because it takes time to learn about the baby and well she's just so steady happy easy with Stephen and I'm suffering from a lot of depression like a lot which she isn't at least I don't think so I'm not sure but she'd probably have told me if she were right she'd definitely have told me absolutely without a doubt so therefore she's not and I'm in like a rebound kind of thing it's not so easy to be pulled in all different directions like I have to make a big decision about what I'm going to do and I need a lot of help what has Mavis had to decide other than having a baby well I don't know but...* shit. This was exactly what she'd done, what she'd *been* doing. Using her low mood to justify her poor behavior. And vice versa.

Jenmarie bundled all of those thoughts up into a ball and smushed them into the back of a mental drawer. She focused on her breath, she listened to Mavis, and was a good friend, as she hadn't been for a period of time she was gonna go ahead and not try too hard to get clear on. When they were done with the call, she could think about how all of the steps towards psychological stability, talk and meds and *ohm*, they were necessary but not sufficient. She could think about how many ostensible changes she'd made, and how little she'd internalized the lessons or advantages those changes ought to have imparted, and how she'd failed to change her behavior accordingly. She could consider how passively she'd let her treatments wash over her, going limp in the riptide and expecting to be swept towards some kind of greater peace or happiness. She could, and also would, have a panic attack that night, fortunately while lying flat in bed already, and that would *really* get her thinking about how much of this stress was something that was happening to her, and how much she could reasonably say she was doing to herself.

That was later, though. For now, she was a friend to Mavis, which was quite literally the least she could do.

S
T
E
P
S

Something more she could do: finally, at long last, take Mavis' (and Tomjohn's, and Arlene's, and everyone's) advice, perhaps the last such morsel of wisdom her preparturient pal would be imparting for quite some time.

There was no easy or graceful way for Jenmarie to break things off with K.J. Er, perhaps it might have been more accurate to say there was no easy *and* graceful way. Grace was hard won, and Jenmarie was tired. So she asked K.J. to meet her at a coffee shop on Seventh and Fifteenth, treated herself to a latte with *two* sweeteners, and settled in to a window seat, her back facing the street. She didn't want any sunlight reflecting off the mostly-glass buildings opposite the coffee shop and blasting into her eyes. If anybody was going to be squinting during this breakup, by golly it wasn't going to be her.

"I'm really sorry," she told K.J.'s squinting face after it had arrived and gotten a coffee, and then again (and again) as that face went soggy and pressed an increasingly desperate suit. She hardened her heart to his pain, because this was the easiest way. Her apologies, at least, were sincere, their meanings manifold.

Jenmarie let K.J. see himself out, remaining in her seat to read her book. Her eyes slipped down the page without ever finding purchase; this wasn't the book's fault. She couldn't keep her heart from leading her on a breakneck sprint across the entire emotional landscape: the relief, the indescribable *release* of being freed from the millstone of relationship drama (and this time in a manner of her own choosing)! The terror of wondering whether or not this was the right decision, if she hadn't just punted a man with whom she could have been truly happy, simply because that relationship had sprouted in the shadow, nay the *ruins,* of another! The freedom of knowing that her time was now entirely her own! Well, except for her job, and her other friends, and all that! The rest of it though, she could fill with whatever she wanted! Like, uh…well, at least until Mavis had her kid, she could talk to her! And…maybe she could call up some other college pals she hadn't spoken to in a while? Those were still just friends though. She had to fill her time with *her* things, like…hobbies. She would have hobbies and she would use them to fill her time! There. It was settled.

Unable to focus on her book (what else was new), Jenmarie decided to meditate. The café was far too loud for her to fixate on her breathing, so she went home, where her breathing was too loud for her to relax. And besides, the whole enterprise just reminded her of K.J. How unfair, that an ex (which was what he was now, an ex, which presumably meant he'd been a boyfriend before he was an ex, wow, she'd had a boyfriend, what a relief to not know until after the fact, huh, wow!) should monopolize the sensation of equanimity. A bit of googling revealed that there was another way: a walking meditation. Instead of focusing on one's breath, one's regular, automatic footfalls served as the object of focus. The tactile nature of this stimulus appealed to Jenmarie; it was a more full-body experience than mere, dumbass respiration.

In time, this became perhaps her first proper hobby, wandering around just her neighborhood of Prospect-Lefferts to begin with, attention turned inward upon the left right left right left right of her steps, which had the pleasant consequence of freeing up her mind to take in far more of the city than she had before. The absolute ass of Brooklyn wasn't the most exciting place to stroll, however, so she took to using NYU Langone up in Midtown as her point of origin; when Jenmarie had a break from her work, she'd leave Langone and stroll through what she'd otherwise considered to be her very least favorite part of Manhattan (the dreaded Times Square being just a handful of blocks to the northeast). Yet East 39th, that barrage of sounds and smells and shoulders so inimical to human flourishing, became a strange, not-unlovely kaleidoscope when Jenmarie really got into a mindful groove. Instead of simply being annoyed by the sound of a jackhammer, or overwhelmed by the screeching brakes of cars starting and stopping their way down Second, Jenmarie folded those annoyances into the broader spectrum of East 39th at midday. How the cars on Second were mainly dark, whereas those on East 39th were brighter and more varied in hue. How the man passing in the other direction on her left had the telltale scar of cleft palate surgery (which sent her mind scurrying to the angry pink of her own facial flaw, but she knocked her focus back to the left right left right and everything was fine). How the sore-thumb majesty of that terra cotta façade there had apparently required so much work that the architects forgot to put those little spikes at the top to keep pigeons from roosting, which made for a lovely birdshit glaze on the craftsmanship. How this one particular spot on the pavement, no larger than two square feet at most, had the unmistakable whiff of asparagus piss. How the notice for that shy kids (all lowercase, that's how you knew they were a *real* indie band) concert at Brooklyn Steel next month featured the word *investiture,* which was a weird word to see on a flyer like that, and one Jenmarie was almost certain the concert promoter wasn't using properly. How that man slumped against the riot gate asking for change had his hand down the front of his pants and, if he wasn't masturbating with one hand while the other was extended with an open palm, he was at the very least yanking his dingus like it was the cyclic of an out-of-control helicopter. That one, to be fair, she probably would have noticed even if she hadn't been in the midst of a walking meditation. Yes, the kaleidoscope analogy felt apt, yet failed to convey something pivotal about the experience; a kaleidoscope is a small tube through which one peers, to glimpse glittering fractals marshaled into a tight globe, set against a sea of black. Jenmarie's experience was far more expansive than that; indeed, it seemed to recruit her peripheral vision in a way that everyday life failed to. She was experiencing far more, yet the focus rooted at her feet prevented any of the otherwise enraging screeches or beeps or screams or whatever fucking noises this fucking…ok, mind's wandering. Focus on the feet. Left right left right. Phew.

That there should be pleasure in this was ceaselessly baffling to Jenmarie, though Arlene provided a plausible explanation in pointing out that the displaced focus gave Jenmarie a distance from which she felt it safe to observe, even engage, in the same way that one can sometimes best engage with a challenging film or book by accepting the artifice of it. That put a nice bow on things, but Jenmarie didn't think it was entirely accurate. Why that should be the case, she couldn't say; it wasn't as though she had an alternative explanation ready at hand. But what did that matter? She didn't need to *explain* her walking practice to reap the rewards. As a matter of fact, she was concerned that explaining it could well dilute its salubrious charms. Best to leave it alone to work its magic.

Here was Jenmarie at peace, then, padding around New York City in lieu of having a hobby. Peace, of course, isn't a particularly exciting state in which to find a protagonist, and the small dramas of this period are scarcely worth dwelling upon. Errant text appeals from K.J., to which she responded with either polite demurrals (returned several hours later, a not-so-subtle indication as to what sort of tone was implied) or, failing those, clinically-phrased denials. These texts had periods at the end, to let him know she meant business. A text reading "No thank you" left room for hope that tomorrow was another day. "No thank you.", with the period at the end, was as a door slamming over and over for all eternity, without once being opened again. Other dramas included: student loan issues, a tense conversation with her parents conducted via email (the only way she spoke to them anymore), the discovery of a disagreement with Arlene about charter schools of all things that made the following session or two slightly awkward, somehow getting poison ivy (probably one of her patients had the oil on their clothes, or else some woodland nymph had slipped into her bedroom and used her arms as breakdance pads), and most disruptive of all, the birth of Mavis' child, aka Jenmarie's godchild. She (for the child was a *she*) was called Kathleen; Jenmarie made the executive decision that the girl would answer to the nickname Kat, to which Mavis was agreeable. Kat was, like all babies, a cute Guillermo Del Toro fish monster whose personality was limited to the color of the sputum caked on her chest. Mavis loved her. Jenmarie accepted the supremacy of her rival for Mavis' attention. So to fill her time, she walked some more. And some more. And then, after that, yet still more.

She refused to think of this as anything other than a healthy thing to do, even as she came to dedicate nearly every hour not engaged with her work or with therapy to walking, and focusing on her left right left right left right. Well, ok, the thought had occurred to her a few times. The thought that this was perhaps some strange manifestation of a grief and instability she wasn't prepared to face. The thought that she was trying to, if not walk away from her problems, at least wear them out until they hadn't the strength to throw a punch. When her mind wandered to those sorts of thoughts, though, guess the fuck what? Left right left right, and then everything was great again. Not once did this strike her as too much of a good thing, or the fanaticism of a new convert. And if it did...well, that was a thought. Left right.

Here is a map of Manhattan, where she did the majority of her walking. Top-down, the streets laid out in a neat orderly grid. As from the side, so from above: the city seems organized, if only one can view it from a great distance. No matter. Imagine Jenmarie as a bright blue dot, her path marked by a bright blue line. She starts, nearly every day, at NYU Langone on the East River. Most days she wanders west, and then south, away from Times Square. On those days when she feels either more confident or more masochistic (and Arlene would have had quite a time speculating on the relationship between those two moods in Jenmarie, had the latter not grown lax in the regularity of her attending sessions with the former, because after all, why bother spending hundreds of dollars a month when the left right left right was free free free free, right? Left?), Jenmarie would swing up through Times Square, dodging Spongebobs and Spidermen eager for photo ops that would cost you more than they'd spent on their entire costumes. The bright blue line threads through the streets, spreading ever outward from East 39ᵗʰ and First Avenue, until the trains come in to play, allowing Jenmarie to access ever-further reaches of the island. Take the 1 train to SoHo and paint it blue; ride the B to Harlem and pour azure into its veins. Months pass. Jenmarie never misses work, never fails to present herself with precisely the same degree of harried-professional polish that she's always had, so nobody suspects that there's something unusual about their colleague, that she's taken to stomping around the city, mind a furious blank, not going anywhere or looking for anything, just walking and trying as hard as she can to not think about anything. Jenmarie had found her new hobbyhorse, alright: oblivion. Was she happy with this, was she concerned? Neither crossed her mind, not if she could help it. Those were emotional states, right, like enjoyment, left to be crushed. Oops, ha, noticed, but what was the point of noticing something if that didn't change it, when she wanted to change it, she wanted things to change. Left right left right, that was something that changed, always changed, one into the other, left into right into left into right, and so that what she was thinking at any given moment. Left right left right. Even in the halls of the hospital, she had taken to fixating upon her steps. To look at her, of course, one would never know. If anything, they noticed a healthy toning of her form, weight loss subtle enough to be commendable. She accepted their compliments with good cheer, insisting it was all diet, not mentioning her nonstop plodding. That, she might have noted had she not been so invested in the left right, was the first sign that this behavior was entering the realm of the problematic. Concealing one's repetitive activities was a sign of addiction, wasn't it? Not necessarily. Not always. She put this question to Arlene, in one of their increasingly rare sessions, who responded with a degree of concern that Jenmarie felt unprofessional from a licensed therapist. This seemed an acceptable pretense for not seeing Arlene anymore. After that, it was just Jenmarie, the city, and the metronome of her left right left right.

In hindsight – sweet, sweet hindsight – that steady footfall would feel less a timekeeper and more a countdown, thwapping away the seconds until came the more overwhelming obsession into which she would sublimate her identity, by which she would allow herself to be consumed. In hindsight, she would wonder if, in some strange way, she'd *known* she was heading towards the High Tomb from the very beginning. She would wonder if its horrors hadn't been waiting for her, calling to her. If they hadn't been built just for her. In hindsight. Or, put another way, yes, now as before, forever and ever…after it was too late.

C
L
E
A
N

What she would come to think of in a few months' time as the High Tomb first came to her attention as something unworthy of the same. Just one little sideshow amongst the many New York had to offer. Fourth and 57th was what one might euphemistically call a "nice" part of town, which was to say it was prohibitively expensive. The kind of place most commonly populated by businesspeople who walked quickly while staring at their phones, and upon inevitably running in to somebody else, suggested that the other party "watch where [they're] going, asshole." Or, perhaps, by members of Manhattan's considerable indigent population, who had drifted towards the Upper East Side in the mistaken belief that those with money to spare would care to do so. And don't forget the tourists who came loaded down with camera and canteen, as though setting out on a wild safari. They acted like it, too: witness the mixture of fear and amusement with which they engaged the natives.

Jenmarie's kind, in other words, were not often seen in this neck of the woods. This was a place where one kept one's head down, or else held it high from a fifty-second story office window. It was not a neighborhood through which one passed, left right left righting all the while, drinking in the sights and sounds with abandon.

This wasn't sufficient to explain why Jenmarie should have been, as best as she could tell, the first person to notice the High Tomb, or at least to recognize that there was something strange about it. But she would never believe there could be any explanation, plausible or otherwise, for much of what was to come, so it would have to do.

The first time she passed by its story-high marble base, Jenmarie noted the fact that the frontage was absolutely spotless in precisely the same way, and to the same degree, that she noted the color of the gum that had been smushed into the manhole cover on the street in front of it. A detail, nothing more. The same went for the second day she passed it. It was, of course, naturally, when else, on the *third* day that something struck her as odd about the building's cleanliness.

The tower on Fourth and 57th was, like most of the others in the area, very tall. From the second story on up, it was all opaque glass, a latticed web of mirrors that recast the sky as something darker, turning fluffy white clouds into portentous thunderheads. The first story, however, save a single revolving door flanked by two rather pedestrian push-pull apertures, was solid marble. Faux-marble, who was she kidding. Or, scratch that, given the part of town this was, that very well could be real marble. Whatever it was, the material itself wasn't what had slowly but surely caught Jenmarie's attention. It was that the maybe-marble was *immaculate,* like the sculptor had only just set down their chisel. There were no handbills or flyers tacked up, no graffiti tags as there were on the buildings on either flank, not even anybody leaning against the façade and smoking a cigarette. A structure so beautiful, so pure, so untouched, in squalid old Midtown...it was kind of fucked up. No, that didn't really cover it. *Fucked up* was too prosaic, suitable for everything from killing a bee and picking it up in such a way that its stinger jammed into your finger, to watching a movie with your parents that you didn't realize had a graphic sex scene. No, the cleanliness of this building was *uncanny.* Bordering on the surreal. It scarcely computed. It inspired a supernatural, primitive dread in Jenmarie that only deepened as she slowly, carefully approached it. Approached it to do what? To do the only thing she could think to do, of course. Which was all one could ever do.

Pinching the bottom of her white undershirt from beneath her V-neck – which was far too plunging to wear without an undershirt – she stretched the thin cotton/synthetic blend towards the marble, hesitated because of very good reasons she couldn't articulate just then, then pressed it to the side of the building and rubbed. Because it was all she could think to do.

Nothing happened. And why would it? It was just a shirt, just a skyscraper. All that linked them was Jenmarie, her wearing the former and being inexplicably fascinated by the latter. They had no reason to be coming into contact with one another, this skyscraper, this shirt. Like so much else in this city.

So Jenmarie laughed. At herself, mostly. Almost entirely. But then she looked down and stopped laughing. Because if she wasn't very much mistaken, the part of the shirt she'd rubbed on the building appeared whiter than the rest of the fabric around it. Cleaner.

Scientifically-minded as she was, Jenmarie repeated the experiment with different sections of her shirt on the buildings on either side of the marble one. Both façades earned her the expected grey-black smudges on her undershirt. But in none of the three instances, she realized, did she get a funny look from a passerby. Nobody was paying attention.

Jenmarie puzzled over this for a moment that, upon glancing at her phone, turned out to have been seven minutes. Seven minutes of her mind wandering unchecked! Unbelievable. Where had it gone? It frightened her to realize that she didn't know, couldn't account for its whereabouts between the minutes of 3:34 and 3:41 in the PM.

Shaking her head, she got back on her way, left right left righting around town, all the while unable to shake a creeping unease. How could something as clean as that stand in such a crud-crusted city? And flanked by filth, no less! The modesty of the miracle was perhaps what most disturbed her, in the spooky sense as well as more quotidian ones. With mounting frustration, in the days to come she caught her mind drifting back to that eerily spotless slab of marble more and more often. The difficulty of returning her focus to its intended object, be it a biopsy result or bipedal regularity, grew in proportion to the frequency with which it became necessary. Over the course of mere weeks, the blue route of her perambulations lost their freewheeling abandon, becoming more narrowly focused on Midtown. The pristine marble façade of the tower on Fourth and 57th became a Constant, something she made a point of walking by at least once a day, usually more. The time she spent marveling at its sheer impossibility – running a finger gently across its surface, searching in vain for the least imperfection or blemish – increased daily, sucking away the hours she could dedicate to walking until she gave up her first fascination (which at least had some cardiovascular benefits) for a new one.

Nobody ever came to clean it, she marveled. Even as she stood before the building for hours on end, hypnotized by the dim, distorted reflection of the world that the marbling of the, uh, marble seemed to suggest (and was it her, or did the swirl of the stone seem to shift from day to day, hour to hour?), not once did she see anybody come by with a spray bottle and rag. Still more remarkable, though, was that she never saw anybody interface with the building, *period*. Nobody shouldered their way in through the revolving door, or scurried out the side exits. Nobody passing by ever checked out their harried reflection, or even propped themselves up with an outstretched hand as they adjusted their sock. The people walking past, well, who cared about them. They were just noise to Jenmarie, so much noise. But about her most favored skyscraper, their dissonance attained harmony in the key of C, or rather its inverse, as to judge by their behavior none of them could C the building at all. Nor did they seem to C Jenmarie, when she focused her attention on the tower. As a fun little experiment that kept her up all the following night (and gave her a hell of a nightmare the evening next), Jenmarie pressed her hand against the marble and studied it as intently as she could, scrutinizing its caramel tempests, stamping them into her memory, trying to convince herself that she wasn't watching them drift into new forms even now. Once she had so filled her conscious mind with the façade that she could see it – still shifting – with her eyes closed, she stepped backward, slowly, slowly, never taking her eyes from the building. She hadn't gone three steps before the first guy walked in to her, a buttoned-up businessman with a satchel slung over his shoulder, the kind of guy you'd imagine would be either of the *hey watch it* variety, or less plausibly of the *oh I'm so sorry* school. What was inconceivable was that he would be neither, uttering not so much as a single sound to acknowledge his at-speed collision with Jenmarie. The guy just regained his footing and kept on walking. The second person to run into Jenmarie was a woman in a pantsuit. As with the other guy, the woman acted as though she wasn't now stumbling, having just plowed right into someone she apparently hadn't seen. And still *didn't* see. Again and again and again this happened; a total of five people collided with Jenmarie, staggered themselves back to a casual gait, and kept on rolling without so much as a backward glance. Yet when Jenmarie closed her eyes and, to the unsatisfactory degree that she could, banished the marble from her mind, she instantly heard a pair of heels scuffling to her right, accompanied by a suggestion that she "get out of the fucking way."

It would be impossible for Jenmarie to later determine precisely where the line was, at what point she'd taken leave of her good sense and begun down the path the High Tomb had laid for her, just for her. But that day when she'd somehow rendered herself invisible (yet quite evidently not incorporeal) just by thinking about a fucking wall, yeah, that was a pretty good candidate.

Would it have made sense to say that she had fallen for the building's ghoulish charms? That might have been giving the architecture a bit too much credit, but it would certainly capture the unrequited nature of Jenmarie's fixation.

She had never seriously entertained the idea that she might have an addictive personality, because deep down Jenmarie knew that to do so would be to open the door to some rather unentertaining truths. Where it stood: she had good impulse control, she felt, and had the honesty to admit that she likely needed to exercise it more than others might. Hers was a life of cravings denied, of wanting all of the bad things quite desperately, and heroically struggling to stay her hand from them. This wasn't to say that she was always, or even often, successful. But where once she'd been a larger girl, she was now a woman of fairly normal size, or as the Fifth Ave types would have it, "plus-sized." Her alcohol consumption was…better, which was to say less, than it had been in the decade-plus since her college experience (and, alright, the months following her divorce). She'd done away with the anonymous one-night stands of that former era as well, though the monogamy thing hadn't exactly panned out the way she'd hoped either. Still: much as she continued to crave, her ability to manage hunger in its various forms was as robust as it had ever been.

All of this would have to serve as a kind of explanation for why Jenmarie failed to recognize the latest, and ultimately most destructive, target of the addictive personality that she most certainly *did* have. As it imparted no apparent reward, no sweet tastes or swirly intoxications, Jenmarie categorized her need to bear daily witness to the immensity of the High Tomb as being something other than a craving. What that might have been was unclear, and ultimately irrelevant to her. To *crave* was to want something bad for you. It was pointless to call an intense desire for a kale salad a *craving,* to her mind. Not that it was technically incorrect. It just wasn't *correct.* And one only *craves* something bad when it makes one feel good, in the short term. So, as burning up her free time fondling a skyscraper in central Manhattan wasn't necessarily making her feel *good* in any appreciable way, it couldn't be *bad*. Therefore, it couldn't be a *craving*. Therefore, it couldn't be an *addiction*, because an addiction was a repeated caving to cravings. Which this wasn't, and so she couldn't, and so it wasn't. QED.

Having studiously constructed a blind spot in which to conceal a rather obvious question (if marveling at the marble didn't make her feel good, even in some eldritch and unfathomable way, then why would she keep coming back, again and again?), Jenmarie kicked a bit more mental sand overtop of it by dreaming up a halfway plausible explanation for her inexplicable obsession. And, to be fair, it was a justification that was true, albeit confused. That she was curious about the building, eager to learn what she could about it, hungry for its secret which even now her rational mind couldn't imagine attributing to anything that wasn't at least a *little* bit creepy, all of this was true. But these were symptoms. The disease was something else entirely.

S
T
O
R
I
E
S

For not a single solitary instant did Jenmarie imagine that Googling the tower on Fourth and 57th would be especially enlightening, at least not in and of itself. Much as she would have loved (and been disappointed) to find a page that calmly and coherently introduced her to the hottest new startup, developers of No-Muss Marble and Invisithink, she was the exact, existential opposite of surprised to discover that no such page existed. What *did* amaze her, though, was that there were no cybersleuths already on the case. She'd expected to find some reddit threads presenting all kinds of screwball theories about how the much-feared Lizard People had designed the building to something something the Prussian educational system and also Q and furthermore ethics in video game journalism. Not that she'd have been able to read said theories, reddit having been designed, as far she could tell, by the same sadist who'd designed customer service phone trees for cable companies. But she'd figured those theories would be out there, and that would have been a relief, in some strange way. It would have meant she wasn't alone. Failing that, she would have been quite happy to discover something that was similar to, but not, a support group for those who had fallen under the building's long, dark shadow. Something to feel less, yes, ok, there it was again, *alone*. But all things recurred, it seemed: no such group existed.

She spent three days revising and refining her search, digging into the depths of the web, going so far as to consider venturing onto the Dark Web, which she knew was a thing but still somehow failed to wholly accept was *really* a thing, and not just a convenience developed by and for hack thriller writers. This, for the moment, was a bridge she would not cross; she couldn't even consider the idea without also wondering how the boys from the FBI would knock on her door. She figured it'd be a big *BANG BANG BANG* with the pinky-side of a fist, but perhaps they'd realize they were dealing with a personage slightly less formidable than demanded the triple *BANG*, and so go for a civil *knock knock knock*, but of course they would have to add some menace to it, so they would knock seven or eight times, because anything above five knocks is always, without fail, bad news.

So, no dark web, but for three days every other stone was overturned, every other lead pursued to its end. And yet, but still, somehow, on the whole wide wild worthless web, Jenmarie found not a single mention of the tower on Fourth and 57th.

Not. One.

This was perhaps the most flummoxing wonder the building had yet shown her. How was this even possible? How could she be the *only person in recorded history* to have ever noticed this big weird fucking self-cleaning skyscraper in the middle of Manhattan, a location fairly well known for the cost of its real estate, amongst many other things? Immediately her mind went whirling off in directions that would have made any of those hack thriller authors proud, not to mention wealthy. Conspiracy! Cover-ups! Web page scrubs! Heads covered in black bags! Cars driving very fast! Unshaven men screaming "THERE'S NO TIME!" Yet each of these visions seemed far too…hm…*small* was the word that Jenmarie settled on, and it felt right. That the building was owned and operated by government spooks would have made for a fun little potboiler, she supposed, but it was parochial in a way that didn't satisfy. Of course, *unsatisfying* was far from a sufficient rationale for ruling out the possibility, so Jenmarie bit the bullet and looked up how to access the Dark Web (she did her "how do I access the dark web" search, which she quickly amended to "how do I access the dark web but just for research," on Bing, because she assumed that the NSA, like everybody else, had forgotten that Bing was a thing). Fortunately, there was a tremendously helpful article on Tech-Advisor, brazenly titled "What Is The Dark Web And How To Access It." Just as prescribed, Jenmarie used Tor to spoof her IP, which was a goofy-ass bit of jargon that translated (and here one of the unshaven men might have shouted "speak English!" at a dweeb on a laptop) to 'she accessed the Dark Web in a way that would make it hard for anybody to know about it'. Why wasn't the jargon for the Dark Web cooler? Well, come to think of it, "Dark Web" wasn't exactly driving the needle to the right as far as *cool* went, so perhaps the lingo fit. At any rate, she cruised the nether recesses of the internet, trying very hard to do her research without accidentally seeing anything that might make it harder to get to sleep than the spotless marble already had, and in so doing, put paid to her intuition re: government coverup conspiracies. That the tower on Fourth and 57th received not a single mention on the…Light Web (?) left the door open for human-sized perfidy; that the Dark Web was just as silent on the matter of the marble all but confirmed a second intuition that Jenmarie had had, recognized, tried to dismiss, tried to at least *ignore*, and then ultimately been forced to tolerate, if not embrace.

Whether or not there was something sinister about the tower (and she was inclined towards thinking that there probably was, though there were really no grounds to do so), there was very little about it that was truly human-sized.

She was perhaps the only person on the planet, in history, ever to have noticed that…but wait a second, how was that possible? In *history?* The building couldn't be more than, what, seventy years old? When did they start stacking that many stories on top of each other? The tower couldn't have been there forever, and something had to have been there before it.

Maybe somebody somewhere on the damn internet would have something to say about *that*, eh?

At once exhausted and elated at having a new tail to chase, Jenmarie squirted some moisturizing drops in her eyes (it felt as though her screen was searing them right out of their sockets), stretched out her wrists for a solid three seconds each, and got back to work.

Two bottles of eyedrops later, Jenmarie felt like she was sitting on top of a landmine. She needed to tell somebody what she'd found. The enormity of this building's mystery had led her to privately christen it The Citadel, a name at which she'd arrived for no reason other than it sounded cool, and she had to call it *something*. Blame the thesaurus; it offered no acceptably epic synonyms for 'building,' and she sure wasn't about to call it The Building. The Building was the name for a pretentious Chelsea speakeasy. The Tower had too much literary baggage, from King's Dark to Tolkien's Two, which put her in mind of Manhattan's ill-fated Twins, which made her think of Tuesday tragedies again, and all things led back to Eddie. Nope, no thanks. What remained that hadn't already been taken? The Keep? Wilson already used it. The Monolith? Clarke. The Pillar? Follett, though that was enough of a stretch that The Pillar had a solid run in the 'maybe' column. Ooh, The Column? The implication that it was holding up something larger was certainly appealing. What was it holding up? Oooh, spooky! In the end, though, only one word seemed acceptably open-ended, yet sufficiently portentous. Giving the structure (The Structure? Nah, that sounded like some Brené Brown self-help checklist) the smack of holiness, to someone or dun dun dun some*thing*, just felt right to Jenmarie. Failing that, The Citadel was the only one that got stuck in her head and bounced around like a bat trying to find its way back out.

(Later, of course, when The Citadel had quietly yielded the role of sobriquet to the words *High* and *Tomb,* Jenmarie would marvel at her ever having been so cavalier about the edifice. She certainly wouldn't have been, had she appreciated the true nature of what she was bumbling in to.)

So The Citadel it was to her, and The Citadel it would be to others. After all, now she had named the thing, put words to it, and what use were words within a single skull? Words were meant to carry information from mouths to ears, from minds to eyes! And The Citadel wasn't the only word she had swirling around her noggin. In the month since she'd changed her investigatory tack and taken a run at the history of The Citadel's plot, she'd scooped up such a stockpile of words, which she then fashioned and refashioned into conjectures which were quickly rearticulated and glazed with the shellac of facthood. Facts! She had facts now! And those facts were made up of words rather than knowledge, which meant they needed to be shared.

With whom, though, should she share these facts? Her first choice was Mavis, obviously, but Mavis was too busy being a mother. That motherhood should prevent her from video chatting with Jenmarie was perplexing to the latter. Wouldn't she already be spending all day in bed, exhausted from, ah, *not* having spent all day in bed? Apparently not. Mavis was on the move, and hadn't the time for any particularly in-depth conversations with her best friend. Which got Jenmarie thinking; what if she wasn't Mavis' best friend? What if Mavis was *her* best friend, but she wasn't Mavis'? It was a thought that could be dismissed as mere middle school bullshit, but that didn't make it sting any less.

Move on, then. Who else to burden with the dreadful presence of The Citadel? Her thoughts turned once again to the lack of any social groups, which was to say support groups, by and for people whose minds had been warped by the building. So she tried to start one, but advertising a group for those who had been distressed by an unsettling edifice on Fourth and 57th got her cranks, pranksters, and a whole mess of people who were properly pissed about all things Trump, so much so that they forgot his cornea-scorching tower was on *Fifth*. A more proactive approach, i.e. pasting flyers around town, got her nothing except a talking-to from a police officer who seemed more tickled than ticked off to be enforcing the POST NO BILLS ordinance.

Strangers would be of no help, then. Yet Jenmarie needed release, the catharsis of communication. So the dilemma remained: who to saddle with the Citadel's existence? Her siblings? Harmon, rest his soul, had had the least time for bullshit. He might have been a good one, but, alas, he was no longer anyone. Melody was…well, when had Jenmarie last spoken to her sister? Melody would have no context from which to make sense of her sister's ramblings about a shuddersome skyscraper…or, indeed, of anything else about her. It had been *such* a long time, after all. So, not her. How about Tomjohn? Jenmarie had unburdened herself to her baby brother plenty of times, and Tomjohn certainly had no problem casting himself as a *truthteller*, in the fashion of those for whom honesty and bullying were distinguishable only by how often one used to word "dumbass" (a non-zero figure in both cases). But for as many ways in which he and Jenmarie had self-incriminated on their late-night calls, and mutually at that, this all struck her as a bridge too far for Tomjohn. Because he genuinely cared about her, and so she had no doubt that the second she got done raving about what she'd discovered, he would start phoning the other Bells to voice his concern. No good, that. So who else? Lenny had either blocked Jenmarie's number or was somewhere without reception (she didn't like how the sharp end of Occam's razor touched down on that second option). So who was left? Who did Jenmarie know whose time she could take without feeling too bad about it, who was an excellent listener and adequate conversationalist, who cared enough to hear Jenmarie out but whose concern couldn't come back to bite her in any meaningful way, who was K.J., obviously it was going to be K.J.

How to reopen that door, though? She'd slammed it rather hard in his face, obviously failing to anticipate that she would hope to claw her way back through it just a few months later. The last words she'd spoken to him were a rejection of his entreaties for lunch, or a drink, or a cup of coffee. This had been done over text, but what constituted 'speaking' was an ever-expanding catchall amongst her generation, so it counted.

In initiating K.J. into the wild world of The Citadel, though, she wanted to speak with him in the archaic, pre-textual sense of the word. Face to face. In person. At kissing distance. No! The last thing she needed was to start this up again, to plunge herself back into the dramatics that attended all relationships in human history (and probably the history of their precursors too, all the way back to their collective flat-headed fishhood). Since when had a relationship ever made anybody happy, long-term? Never. Not once. There were no examples. People who said they were happy in relationships were liars. Jenmarie was so much happier now that she was single, that was just a *fact*. So she would have K.J. meet her in a public coffee shop, in the middle of the afternoon. This was to curtail her own impulses, her own *cravings*, as much as to forestall any upon which K.J. might try to act. For attempting to chip away at, and so unwittingly enhancing, the mystique of The Citadel had a curious, almost aphrodisiacal effect on Jenmarie. That was perhaps the wrong word (if it was a word at all), but she couldn't think of a better one. It wasn't mere sex that Jenmarie felt herself craving as she hunched nearer and nearer her computer screen, day after day. It was chocolate and whiskey and carbs and wine and all of the bad things, well obviously the bad things because they were cravings, but these were *powerful* urges, so strong that she sometimes felt her hold on self-control to be of the skin-of-her-teeth variety. The Citadel unleashed and intensified her desires, all the while presenting her with the means of moderating them: spend more time on The Citadel. Keep digging. Keep looking. Keep reading. Keep hunting. Hell, maybe The Keep wasn't such a wrong-headed name for the place after all. Particularly if one teased out the Wilson connection; there was, after all, something vampiric about the hold the building had on her, how its push-pull seductions masked the disparity between the exactions and the endowments. This naturally drummed up images of her biting K.J. (leaving a lopsided imprint in his neck, thanks to a chipped fang) and turning him into another devotee of The Citadel, a research partner, a whaddyacallit. The guy who helps the vampire find new victims. Where was this metaphor going? Too far afield. The point was, K.J. was a biter. Not that that was relevant, or mattered.

So she texted the biter and told him she wanted to talk with him. Later that night, she had the presence of mind to whisper "whoops" to herself as K.J. removed the condom and carried it to the bathroom like a vial of highly corrosive acid.

The next morning, over coffee, she brought him up to speed on The Citadel. Her initial puzzlement over it, the shifting swirls in the marble, focusing upon which rendered one some kind of invisible, all of it. She had braced herself to be goggled at as a loon, and so was unnerved to find K.J. nodding along, asking questions, engaged every step of the way. Either he was so credulous as to be unflappable (how to shock a man, after all, for whom all things were possible?), or he was so disturbed by the evident insanity of the woman with whom he'd just shared a bed that he was rolling with the punches until such time as he could make a safe getaway. As it became more and more apparent that this latter interpretation was the correct one (the tell being when K.J. slipped up and asked her how she *thought* she'd noticed that the patterns in the marble were shifting, only to quickly and clumsily repeat himself without the underhanded swipe at her psychological credibility), her tone became slightly more desperate. "Just come take a look at it with me," she implored him. "I'll buy you another cup of coffee, we'll walk by it, and if you don't think anything is odd or off about it, then, I don't know, I'll go see a therapist."

K.J.'s eyebrows wiggled and curled – another tell. "…I thought you were already seeing a therapist?"

"I was," Jenmarie sighed. "But I stopped."

"Why?"

I started walking was not a good answer, even if it was the real one. So she lied and said it had been too expensive. Maybe K.J. bought it, maybe he didn't. Didn't matter. Either way, it was enough to get him off his ass and heading uptown on the F. On the way, she explained what she'd discovered about the plot of land upon which The Citadel now stood. The New York Public Library had been an invaluable resource, having compiled a tremendously helpful list of books on the architectural history of the city. Using these, as well as a few inquiries to the Landmarks Preservation Commission, the Neighborhood Preservation Center, and a variety of architectural firms around the city, she had been able to determine that The Citadel couldn't reasonably have existed and gone unnoticed until very, *very* recently. It was sixty-two stories tall (she'd counted, of course). In 1908, the Singer Building at the south end of the island was the tallest building in *the world*, and that was only forty-seven stories tall. It was but four miles from The Citadel – hardly adequate to camouflage a skyscraper trying to fly under the radar. Five years later the Woolworth Building shot up in the same part of town, dwarfing the Singer at fifty-seven stories. The tallest in New York still wasn't tall enough to shade the Citadel. It wasn't until the Bank of Manhattan Trust Building (which was now, unfortunately, The Trump Building, not to be confused with Trump Tower, though the former's lack of gaudy gold typography made the distinction clear enough) rose to its seventy-one stories in 1930, snatching the title of World's Tallest Building in the process, that Manhattan saw any structures larger than The Citadel. Once again, though, the problem of proximity: The Bank of Manhattan Trust Building was four miles southwest of The Citadel. It was plausible that the latter could have appeared – as opposed to having been *constructed*, which Jenmarie found unlikely – as early as 1930 without attracting the sort of attention that apparently hypnotized one and made one invisible (hearing the absurdity of that escaping her mouth so matter-of-factly, Jenmarie first opted to backpedal by shrugging and saying "and probably a bunch of other magical shit, ha, ha," and when that did nothing to soften K.J.'s features, she added, "I'm not crazy," which, go figure, didn't work either), but at that point the tallest buildings in the vicinity of Fourth and 57th were the Fuller Building on Madison (completed in 1929, but only forty-two stories tall) and the Hotel Sherry-Netherland on Fifth (finished in 1927, but a measly forty stories). Even when Trump Tower went up in 1983, reaching no more than fifty-eight stories above the street (despite what its namesake may have claimed in pursuit of political office), there was nothing as tall as The Citadel within a three block radius. At long last, in 2011, the boxy behemoth of 432 Park Avenue would take its place as the second tallest building in the city at eighty-one stories, looming over everything around it, which included The Citadel. "See?" she concluded.

K.J. blinked himself back from whatever ledge his attention had waddled up to. "…huh?"

Jenmarie sighed. "Until 1930, the Citadel would have been the tallest building in the city. I've gone digging through a bunch of old photos from around that time, ones that show the skyline. There's this book by two guys with names, I can't remember right now, they were funny names, but it covers thirty-five to fifty-five. The book. They aren't exactly labeled, the *pictures* in the book I mean, they're not labeled like 'here's the part of the skyline we're looking at', but I could use, uh, I *used* some old real estate atlases and online databases to suss out some approximations based on the buildings I *could* see. The shots with the Fourth and 57th neighborhood in the background? No Citadel. Clear sky. So I feel pretty confident saying that there was no Citadel to speak of as late as 1955. Now, the other point that I'm saying, and it's really all in the numbers, I think the data speaks for itself, or themselves, data is plural right? Whatever, and, um, but prior to 2011 the Citadel would have stood out for being the tallest building in the neighborhood. It's easy to ignore now because it's just one more big thing among the other big things, but before 432 Park went up, how would nobody look at the tallest building around and wonder, gosh, why doesn't anybody know what that is? See what I'm saying?"

K.J. narrowed his eyes at the floor of the F train. "You're saying…you think it was built in 2011?"

"I don't think it was built."

"…then what? It just sprang up? Grew out of the pavement?"

She shrugged. "I don't know. What I *do* know is, Fifth and 57th, right next door, where Trump Tower is, that's one of the busiest thoroughfares in the city. There are all kinds of pictures and videos you can find of that intersection, from all different angles. Instagram hashtags are especially helpful for that, there's all sorts of bougie bullshit there that people love to brag about being just even *near*. Hashtag Four Seasons, Hashtag Tiffany's, Hashtag St. Regis. Then you've got the Spanish consulate over on Lexington, 432 Park, and I really wish I didn't have to keep saying his stupid name but Trump Tower, and the Seagram further down on Park. All kinds of touristy stuff that gets snapped, from the street, from the top floors, everywhere in between. You can piece together collages of the area's skyline, well, not *you*, not like you *couldn't* I mean, but you wouldn't, anybody could though if they wanted to, which I did, so, uh, I did, and I got pretty comprehensive looks at which buildings were up and which weren't. I've got whole panoramas stitched together as far back as 2007, and I've got in-progress ones from as early as 2002."

K.J. blinked, very, very slowly. "...and? When does the, uh, *The Citadel* show up?"

Jenmarie grinned, bouncing on her feet like a toddler after nap time (had she a mirror, she might have noticed the similarity to how Arlene celebrated getting an especially juicy bit of trauma on the ropes). "Well, now, that's a question, isn't it? I mean, it's *the* question, but it's got more than one answer. Because," she pulled out her phone and started scrolling through photos, "because, look, I'll show you – the first time I noticed it in photos was in 2012. One year after 432 Park went up! Almost like it was just waiting for something taller to show up and make it safe to grow, right?" Jenmarie wasn't so far gone that she couldn't hear her rhetorical *right?*, a pseudointellectual vocal tic she despised perhaps more than any other. But, oh *h-well* (okay, not *any* other), it was too late now, perhaps she just needed to accustom herself to being the kind of person who says *right?* in the middle of explaining something. "Gah," she continued, "where are these pictures?"

She was aware of, or maybe just imagined, K.J. stealing a glance over her shoulder as she scrolled through her patchwork panoramas of yesteryear's skyline. "...ah-" he started to say, but Jenmarie quickly cut him off with "well, anyway, I'll find them later." She stuffed her phone back into her pocket and summarized her findings for him: "2012 was the first year I could find photos of The Citadel, at *first*. But then I thought, gosh, I'm only looking for it as being a head or two taller than just about anything else in the area. What happens if I, and I can't remember why I first thought to do this but it just sort of *came* to me, what happens if I look down a little bit and look for it *below* the then-highest buildings in the area, from *before* 2011? At first I couldn't be sure what I was seeing because it's so nondescript, you saw it, well, you *will* see it, it could be any building basically, which I bet is the point, but I made a very careful survey of all the photos and the building itself, I went up to the top of 432 Park and got a really good look at it, and don't look at me like that, I know, but just buckle up, hold on to your butt because I'm about to tell you, uh, I am *now* telling you, that The Citadel is getting taller. It's growing! I looked for a slightly smaller version of it, and and, and I've spotted it as far back as 2006…but back then it was *only thirty-nine stories tall!* Yet there's never any construction equipment in any of the photos, no cranes or pulleys or little grate elevators, whatever, I don't know what other stuff you'd need to make a building taller but I know you'd need *something*. So I was looking for any kind of proprietorial history of the plot, or construction contracts, which was why I was calling up those architectural firms like I said, and as far as every firm in the city is concerned, nobody has ever so much as touched that property, and as far as the city seems to be concerned, nobody owns it. On paper, it doesn't even exist!"

"Jenmarie."

"What?"

K.J. looked at her for a long time, long enough that the train on which they rode had time to screech into 42nd Street (that screech being a steady flow of direct current getting chopped into alternating current, that was something Jenmarie had learned by accident in the course of her research, which spoke to either her investigative breadth, or else a lack of focus), dislodge some passengers while taking on others, have one of the incoming passengers hold the door for their friends, much to the audible frustration of the other passengers and conductor, until finally the doors closed and the train continued shrieking its way uptown – all of this happened before K.J. said his piece, which Jenmarie could see coming from miles away, and so decided not to let him say.

"You think I'm crazy," she said.

He simply stared at her, luxuriating in one of those maddeningly long pauses of his. K.J. Hanifan, live on location. "I'm just wondering," he finally offered, "when's the last time you slept."

"I get enough sleep," Jenmarie replied at once.

"…that's not what I asked."

Jenmarie, as she often did when she felt uncomfortable on the subway, made a formal study of the ads running along the upper edges of the siding, just below the ceiling. Get my degree online in two years? You don't say! "You think I'm manic or something."

"You've been having panic attacks."

She glared at him – had she told him that? She probably had. Why had she told him that? "All I'm asking is for you to just… keep an open mind until you see this building. If you look at it and think it's just a normal building, that I'm totally nuts and making all of this up, then you and I will go straight to the nearest psych ward and I'll check myself in. I mean that. I mean that more than I've ever meant anything, because I know that I'm not crazy more certainly than I've ever known anything." She returned her eyes to the ads running above their heads. Get those damages you're entitled to, order out with the city's number one delivery app, wear this watch that the famous man on the boat has. "You'll see," Jenmarie mumbled, scanning her eyes across the colorful corporate commandments. "You'll see the Citadel, or fine, we can call it The Building, whatever, I just wanted to give it a creepy name. Anyway, you'll see it, *feel* it, and before I can even show you the pictures you'll believe everything I just told you." Finally, she lowered her gaze to K.J. once more.

"I hope you're right," was all K.J. had to say to that, after not much of a pause at all.

Jenmarie lifted her eyes back to the ads once more. See the new Amazon original series. Get a better apartment. Cut the cord.

They got off at Sixth and 57th and walked (though Jenmarie, suddenly anxious that perhaps she ought to have hedged her bets a *tiny* bit with the whole 'off I go to the loony bin' line, was intermittently hustling out of nervous energy and dragging ass to buy the time she'd need to think of a suitable way to walk that gambit back) east towards Fourth. Her heart simultaneously in her throat and her intestines, Jenmarie grabbed K.J.'s hand, dragged him right up to the marble façade of The Citadel (forgetting her planned theatricalities, the first of which would have been stopping him on the far curb and playing the 'do you notice anything unusual' game, fishing for the answer of 'boy, that sure is a clean building'), and planted his hand on the glacial swirls.

The moment his hand touched the marble, she saw his face change. That slackening of his features, the dangling jaw and sloping eyebrows, provided perhaps the very first taste of deep, unfettered vindication she'd ever experienced.

He felt it. And as he stepped slowly backwards, focusing on the marble which moved just as she'd described…he vanished. Only that wasn't quite right. His form still hung in the air, nearly visible if she squinted and strained. But if she let her attention drift to something else, K.J. vanished. Even though he didn't. He was there and he wasn't. She couldn't see through him – it wasn't as though he were a translucent blue force ghost or something – yet he was too insubstantial to fix her vision upon.

So, at her back though the building now was, she brought The Citadel up in her mind's eye and focused on that as hard as she could. And suddenly, there again was K.J., eyes near to falling out of his head as passersby crashed into him from both sides as casually as if they were hip-popping their way through a stubborn turnstile.

"K.J.," she called, somehow knowing that, fixated on The Citadel as she remained, only K.J. would hear her voice.

He goggled at her and nodded. Jenmarie grinned.

C
A
R
E

K.J. frowned at her and shook his head. Jenmarie frowned right back.

"The fuck are you talking about?" she sputtered over the pre-happy hour beers she and K.J. felt they'd had no choice but to get at two in the afternoon. "Do you not believe me now? Are you…did you *un*believe me?"

K.J. shook his head even more enthusiastically. "It's the opposite. I believe every word you said." Which, of course he did, now that he'd seen all of the pictures Jenmarie had told him about, detailing the quite literal rise of The Citadel. "Which is precisely why I really, truly believe we should leave this alone."

Unbelievable. She'd shown him something that nobody on the entire internet, and therefore nobody in the whole entire universe, had ever noticed before. A squeaky-clean skyscraper punching its way up out of the ground in the middle of Manhattan, forging itself into ever-greater being, story by story by story. And everybody had just walked right on by, because Manhattan was a head-down kind of city; the only people who had the right to stand tall were buildings. Even the little humans on the very top floors of those buildings, they kept their heads down too, thinking themselves powerful for being able to look down upon the not-so-great unwashed. But cowed was cowed, and all served at the pleasure of their edifice. Yeah, Manhattan had an Edifice Complex.

"They all just assumed it was supposed to be there," she continued her own thought without letting K.J. in on the bits that had never escaped her skull. "Everybody ignored it like they ignore everything in the city that doesn't mean anything to them, which is fucking most of it. But, you know, what's the alternative? How could you sift through all the noise, and colors, and, and people and find any kind of meaning in it? The only way to get from one day to the next is to tune all that out. And since nobody ever had anything to do with The Citadel, nobody bothered to wonder what it was doing there, or what the fuck it was." She leaned forward. "The doors don't open, K.J. I've tried them. It's like they're…stage props, painted and glued onto door-shaped scenery."

Pursing his lips, K.J. took a hearty pull of his beer, and then another large enough to kill the round. He lifted a finger and spun it at the bartender, as he'd likely seen in a Humphrey Bogart movie or something, but the bartender apparently hadn't seen those movies, and so replied with a quizzical buffalo grunt. K.J. clarified that he wanted another round for himself and the lady, a request to which the bartender assented whilst wondering in a stage whisper why K.J. hadn't just said that to begin with.

Sighing, the would-be Bogey turned back to Jenmarie. "…this is what I'm talking about. You just started saying something that was I guess relevant to what you were thinking, but from my perspective, you sound a bit bonkers. I know," he raised his palms as though approaching a feral animal to serve it a court summons, "I know you're not. I'm on your side, I saw it too, I *felt* it, I know you're telling the truth. I can say all of that and I *still* worry you're slipping into something…unpleasant. Psychologically." Jenmarie opened her mouth, but K.J. pressed his point with uncharacteristic adamancy, leaning towards her on his stool and waggling his right pointer finger. "I mean, here's what I'm asking you, I guess. Why? Why is this so important to you? There's something creepy about the building, I am *fully* on board with that. But the, ok, the *Citadel* isn't hurting anybody. It's just this weird, crazy building growing against the laws of nature or logic or the universe or whatever. Which, then I'm wondering…well, why do you care?"

Jenmarie thought about that for a bit too long. "If you believed me," she finally snapped as the bartender delivered a fresh round, "you wouldn't be asking me that. Thanks," she added to the bartender, who was already out of earshot.

"I'm asking you *because* I believe you. Because th-"

"So you need me to explain why I care about the evil mystery skyscraper in the cent-"

"Evil's a big word."

"It's a big fucking building."

"Right," K.J. agreed, "it is. The whole thing is *big*. That's what I'm telling you. Th-"

"If you turn this into me somehow proving your point for you, I'm gonna…I'm gonna lose it, K.J."

The classic K.J. tape delay. "That's not what I'm doing," he finally mumbled in a way that implied the word *anymore*. "I'm just saying, this is such a big thing to be worrying about by yourself. It's like worrying about global warming by yourself. Where's that gonna get you?"

"That's why I'm telling you."

"Right, but what am I gonna do about it too, you know? You should call up whoever, CERN or MIT or whoever, and let them work on it. I don't s-"

"I didn't call them because I thought if *you* don't believe me, nobody will."

K.J. took another long pause, glancing down at his feet as he did. He sighed, opened his mouth, then closed it again.

"What?" Jenmarie asked.

At the end of what was either a second pause, or else a continuation of the first, K.J. finally said "I don't know you that well."

Jenmarie's nose suddenly itched, but she decided that scratching at it would be a show of weakness. Torn, she settled for twitching her upper lip like she was auditioning for *Kenneth Branagh's Bewitched*. "That doesn't have anything to do with what I'm saying," she growled.

"*I'm* just saying, I don't see why me believing or not you matters that much. I don't see why you, uh…why you care, to be honest. You…I mean, you dumped me."

"…that doesn't have *anything* to do with what *I'm* saying, though," she reiterated, a plaintive note creeping in to her voice.

"Okay," was all K.J. said to that.

They sat in silence for nearly a full minute, neither so much as reaching for their beer. Despite both very much wanting to.

"I feel like if I knew you better," K.J. finally whispered, "I'd be worried about you."

Jenmarie's twitch migrated up to her left eye. "Does that mean you're not?"

"...do you want me to be?"

"No."

K.J. laughed, though clearly not from a mirthful place. "I'm so confused. What do you want out of this?"

Jenmarie sniffed, then lifted her drink and took a sip. "I didn't *dump* you," she mumbled into her glass.

"That's not what I'm talking about anymore. And you did."

"No."

"Yes."

Jenmarie shook her head. "I stopped seeing you. I didn't *dump* you."

"You did, but that's n-"

"I *didn't.*"

"That's not the point."

"So what is, then?"

"I'm just really confused about what you want from me right now."

"Yeah, well, sorry I'm not making *perfect sense*. Sorry I'm not making absolutely *perfect sense* telling you about this weird building that doesn't even make any sense either."

K.J. leaned forward. He started to extend his hand, as though to reach for hers, then thought better of it. Whatever the *it* had been. He thought better of that. "If it doesn't make sense, then there's no point worrying about it. Just let the building be." He thought better of his better thinking, and reached out for Jenmarie's hand. She let him take it. "It's not hurting you. It's not like it landed on your family and now you have to get revenge. You were getting along just fine before you found it."

"I wasn't getting along *just fine.*"

135

"That didn't have anything to do with The Citadel though."

Jenmarie pinched her lips, a look of glass-shattering fury sweeping across her face, before vanishing to that crowded red room where all of her most corrosive thoughts awaited their encore. She'd spend the foreseeable future imagining all of the punchy ripostes she might have offered here. She'd imagine saying them. She'd imagine the satisfaction of having said them.

For now, though, she only nodded gloomily.

K.J. had the decency to look contrite about what he'd said. But he didn't say *sorry.*

"I think it's something bad," Jenmarie monotoned. "Something evil."

"Yeah, you mentioned that. But thus far, it seems like it's been pretty damn neutral. Really, it could just as easily be something good."

"Good things," Jenmarie explained, as though to a child, "aren't usually creepy."

"So, fine, so let's say it's bad. Or, sorry, *evil.* What the fuck do you think you're going to do about it?"

Jenmarie took a deep breath through her nose and ducked her head slightly.

Before she had a chance to respond, K.J. steamed onwards, the hard edge of his tone belying a heavy weight lifting from his chest: "if you think you're saving the world or something, that's an excuse that's, for one thing, not based on the evidence you're so fond of referencing, and I'm not trying to denigrate your research, you've done a hell of a job. But, for another thing, the way you're acting isn't the way somebody who genuinely believes the city, or the country, or the world or *whatever* is in mortal danger, would act. You're acting..." he paused, wincing at the thought as though it were caught in his throat.

"How am I acting?" Jenmarie inquired, without heat or malice, as casually as though she were asking after the name of a song heard blaring from a passing car.

K.J. sighed. "Forget it."

"No, please." Her tone sharpened. "Tell me. How am I acting?"

After what both of them must have known would be the final tape delay Jenmarie would ever sit through, K.J. said "I guess I should say, I don't think you're acting at all. I think this is you. This is who you are."

It was a solid thirty seconds before Jenmaire could bring herself to say "you're right. You don't know me that well."

K.J. just shrugged again. It was clear enough he had more to say, and just as clear he'd no intention of saying it.

Jenmarie got up, closed out her tab, and left without saying goodbye.

L
E
V
E
R

Beyond pegging The Citadel's arrival at sometime near the beginning of the 21st century, Jenmarie's research revealed precious little of value (if, indeed, dating it to a few years ago could be considered *valuable,* not that Jenmarie had ever found much of value in dating, thank you, tip your waitress, take my wife, etc.). There were no records that she, or any of the local historians she contacted on the mostly-false pretense of being an amateur journalist, could dig up pertaining to the property's stewards at any point in the city's history. From the moment the corner of Fourth and 57th first appeared on the Commissioner's Plan of 1811, along with the bulk of Manhattan's grid, all the way to the present…there was nothing.

So what about further back, then? Well, prior to being designated as a street corner, the spot that would serve as the foundation for that dreadful edifice was surely just a bush or a tree or some shit. There would be nothing to distinguish it from any of the other bushes or trees, and so attempting to chart its history back beyond the Plan was little more than a test of Jenmarie's steadily fraying patience. The Colonists who once lived there weren't much help either, neglecting to leave behind any convenient folklore about a tree that never stops growing, or a pile of rocks that rattled on still evenings. The Lenape who inhabited the island before that offered just as little guidance. Was a straightforward map indicating some sacred burial grounds too much to ask? X marks the restive spirit?

Apparently, yes. And thus, after eight months of slamming her head against books and computer screens and historians, she was forced to concede that academia had failed her. So, what now?

"Um," this would-be hotshot named Trent (of course) said to her, "that's not possible."

"You're saying you can't do it?" Jenmarie fired back.

"Nnnno, I'm saying it's illegal. They passed a law in 2016. You can't take a tourist chopper over the city anymore. And even if I could, landing on a building without a pad is gonna be just about impossible."

"So what you're saying," Jenmarie reiterated to Trent, aka the fifteenth helicopter pilot she'd tried to convince to take her up to the top of The Citadel, "is that you're not a good enough pilot, or a brave enough man, to pull it off."

"Nnnno, I'm saying maybe there's a reason they won't just let you in the front door."

So it had gone with all of the chopper pilots Jenmarie had tried, and so it went. It was a simple request, accompanied by the promise of generous remuneration! Yet nobody would take her up over The Citadel and let her disembark – they didn't even want to hover over the roof and drop a rope ladder or anything! Nothing! Weren't chopper pilots supposed to be renegades at heart? Weren't they the bikers of the sky? Wasn't that why they called motorcycles 'choppers'?

If not from above, then what of below? Jenmarie pored over every map she could find that detailed Manhattan's underground infrastructure, which was limited to the MTA subway maps. For fairly obvious reasons, information about sewer lines and water mains was harder to come by; Jenmarie sent out a blast of emails to various personages in the NYC Municipal Water Finance Authority and NYC Water Board, and received nothing but a few curt dismissals of her curiosity. So it wasn't just the Lenape who weren't interested in sharing their maps! Which, on second thought, they probably hadn't had. Still! The more things change, eh?

Did it occur to Jenmarie, somewhere in here, to mix up an explosive and plant it in front of the fake doors to The Citadel? Did she dream of blasting it open like a bank vault? Yes, yes, yes. Of course she did. But if her frenzied and, she would reluctantly concede, ill-advised missives to the city's water authorities hadn't already landed her on some kind of watch list, adding "how to make a bomb" to her search history undoubtedly would. She did recall that K.J. had once told her a rather compelling story about working at a C4 plant, or storage depot, or *something*, and she got three-quarters of the way to calling him and asking if he might not be able to get a hold of some for her before realizing that if she did that, she might well cut out the middle man and call for the funny farmers and their butterfly nets herself. Besides, fuck him. He didn't understand what she was doing here. Why it was important. He didn't understand *her*. Which made him unworthy of providing her with plastic explosives.

So she dedicated herself to devising less incendiary means of effecting entry, including but not limited to: tracking down the payphone nearest The Citadel, which as far as she could tell was up on 66th and all the way over on West End Avenue, just about the other side of the island. Luckily it was one of those vintage booth-style ones with the door, so Jenmarie was able to shut herself in and imagine she was Clark Kent spinning around so fast his briefs wound up on the outside. Instead of becoming Superman, though, she called 911 and reported a fire in "the big tower on Fourth and 57th, the one with the two-story marble façade that moves when you look at it too long. Huh? I didn't say that. You're hearing things. Hurry, there's, uh…fire alarm!" And then she was running to the cab she'd hired to wait for her around the corner, telling him to step on it to Trump Tower on Fifth (she didn't want to get dropped off *right* in front of the ass-embling fire department) and that there was an extra thirty-five bucks in it for him if he could beat Google Maps' estimated ten minute drive by at least three. He did her one better, getting her to Fifth and 57th a mere six minutes after she'd placed the call to the fire department, giving her just enough time to galumph over to the bougie leathergoods store across the street and position herself at the window, as if she would have been caught *dead* lugging that stupid fucking purse they'd put on a plinth here around town. Perhaps they'd put it there to deter would-be burglars. That was the only explanation Jenmarie could think of for…that thought slipped off the rickety rope bridge that had become Jenmarie's attention span and plummeted into a deep, dark gulley. The fire department was here, trucks howling and flashing like two nubile freshmen on their first spring break. Seven decidedly un-hunky firemen piled out of the trucks, looked at The Citadel…and then looked away. Only they didn't really look away – it was as though their heads had been turned, *pushed* away. Gently, yes, but pushed all the same, as one might deflect a lover's advances if the mood wasn't quite right. They were hardly there for three minutes before they piled back into their trucks. Jenmarie had to wrestle down the impulse to dash across the street and scream something to the effect of "BUT MY BABY IS IN THERE," something to get them back out of their fucking trucks and into the fucking building, or at least *trying* to pry the door open, so she could see what happened when somebody took a crowbar to it without having to do so herself. Ultimately, though, she suppressed the urge, because she had great impulse control and did not give in to her cravings and was very much on top of her life and everything was going well and also great and good. Great!

So she Binged "how to make a bomb," once again appending "for research." She found numerous options, all of which sounded too dangerous. Which made sense now that she was staring the directions in the face, of course, but in her naivety she'd assumed that bombs were only a threat when you pushed the button or flipped the switch or depressed the plunger or whatever. What a waste *that* search turned out to be, particularly as it led her to search things like "how to tell if I'm on a government watch list," which led her to an article called "how to get off a government watch list," which averred that one of the best ways to get *on* a government watch list was to search for ways to get *off* of one. One suggestion for determining whether or not one was on a list was to apply for loans and see if the applications were denied or delayed for no reason. So she applied for two personal loans, both of which ground through the bureaucratic gears with considerable lassitude. That wasn't inherently suspicious though, because Jenmarie had fairly rotten credit thanks to the massive debt she'd racked up effecting her escape from the agrarian comforts of Tennessee, where never once had she placed a fraudulent call to the fire department, Binged bomb-making tips, or landed herself on a government watch list (maybe). But fine. Whatever. Maybe she was on a watch list, maybe she wasn't. What was it to her? It *wasn't*, that was what it was, which was *wasn't*. So, fuck it.

Yeah. Fuck it. Here was Jenmarie Bell at thirty-three and her wit's end, taking the train to the nearest hardware store, some mom and pop outfit called Quality Equipment, and buying the biggest crowbar they had, crowbars were the best way to open things up and that was what she needed, she needed to open a thing up, and furthermore because fuck it. She stood on the train ride there, and stood on the way back, even though there were seats available, because fuck it. What was she thinking about, white-knuckling the crowbar in her right hand and the central pole of the F train in her left? Nothing, that's what. There was nothing to think about, so she thought about nothing. Thinking didn't enter into it, anyway. Where had thinking gotten her? On a federal fucking watch list, that was where, probably, maybe, who knew, except she did, definitely, she knew.

For the briefest of brief moments a something pierced the nothing, a stray person-shaped thought that could have been *anybody*, Mavis or Eddie or Arlene or K.J. or come to think of it even Jenmarie herself, but ultimately it was a shape without features, which meant it wasn't much fucking good to her, and even if it *had* had features, Jenmarie would have had no use for them, so the thought was banished and nothingness reigned.

Then everythingness conquered and deposed the quiet tyranny of distraction. Cars honking for no reason as they glide smoothly down the street, people weeping into their phones (why oh why did half the people walking around Manhattan on their phones insist on weeping and wailing into them?), garbage rotting in nose-high piles, bus brakes screeching, jackhammers pounding, dogs snarling, music blaring, tides rising, hopes crumbling, trumpets blowing, walls crumbling, snakes devouring seas, moons crashing into planets, mountains moving not towards but away, the mountain will not come to Muhammad and Muhammad will never reach the mountain you see, which perhaps explains the Medina-era grouchies. And at the end of it all the ash and the vine, the ash brown and the vine green and the vine red and the ash black now dust, blowing away while the vine still stands, will stand, will always stand, can never fall, can *certainly* never be toppled. It's a mighty fucking vine. You see.

Now listen. Amidst the din, there is silence, even still.

Jenmarie made no effort to disguise her approach; she walked right up to The Citadel's fake doors, specifically the push-pull piece of shit on the left, and jammed the crowbar between the fake plastic setting of the fake glass and the fake frame itself.

What followed wasn't a matter of perspective: it was *the* matter of perspective.

T
O
M
B

Lives shift in jellyfish. Squish!

Jenmarie is inside of a jellyfish. No, that's not right. Don't be ridiculous. Jenmarie is inside of one hundred jellyfish, all in a row, like an invertebrate conga line, or the longest, fleshiest concertina ever assembled. No, not assembled – *birthed* seems nearer the mark. All around her are folds, flaps, ridges, covered in some viscous slime she's yet to touch, because she's sort of what would you say, floating? Swimming through this tunnel, pulsing, expanding, contracting, some sort of what would you call it, peristalsis? Like she's been devoured by a giant and this is its what, gullet? Or its intestines? Too early for the intestines, or perhaps that's hopelessly anthropocentric of her. If another entity wishes to have its intestines come before the throat, who is she to judge?

Dinner, it seems. Lunch. Or just a snack. Devoured all the same.

The yielding ribs of wherever she is hide a light from her, a light which surrounds the passage but does not enter it. At either end, her path vanishes into darkness. How's this for an express ride to the afterlife, then? No light at either end of the tunnel, but plenty outside of it! Is this where she is, then? Has assaulting the Citadel resulted in her demise? Had she angered it to such an extent that it grew an arm, reached down, and gobbled her up? Or maybe that's why she's started at the guttyworks – the fake door was the anus, and The Citadel took her like a suppository. Ha ha, ho ho! No! Why? What is the purpose? She can't be dead. She can still feel. Granted, unfeelingness as a metric for death is just one of those things people have decided upon arbitrarily, probably so they didn't feel rotten about burying or burning their loved ones. Aren't there some cultures that believe the body retains the ability to feel for a time after death? How would that work? How does anything work? It doesn't. Nothing works. Oh gosh, what if by hitting The Citadel, she'd destroyed the entire world, or the universe, and yet in so doing had saved herself, the Citadel had saved her, and now here she is in its bodyhorror ark, the sole citizen of her turkey-link galaxy? Ha ha, now who's being anthropocentric?! Still her. Who else could be? Who else is there?

She's losing her mind. Focus, she says to herself, which doesn't work because it never works, when has that ever worked. Never, that's when. Which might be when she is too. This is Never. Certainly checks out. Reflexively, she reaches into her pocket and pulls out her phone to look at the clock. The phone is in her pocket, and still works. There's just no service. No time. What, no Wi-Fi? She cackles to herself as she thumbs through to settings and sees that there is, in fact, no Wi-Fi here in Never. Now she stops laughing because the phone in her pocket has convinced her, more than the input of her senses, and the fact of her thinking, that she is alive, that Never is perhaps not Never but Sometime and Somewhere. She takes a picture with her phone camera, and then a video, all of which come up black, this place is camera shy it seems, not ready for its close-up. So, cackling once again, she flips it to selfie mode and takes the first selfie she's ever taken in her entire life, she's been in ones other people had taken but this is the first *she's* taken, in her life, if indeed she is still alive, which she is, she knows she is because she's just worked that out, why aren't you paying attention, ha ha, hee hee, she's alive and well, you see? The dead do not laugh except in cut-rate horror stories. Laughter is for the living. Yet she sees in the selfie that there are tears on her face, that's all she sees, an image of her soggy face in a sea of perfect dark. But that's ok, because crying is basically the same as laughing, just in advance, because when something tragic happens everybody says some day we'll look back on this and laugh, but the body says nah dude I'm gonna get a head start and laugh about it now, it's just the heart that doesn't want to laugh, but the brain does because the brain is the body but the body is not the mind and the mind is not the brain it's really not that complicated, it's really very simple. What's the heart? Is that what's pulsing and humming outside the tunnel? No clue, but not the what but the where, the *here*, that's the where! What?

Squish!

To think on her surroundings is to change them. Perhaps it's like seeing the pattern, spotting the face in the woodgrain. Perhaps it's not like that at all. Perhaps it's like something else entirely. This is a land of perhaps, but the nearest thing to a certainty Jenmarie has is that in the folds of the accordion, the give in the ribs, the space between the jellyfish, there are glimpses of worlds beyond. Landscapes without distance, perspective collapsing into a single point, peaks and valleys coexisting in precisely the same space, rivers spraying every which way and deserts searing the air into ghostly bacon strips, together forever, never apart, yet one untouched by the other. With each pulse of the tunnel, each silent contraction and release that seems accompanied by a hushed *whmm* noise but, upon closer inspection, is perhaps (perhaps!) passing in silence, leaving Jenmarie's mind to supply the sound, with each of these squishy squeezes the scenery changes, the pinhead universe regenerates. Are they being improved, or are they decaying? Their tendency, she intuits, she somehow *knows,* is towards perfection. But what kind of perfection? There are, after all, so many different kinds.

Silence. Yes, this, wherever whenever whatever this place is, is silent. The sounds are coming from inside Jenmarie's head. The calls are coming from inside the house, hee hee, ha ha. She's sure of this. Of hee hee ha ha, she is certain. It is the only fixéd truth, in the Land of the Jellyfish.

Until wow, and then what's this, suddenly gee whiz, Jenmarie is no longer in the tunnel of slug. Did anything materialize from the darkness at either end? She doesn't think so. She hadn't seen anything. Simply, now, at once, no fanfare, no heads up, just plop, she's out of the tunnel and standing on what. Standing on something. What something? Some sort of something. Or other. Some something or other. Standing. Not floating. Much less mystical, but that's fine. That's alright. It's nice to stand, sometimes.

Look down, then. Look. The surface upon which her feet are, sigh, standing but not, of course, touching, so yes we haven't rid ourselves of the mystical quite yet, no, there's still some spooky shit left in store, at any rate the surface, the material, the floor so to speak, is of the same marble as the façade of the building. The pattern swirl oh let's call it marbling of the marble moves far more quickly in here, no mistaking what it's up to, it's curling like the smoke that peels off rotting mulch, like a thick mist sliding up an embankment, like snakes thrown from the loft of the barn. Yet in flashes of deadlight she can see now, she can know without having to be told, that this isn't marble. It's something different, made to look like marble. And yes, it was made. There is intention behind it. She knows. How does she know? She does. Just look at it. How? There is no light. No light above, no light below. No light on either side, if we're being thorough. But no darkness, either. No shadow. Not a single shadow anywhere here. She looks down at her hand, folds her fingers over her palm and sees them casting no pall across her lifeline, across the nooks and crannies she'd once scrutinized in others, that was her thing for a few months back in middle school, she'd learned how to "read palms" and used this as an excuse to take up boys' hands in her own and feel their warmth, sometimes feel them trembling, for they were just as nervous as she, just as elated by the touch of another...

Light below. Yes, *light*. Below. Which puts her above. Above what? Above below, duh. How can she see below? The light shines through the marble that isn't marble. So what's above, then? Nothing. Nothing is above. She reaches up and touches nothing, thick and viscous nothing, like fresh maple syrup. Mmm. It doesn't smell like fresh maple syrup, though. Doesn't smell like anything. She's got her fingers nearly inside her nostrils now, and nothing. As for a taste test, she'll avail herself of the context clues and guess that the goop won't taste much like fresh maple syrup either. No smell, no taste, no sound. Thinking more on her sensations, there's no temperature in here. No touch. She

151

can see her feet on the not-so-marble, yet she can't *feel* them. She can remember what a flat surface feels like against the soles of her feet, and she catches herself lugging the memory up from storage and draping it over this moment, if it is indeed a moment. But it takes hardly any work to recognize that recollection for what it is. Here, now, as for this, in the current maybe-moment: no touch.

So: below. The light. The light that is unmistakably a light slicing through something that's other than darkness but not quite light. How to get down to it? Why, the stairs, of course. The staircase over there. Where's there? It's here, now. Were the stairs always there? No, of course not. It's more than the marbling that shifts and slithers. Architecture is febrile, it's got moods. How does she know this? It's alive. It was constructed. It's a jellyfish.

Ok. So she goes down the stairs. It's a long way down. Down down down, surrounded by what appears to be, but isn't, marble. She remembers sensations for herself, knowing full well she's experiencing none of them, yet powerless to do anything *but* experience them. The cold of the stone, the echoing of her footsteps through the tall, tiny, cavernous, claustrophobic cellar steps from the attic of the universe (yes all at once, it can be all things to one person at one time, all the time), the jolt of her feet landing on the next rise down, the taste of fresh maple syrup (this one less in response to an immediate stimulus, more wishful thinking). It puts her in mind of a grand tomb, something in which an emperor would have had himself, well, entombed, probably with his wife and horses and entire army, hell, why not the entire empire, the people and the property alike, because when you're emperor what's the difference, one by one, single file, no rush, into the tomb you go, of course we have room, can't you see how far down it goes (forever), can't you see how much room we have (for everyone)? There's room in the tomb, come on in. It's a deep tomb, one she entered on the ground floor, yet one in which ascent is impossible. Down is the only way to go. Had the tunnel, the esophagus, the intestines dropped her where she entered, though? Or had it been as an elevator, rushing her to the top? Does she feel like she is high up off the Earth, or moving deeper and deeper into it? Does it matter? Can she say? Yes and no. But in what order? The tomb is either deep, or it is high. And that little part of her brain that has yet to break, the same one that had dubbed this place The Citadel for no reason beyond it's sounding cool, somehow the only subsection of her brain still functioning, that peaceful piece of mind stirs and decides that the tomb is high, because a High Tomb sounds cooler than a Deep Tomb. And thus, the ontology of the space is established. It is high, not deep, and nothing can persuade her otherwise.

She can feel the Tomb approve. This is no more its name than the Citadel was, yet these are words to which it will answer. The High Tomb. It will answer.

Suddenly, after years and years of descent, Jenmarie reaches the light. The light isn't a light, it's not light at all, but it's lightier than the not-light-not-dark of the not-light-light. Jenmarie looks at it and squints, not because she needs to but because that is what one does at things one does not understand. One squints. So, being one faced with the unknown, Jenmarie squints. She looks up and sees the path by which she'd descended still open to her. She looks down and sees the same path spiraling down down *way* down. To her flanks, on this level, there is nothing save the light. Save the light, all is as it has been. So it's obvious, then, isn't it? What she has to do? Is obvious? No? She must step into the light. This is what is needed from her. Demanded, even? No. No? Yes to no. It feels too…polite. An offering. A gift. Here is the light, save it. Save the light. It doesn't need you, but it will have you all the same. So Jenmarie takes a step towards it, and then another, and then another, and then she's in it. And then she's in a jellyfish tunnel, light here but darkness at either end, with impossible worlds to either side. Floating drifting shuffling through silence. Perfect silence, so perfect she has no choice but to project imperfections upon it. Squishes of the gelatinous décor, shushing sounds from the shifting fabric of her clothes, a heartbeat, either hers or the one flexing the folds of the tunnel. And

T
H
E
N

She was holding a child's hand in hers, bent so low her forehead was nearly resting upon the palm. Jenmarie looked up and locked eyes with her middle school crush (well, third crush from the top). She couldn't recall his name, but that was the last thing on her mind just then. The *first* thing on her mind was the fact that her third-best middle school crush was precisely as she'd remembered him, prior to his moving away in the eighth grade. I.e., a middle-schooler.

Jenmarie looked down at herself to discover that she, too, was a middle schooler. She was wearing some stupid fucking tie-dye shirt, because, wow, she'd completely forgotten about this but in her middle-school years she had worked summers at Camp Cherokee, which now that she thought about it was a little fucked up because there were totem poles and teepees everywhere, Native American minstrelry run by for and about white kids it seemed, it wasn't part of the mission statement but it was the *de facto* rule, anyway Camp Cherokee, where once she had been a camper but now returned as a junior counselor, but being too young for real responsibilities she was only ever given rather low-stakes supervisory tasks, and her favorite was overseeing the tie-dying, which, worst case scenario, a kid spilled the ink on themselves, or couldn't figure out how to tie the shirt properly, it was really just the two steps, tie and dye, and if some little dipshit found a way to tie and then die, well, perhaps that was a kind of Darwinism at work, and anyway, one of those little dipshits who had actually been fairly sweet was a kid named, what was it, maybe Luke? Call him Luke, why not, Luke had had a crush on her, as young boys always go for older girls, whereas older men always go for younger women, but as a young boy Luke was into the older girl, which was to say middle-school-aged Jenmarie, and so he tried to tie-die (whoops, dye) her a shirt that was purple (her favorite color at the time) with a big pink heart in the middle, but as there were neither purple nor pink dyes, Luke had tried to combine blue and red for the former, and, more poignantly, red and yellow for the latter. The result was not what Luke had intended at all, and so it was with tears in his eyes that he'd handed her the shirt, at which point he'd run weeping into the woods, prompting a minor manhunt (er, boyhunt) to retrieve him. Jenmarie had found the whole display rather pitiful, yet endearing enough to engender a protectiveness toward the boy's feelings. So as the other campers taunted him, Jenmarie wore the shirt Luke had made her every single day for the remainder of the week, over which time she'd come to appreciate it, apparently enough to wear it to school, which she didn't remember doing, and apparently enough to have it on as she grabbed the tiny little hand of her third-top crush in middle school in, what year would this have been? 1999? 2000?

"Oh, fuck me," she whispered to her third-top crush.

Her third-top crush wrinkled his nose and glanced nervously towards the teacher.

"Jenmarie!" the teacher – Mrs. Carmody, that was her name, wow, who would have thought Jenmarie still had that name rattling around her head, who would have known it would come in handy like this – shouted. She had good ears, huh? Mrs. Carmody? "What kind of language is that?"

Slowly, Jenmarie lifted her gaze from the child's hand she held in hers, which was also a child's hand, hers was the hand of a child which naturally, logically, inevitably implied that the rest of the body attached to the hand, *her* hand, was a child's, she was a child, it was 1999 or 2000 and what the fuck, this was the work of the Tomb? Turning people into kiddies again?!

"I'm a fucking *child!*" Jenmarie shouted.

Mrs. Carmody looked as though she was caught between reprimanding little Jenmarie Bell, and running as far away from her as she possibly could.

Jenmarie grasped for some thought by which to steady herself, to prove that this wasn't a dream, that she hadn't imagined her adulthood, and came back with a handful of all the wrong ones: "On September 11, 2001," she reminded herself, shocked at how small and high her voice was, frustrated at how little gravity she could muster with it, but hey, at least she wasn't screaming anymore, "planes will fly into the twin towers in New York, and one will hit the Pentagon. And in 2008 there's going to be a massive economic crash when the housing bubble bursts. And Donald Trump is going to be president! There's so much horrible stuff that hasn't happened yet." She looked up at her third-top crush, who was staring at his palm as though his fingers had just turned into pickles and Jenmarie had taken a bite. "What's your name?" she asked him. *h-What* h-was what came out of her mouth. Ah, shit. At this age, still being in Tennessee, she'd yet to even *begun* ironing the twang from her voice.

"Huh?" Huh asked.

"I can't remember your name." *Ah cain't.* Fuck.

Huh looked at what few lines his palm had to offer. "Where does it say about the airplane bubbles?"

Mrs. Carmody, who Jenmarie briefly thought might be eight feet tall before remembering that she herself had yet to reach her full height (late bloomer, she'd been – or, perhaps it would be more apt to say, she *is*), stormed over. "Ms. Bell," she began, because ah yes, it was all coming back now, Mrs. Carmody's favorite intimidation technique was to revert to formalities, as though addressing the children thusly would inspire some greater sense of responsibility in them. With the benefit of hindsight, knowing that teachers were far more cynical creatures than she, as a student, had suspected, she wondered if Mrs. Carmody knew, or at least suspected, how the students mocked her behind her back for this, referring to her as *Ms. Mrs. Carmody.* "What on Earth," she continued, "are you talking about?"

Jenmarie looked up at her teacher, stunned at how calm she felt, how logical this all seemed. Perhaps it was shock numbing the horror, or perhaps she'd yet to accept that this, like the High Tomb itself, was no dream, no hallucination, but a thing that was actually happening to her, right now, which was twenty years ago as of a few hours ago, but was now, well, *now*. But how to explain this to Mrs. Carmody?

"I think I got *17 Again*'d," she whimpered, feeling the fact overwhelm her the moment she turned to face it. So she gulped loudly enough to fill out the hollow yawning inside her chest with echo and asked, "has *17 Again* come out yet?"

Mrs. Carmody's mouth dropped open, ever so slightly, another little tic Jenmarie had completely forgotten about. It was the tell that she didn't know the answer to a question a student was asking – a lapse in knowledge being something to which Mrs. Carmody would never, ever admit.

"The movie," Jenmarie continued, having no interest in watching her teacher flail for a way to respond – she could feel the hollow peeling itself open, wider and wider…

From the way that Mrs. Carmody said "ah yes, the movie, I wasn't sure what you were talking about," Jenmarie knew that it hadn't come out yet. Maybe Zac Efron hadn't even been born yet. No, that couldn't be. Of course he'd been born. He just wasn't a *thing* yet. Or maybe he was? Hadn't he been a child star? Not the point!

"Ok," Jenmarie tried again, "what about *Big?* The Tom Hanks one?"

On surer ground here, Mrs. Carmody nodded enthusiastically. "Of course. I've seen *Big.* It's great." She narrowed her eyes. "Have *you* s-"

"Sure is," Jenmarie agreed. "Well, I think I've kind of reverse-*Big*'d. Except instead of turning me into a kid in 2019, which was when I was, it just sent my mind backward in time. So I'm kind of from the future, I guess, or at least my brain is. Sorry, didn't realize I was gonna scream like that, sorry. But there was this creepy building in New York, that's where I live, er, where I was living as an adult…in New York, not in the creepy building, but anyway I was doing my oncology fellowship at NYU, doing pretty fucking well for, sorry, I know, *freaking* well for myself in

159

terms of, like, I was good at my job at least, but you know, maybe
not the other stuff, anyway, and so I got a little bit too wrapped
up in this creepy building, which, you know, I guess I see that
now, being a thirteen-year-old again has given me some perspective I guess you could say, a bit of distance, I went through a
pretty nasty divorce and I maybe spiraled a little bit, but, huh,
huh, oh gosh, wow, how long have I been crying? I swear I'm
not sad, I guess I'm just a little overwhelmed because now I'm in
the past again because listen I went into the creepy building with
a crowbar and it was made of marble that moved, well the marble
didn't move but the patterns on it did, and gosh this all sounds
pretty silly in this stupid fucking, sorry, accent I've got, no offense to yours Mrs. Carmody, everybody is free to sound how they
wanna sound but I personally think it's fucking stupid, I know, I
know, anyway, I said sorry already, Jesus. Sorry. But what I'm
trying to tell you is I, hah, huh," she took the tissue her third-top
crush had procured for her with his left hand, his right still being
held prisoner by Jenmarie's left as she grabbed the tissue with
her right and honked into it, "what I'm trying to tell you is I was
in the tower, I went through this jellyfish sphincter thing, and
I'm being glib now because I know that's not what it was but it
was *something* alright, but it didn't have smell or sound or feeling,
it was just this this this *thing,* and it dropped me in a big tower
and then and it was like a tomb, like a tower tomb, a High Tomb,
and then," another honk into the already soiled tissue, which left
her with a coating of mucus on the tip of her nose, "aw jeez,
could I get another tissue? Thanks." Wipe, honk. "Aw jeeze,
could I g…thanks." Wipe, honk. "Anyway what I'm saying is I
was in the tower and I thought about this memory, I mean not
honking and blowing my nose because I didn't remember this
because it hadn't happened before, I meant me reading the palm

of a kid I had a crush on, which, don't make that face, I don't have a crush on you anymore, I'm a thirty-three year old divorcee for fuck's sake, you're young enough to be my son if I'd had a kid in my twenties, but I remembered this and a light came on below me in the tower, only it wasn't a light, but I went towards that and went through another jellyfish and now I'm here in the past. We should all invest in the companies that I know will be successful in the future. Apple!" And then she resumed screaming as the hollow swallowed her, gobbled her from the inside out, pitched her into an abyss of which she was both the boundary and the bottomless deep.

So Mrs. Carmody called for the principal, who personally escorted Jenmarie (who had graduated from 'screaming and seizing' to 'choked sputtering and middle-distance staring') to the guidance counselor's office. The guidance counselor was called Ms. Bullshea, which an earthier student body would most certainly have twisted into Ms. Bullshit. But these were sheltered suburban children for whom imagination was the thing LeVar Burton walked you through on television, and so Ms. Bullshea was dubbed Ms. Bulbshape, despite the fact that she cut an almost worryingly trim figure. Jenmarie sat outside, listening to the principal, whose name escaped her, trying to convince a discomfited Ms. Bullshea that as school counselor she was indeed qualified to deal with this girl's problems, counselor was right in the job title, and besides, if there was anything little Jenmarie needed just then it was *guidance*, well, guidance and maybe some sort of horse tranquilizer because the way she swung from gibbering frenzy to perfect catatonia and back was *incredibly* upsetting and it'd have been terrific if they could just make her go to sleep, not that that was, you know, that wasn't school policy, just, Jesus, it was freaky, but anyway, they just needed to buy time until her parents came. They had both been contacted and were on their way.

That was a suitable smelling salt for Jenmarie. Her parents were on their way. God, she hadn't spoken to her parents in *years*, not because of any grand falling out they'd had, or some cataclysmic rift that had yawned open between them, but more because, well, she'd forgotten why, but there was certainly a why and it was highly plausible and persuasive. She was grown, she'd gotten busy, regular calls had become semi-regular had become sporadic had become a thing of the past. Yeah, that was it. Her first impulse, then, was to insist that her parents be called off, this was hardly the context in which to host a grand reunion, but the twofold stupidity of such a thought quickly revealed itself to her. The more obvious prong was that here, now, it had not been years since she'd seen her parents. It had been hours. More troubling was the second objection; that she was well and truly fucked here. She, or her consciousness anyway, had been sent back in time, into her old body. Somehow. *Twenty years* in the past. Did that mean she was stuck here now? Did she have to live through her adolescence again, live through *puberty* (and the late bloom that had so humiliated her), take all the tests, apply to all the colleges, go through school, through fucking *residency*…did she have to do all of this shit over again?!? Was she doomed to do it all again? Maybe this was some transdimensional Being's idea of doing her a solid. Take the fruits of life's brutal pedagogy and uh, mix up a different sort of smoothie with them. Or…whatever. A metaphysical mulligan, was that what somebody, or that dun dun dun some*thing,* was trying to give her?

Well, shit, that was awfully generous, but not something in which she was interested. How to re-gift, then?

The High Tomb. She had come down to get here – it was a

simple matter of getting back to it, forcing her way inside once again, and going back up to where she'd come from. Only that wouldn't work, would it? She'd seen too many time travel movies to expect that it would. In the time between now and whenever she could convince her parents to take her to New York, a place she knew they had absolutely no interest in going, she would make different decisions than she had in her first go-around as a thirteen-year-old, set different balls rolling, recruit different butterflies into flapping up different hurricanes. No matter how careful she tried to be, even if she could hypothetically obtain a diagram of her past-now-present, instructing her precisely where to put her feet and what to say and when to breathe, the mere fact of her returning with different knowledge was sure to cause a disturbance akin to dragging three elephants onto a space shuttle just prior to liftoff. All the fine-tuned measurements in the world wouldn't keep things from getting *Challenger*-esque, which, come to think of it, "what day is it?" Jenmarie asked.

"Tuesday," Ms. Bullshea replied, visibly suspicious of Jenmarie's sudden-onset lucidity.

Jenmarie shook her head and made some wet gasping noises that were byproducts of mirth or grief, she couldn't be sure which. And what was the difference. "Of course it is."

So if she went back to the High Tomb and walked back up, assuming she were in, what, a new timeline let's say, she would be returning to a 2019 that was fundamentally different from the one she'd left. Well, that was a little too grandiose – her impact on the world at large was bound to be vanishingly small, if indeed she'd left any sort of legacy that could rise to meet a word as powerful as 'impact.' 2019 would be just as she'd left it, then, but her place within it would be fundamentally different. Most notably in her apparent absence between, uh, "what year is it?" she asked, eliciting a suitably baffled pause from Ms. Bullshea, in which she made a face that was something between concern for the child's well-being and frustration at having one more thing to explain to the parents. It emerged that the year was indeed 1999, which ok, let's say she got back to the High Tomb this year, and let's say the High Tomb still existed, er, existed *yet*, if that was, well, anyway, and furthermore let's say she was able to crowbar her way back in. Where would she go? Was it only her consciousness that moved through time? In 2019, her *old* 2019, for example, had she vanished? Had her body crumpled lifelessly to the ground at the corner of Fourth and 57th, and was it as invisible to passersby as the High Tomb itself was? What would happen to new 1999 Jenmarie if she got back into the High Tomb and launched herself twenty years into the future? Would she pop out in 2019 to find she'd been considered a missing person? Or if the body was the vessel, and the Tomb had simply plucked her consciousness from it to be shuffled about through time and space, what would happen if she'd been declared dead, and had been buried or burned? Would she be dropped back into her body in 2019 to find herself sealed in an altogether narrower tomb, a casket she'd claw vainly at for a few fleeting moments (or maybe, you know, *days)* before she finally died a proper death? Or would her mind find no body to which to return, and so, what, float freely through the aether, perhaps fucking off to find whoever, *what*ever, had constructed the High Tomb and so *destroyed her life?*

Suddenly a piece of the future imposed itself upon the past, and things became, for the moment, quite a bit simpler for Jenmarie: she had a panic attack twenty years ahead of schedule. The universe, which had in the past few hours become far too large to bother with something as puny as a human, obligingly collapsed into a more comprehensible sort of nothing, shrinking and shrinking until all that was left was Jenmarie's right cheek, and the high-pile carpet of Ms. Bullshea's office.

F
O
L
K
S

She awoke to the faces of her mother and father, far younger than she remembered them. The thought that it was Jenmarie herself who had so aged them in the years leading up to their lapse in communication slammed into her like a wrecking ball into a children's hospital, which put her in mind of that stupid song, the wrecking ball did, not the other bit, but she very quickly realized that said stupid song hadn't been written yet, or at least it hadn't been recorded, sometimes these songs were written and tucked into a drawer for years before they saw the light of day, but well and at any rate, there would be no songs about wrecking balls on the radio any time soon, so maybe there were *some* perks to being blasted back into one's adolescent body.

"Why is this happening to me?" Jenmarie heard herself ask in a high, brittle voice.

"Oh, baby," Mom cooed, which made Jenmarie cry harder than she had since her divorce. Which wouldn't be for another nineteen-odd years now. Which, in point of fact, wouldn't be happening at all, unless she could somehow manage to tread the precise path by which she'd met, befriended, fallen for, and then out with, Eddie. Yeah, her current predicament *could* be considered a second chance, a new lease on life, and other nonsense of that nature. Which ought to have been a relief. But it was only now, staring down the fast-fading prints on the path still before her, that she recognized the small torch she'd been shielding in the back of her mind, away from the tempests of fury and shame, a flame she had hoped might one day find kindling and regain its former glory, its incomparable warmth, its gorgeous light. She'd believed, in a way she could never have articulated and would have, in fact, denied ferociously, that there might have been a reconciliation to play out with Eddie, that if only she could get her head screwed back on, if only she could figure her shit out and change accordingly, then she might be able to show him *how* she'd changed, and make it work. The joke was on her, of course, because she was going to get half of her wish. She was going to change whether she wanted to or not; she was going to have more time than she'd bargained for to figure her shit out. By the time she was thirty-three again, she'd be fifty-three. Her *mind* would be, at least, but the mind was inseparable from the physical brain, which was subject to all manner of squirts and pulses that were themselves dictated by glands and hormones, or maybe the hormones *were* the squirts? Point was, would having a fifty-three year-old mind matter if her body were still pumping her brain full of thirty-three year-old juices? She hoped not; that way, she could write off her sudden wistful longing for Eddie as a by-product of her second pubescence. The truth, though, was likely something more complicated. Oh, who was she kidding. Of *course* it wasn't more complicated. The explanation was simple: it was to shrug, stick out one's lips, run a finger up and down over them to make a *bh-bh-bh-bh-bh* noise, and then soil one's trousers.

Heroically, she managed to keep herself from doing this. What she did instead was press her head back into the pillow (there was a pillow under her head, where was she, the nurses' office, no the hospital, the school had no doubt wanted shut of the problem child as quickly as possible, Ms. Bullshea probably would have just slid Jenmarie out the window and called it a day if she could have), screw her eyes shut, and find new depths from which to dredge up thick, oily tears. She'd wanted a second chance, she hadn't known it but she had, wanted the second chance that was, not known it, that wasn't what she had, that was what she hadn't. Well, here it was. Her metaphysical mulligan. She didn't want it. If she'd known what it would mean, where it would lead, she'd never have followed the memory of her third-top crush's soft, pink-ass little palm that didn't even have any lines on it to speak of, the kid had yet to turn that hand to anything more strenuous than slapping at his little dingus, trying to work out the cheat code his friends had told him about – and good god, that reminded her, she wouldn't be able to have sex with anyone for at least five years; even if it were *legal* to have sex with another minor, as she was now herself a minor, that would only be on a technicality, and besides, to even consider the abominable act was enough to parch her for the foreseeable future, and the odds of finding a man her "own age," which was to say in his thirties, who was willing to have sex with a minor were, come to think of it, pretty good, but she sure as hell didn't want to sleep with a grown man who was interested in sleeping with a child...whatever, point was, if she'd known where the High Tomb would lead, she'd have chosen a checkpoint nearer her own time, sliding back downstream just far enough to head off the troubles with Eddie at the pass. But what if she'd done that, only to discover that the troubles were inevitable, that all choices would lead to her alone, miserable, and only intermittently conscious between panic attacks?

That was nearly enough to send her back under, but she stayed afloat by fixing her gaze on her parents' faces and thinking about how happy she'd have been to have never seen them again, because why, what had they done, it wasn't what they'd done was it, it was who they were, they were the shameful south, they were the twang in Jenmarie's voice, they were the contradiction of her cosmopolitan pretensions, that was their sin, that was what they'd done, which wasn't anything, they hadn't done anything, it was she who had done, done to them, done what, done *wrong*, she had wronged them by pushing them away, pushing herself away, for no other reason than she didn't want to be them, but being near someone isn't the same as being them, of course not, no, then why had she done it, she'd done it because she hadn't known what else to do maybe, or she'd done it because she'd known it had to be done, even if it didn't. She didn't know and it didn't matter anymore because she hadn't done any of it yet. Would she again? Impossible to say. But she would find out. Slowly, agonizingly, in real time, one grain of sand slipping through the glass bottleneck at a time, plop plop plop, she would live her youth over again, and she would find out.

"Hi Mom," she said to her Mom.

"Hi Dad," she said to her Dad.

And then she started crying again, but her parents didn't cry.

They didn't understand why they should have. It had only been this morning they'd last seen their daughter, after all. But what truly sent Jenmarie off the deep end was considering not what was happening to her, but what had happened to the thirteen-year-old Jenmarie Bell, the one who was the daughter to these two elder Bells, Barry and Carrie. 2019's Jenmarie had overwritten 1999's. Their daughter, as they knew her, was dead. Gone. Erased. No more. They didn't know it, but they had a new daughter, one far more damaged than the original model.

"I wanna go home," she told them.

"We'll be goin' home just as soon as we got some clue of what..." her father trailed off, glancing towards his wife, who was Jenmarie's mother, who was currently just a few years north of Jenmarie's age. Her *actual* age.

"We'll be going home soon," her mother filled in.

No, Jenmarie thought. They would be going to *their* home, and taking her with.

She spared a thought for how young her parents were. Only a few years older than she herself was. Had been. Er...whatever. Jenmarie tried to imagine starting a family, raising children. Had she stayed married. Had she never found the Tomb. Oh, how unprepared her parents must have felt. *All* parents. Nobody on the planet had ever been old enough to have children. Which explained why everybody's kids turned out the way they did.

In the interest of speeding her father's clue-getting process along (for there was more waiting than she could bear coming her way), she informed them that she had suffered a vasovagal syncope brought on by stress. A panic attack. What she needed was sertraline and trazodone, started at fifty milligrams per day each, to be scaled up to one hundred milligrams and seventy-five milligrams, respectively. Her parents assured her that she should rest, the doctor would explain everything, to which Jenmarie sighed and assured *them* that doctors couldn't explain nearly as much as they pretended they could. She did not add that she knew this from experience, being a doctor herself. Having been, anyway. Christ, how it chafed! Stripped of her credentials! The antipathy she felt for the nurse who came rolling in to explain that they, ha ha, *couldn't* explain what had happened to Jenmarie was as childish and unproductive as it was undeniable. The young patient asked, not at all patiently, if perhaps a vasovagal syncope brought on by stress might not be a plausible account of her tumble into insensibility. The nurse conceded that it might. Jenmarie looked *very* smugly at her parents, whose apparent indifference to their daughter's diagnostic aptitude fully kneecapped the precocious young Bell's triumph. So she slumped back into the lumpy hospital bed, slouched into the wheelchair they brought around for her, and shot *bolt upright* when Barry brought the car around. The laughter that escaped her was a shrill, lunatic cluck.

"What's wrong?" Carrie wondered.

"I forgot what Dad's car looked like," Jenmarie mumbled. She corrected herself: "Looks."

Barry's car, and so the Bell family's car, was a dinosaur even in the late nineties. It was a Chevy Caprice Classic (a name which could be emphasized any number of ways to mildly amusing effect), a low four-door fossil burdened with a dusky cream paint job and wooden paneling along the bottom. It came with an ashtray in the backseat, for God's sake. Factory standard! It was, Barry joked with a frequency that betrayed an unpleasant truth, a car he'd chosen for its ineffable whiteness. There were roads in Tennessee that he, being quite a bit darker of skin than most of his soft pink neighbors, felt uncomfortable driving down at any time other than high noon, and some of these roads had a habit of sneaking up on him if he made so much as a single wrong turn. The Caprice, then, was a camouflage, a car that only a white suburbanite would be caught dead in – and so, Barry would chuckle joylessly, a car that he hoped a black man would not be caught alive in, and so, well, one can see how that joke ends.

She nearly wondered where her siblings were, before the obvious answer slapped her on the back of the head: still at work. The answer slapped her again, but harder: still at *school*.

It was fascinating, to watch reality swell to fill the holes in her memory with mundanity of this sort, blurring the line between the two kingdoms as it did. It wasn't that she questioned whether or not the whole of her life up to the High Tomb had been a dream, not at all. Simply that, as Chuckey, Tennessee crawled past outside the window of the Caprice Classic, and as Jenmarie noted each forgotten landmark and storefront as just that, *forgotten,* the interior of the Tomb (and all that had come before it) was already taking on the gauziness of a half-remembered dream. Which terrified Jenmarie. What if she should forget her old life, and return fully to this one, only to make precisely the same choices to deliver her once more to the Tomb, running the loop over and over and over for eter…oh, wow, wasn't that where the Wallis Shopping Center used to be? Which was to say, would be? Gosh, that land had been cornfields? Which was to say, were now? Gosh again, but Jenmarie had *completely* forgotten about… that. Yes. That. Jenmarie focused on that, on the *difference* between how things would be and how they now were. It was all she had to link her to her old life, in the future.

Chuckey, Tennessee was, to put it so mildly one was hardly putting it at all, not an urban center. The nearest halfway civilized outpost was Johnson City some twenty miles away, a city named for Andrew Johnson, a man known to history as *who? Lincoln's*

173

veep? Oh yeah, I guess somebody had to finish out the term, huh? But still, there was no shortage of disagreement between the Tennessee before her and the one she had known. These discrepancies could be hard to identify, as they so often took the form of those landmarks by which Jenmarie had oriented herself during her last years in Tennessee (which, lacking these, only deepened her disorientation now). The four-lane highway, for a start, hadn't reached Hotdog Lane – so it was still just a single dirt road that broke from the nearest Interstate (and *that* only got one within five miles of Chuckey), looped around through Limestone, struggled over the train tracks, tore through Greeneville, and *then* rumbled into Chuckey, at which point one could follow another dirt (and then gravel) road to 1137 Hotdog Lane. So it wasn't until Greeneville that Jenmarie realized where they were, or why they were going this way – the four-lane had been lain by the time she'd learned to drive, and so it had been easy to forget that once upon a time the trip home had been far more circuitous. Also absent was The Barn On Bill Dunscomb's Property, a bright red behemoth that would, in about 2004 or 2005, take pride of place atop the hill just behind the bullethole-riddled WELCOME TO CHUCKEY sign, a salutation so on-the-nose Jenmarie could only imagine that it had been the Chamber of Commerce themselves who had taken those potshots at the placard. The Barn on Bill Dunscomb's Property was always referred to thusly, by its full name (The Barn On Bill Dunscomb's Property), until Jenmarie's older brother Harmon turned it into an acronym and made it work for them. Thus The Barn On Bill Dunscomb's Property became The Bobdip, because they were kids in a hurry. Now, though, *this time around*, Jenmarie would be happy to say The Barn On Bill Dunscomb's Property in its entirety. She had time. She had nothing but time.

Those were arguably the most dramatic absences (at least until the one Jenmarie would kick herself ten times over for not catching immediately), but the more attentively she stared outside the window of her dad's Caprice ("Father's Caprice", now there was a great title for a Lifetime movie, even though Lifetime wasn't Lifetime anymore, or wouldn't…oh shit, should she write a famous movie? That'd be a way to get rich, right? She just had to remember a famous movie word for word. Then get an agent, probably. And make sure it was made the same way. Come to think of it, this was a terrible idea, which she immediately dismissed) and watched Tennessee's past pass by, the more she noticed the endless parade of future-shaped holes in the landscape, the past-now-present smears against her memory. Like Gary's Computer Land, with its lamentable window display of red apples surrounding the words "WE SERVICE THEM ALL" spelled in floppy discs, to which a rather standoffish sheet of 8.5 x 11 printer paper was permanently appended, presenting the single, theoretically-clarifying word "MACINTOSH" in truculent black marker thrusts. Alas, Gary's would one day become a music store called Let's Hear It, with the 's' in 'Let's' being made to look like a clef, and which would itself go out of business sometime around 2009, to be replaced by a State Farm agent's offices. Oh, and there was Ties To Meet You, a formalwear rental shop that went under, *will* go under a few years from now when a Men's Wearhouse opens up off the forthcoming four-lane. Ah, and let's not forget to remember the plinth in Limestone that will stand empty by 2017, when a push from the historically Unionist eastern side of the state (where Chuckey was located) to remove a statue of the confederate war hero by the tragic name of Gideon J. Pillow – a man hailing from the seditious center of Tennessee – and replace him with the likeness of someone from the Volunteer State who maybe *wasn't* a hate monster on the wrong side of history eventually devolved into a compromise by which the pedestal would remain empty, the Pillow statue would be shuttled off to a museum (TBD), and no taxpayer money would be spent casting a tribute to someone those dirty liberals found acceptable, who would probably not only be a woman but a black as well, *yuck*, no thanks, yee-haw, etc. anyway, that was all to come, but for now, there was Brigadier General Pillow in the bronze, protecting his little corner of town with saber drawn and expression confused. This was technically not an absence but a presence, though Jenmarie would argue that the statue's presence detracted, and so was, in its way, an absence. Hers had become a life of technicalities, so why the fuck not, huh? If that wasn't acceptable, though, there was always the empty storefront that would, sometime around 2006 or 2007, near about the last time Jenmarie would physically come down here, transform into Everyday Living, an atypically trendy coffee joint for the area that seemed to have been destined for Los Angeles and somehow gotten lost, settling (in so many ways) for the small center of Greeneville, which after attempting to branch out into small-scale retail merchandising of their signature roasts would enter a protracted legal battle with Kroger, whose house brand was also called Everyday Living, a dispute that the lowly café couldn't afford to prolong, and so settled by changing their name to Many Days Living, a purely superficial rebranding which nonetheless took a bite out of their clientele (though the Dunkin Donuts, which this far south was downright exotic, that went up – *will* go up – on that blasted four-lane certainly didn't help matters), resulting in the spot's once again becoming an empty storefront in 2010, which *was* the last time Jenmarie ever came down here. It had occurred to her that it was perhaps the sight of that abandoned façade, the words MANY DAYS LIVING existing only as ghostly outlines etched into the edifice itself, where they had been installed with more optimism than a town like Greeneville could rightly sustain, that had been the last straw for Jenmarie, that had pushed her over the edge from gritting her teeth and returning home every few years to throwing her self-sufficiency back in her family's collective face and simply refusing to see them, refusing to even make time for them when they offered to come visit *her*.

Her home, though, her *parents'* home, was largely as she re-membered it. There had been no grand expansions or exterior renovations since 1997, when a single-story mudroom was thrown up, thus freeing the hallway closet space of the washer and dryer, which free space was quickly cluttered up with all of the arcane, hyper-specific culinary paraphernalia Barry and Car-rie had always wanted to buy but never wanted to use. The home, all but complete in '99, was exquisitely middling; it was largely a ground-floor affair, though the left half shot up in what should have been called a finished loft, but which Barry got away with calling the 'second story' for lack of contradiction. The vinyl pan-eling was nearly the same dull ivory of the Caprice's paint job, the roof grey and peeling. The front door was a deep forest green, for some fucking reason, which was its only real distinc-tion amongst the rest of the neighborhood. And what a neigh-borhood; the Bell's place was the third of seven houses plopped along a slow rise of land that, in the middle of the next decade, would be folded into a neighboring borough which, for reasons Jenmarie would at no point in the subsequent twenty years come to understand (not that she would investigate them too thor-oughly), would excite a frenzy of McMansion construction at the top of the hill, raising property values along the slope to such a degree that those sitting on an adjustable-rate mortgage or two would be chased off, leaving homes in such a state of disrepair that the county wouldn't even see fit to condemn them. Such was the staggering disparity that would come to dominate this part of the country, between the monied cityfolks and their millions looking to get "a taste of the country" in one of their seasonal homes, and the people who were just the taste these city slickers sought, themselves unable to taste much of anything save whatever the rich people had most recently driven the heel of their boot into. Why, in 2001, just prior to that Tuesday in September, but just after Jenmarie's younger brother had been born, one would be able to walk out onto the Bell porch and see a doublewide on cement bearings downslope on the right, a single-story clapboard tumbledown across the street, and upslope on the left, two of those identical pre-fab mansions, the gaudiest of which would feature a massive window over the front door that was sized and positioned to be useless for anything besides forcing the neighborhood to have a look at how fucking big their foyer chandelier was. It got egged every Halloween as a matter of course.

That would be in 2001. Just after Jenmarie's youngest brother had been born.

In…two years.

"Oh, no," she gasped from the backseat, managing a scream for the follow-up: "Jesus Fuck! NO!"

"Jenmarie Bell!" her mom snapped. "Watch your mouth!"

I'm a grown-ass woman, she nearly said, along with *Tomjohn hasn't been born yet!* She suppressed both impulses, dreading the further castigations that would come her way as a result of the former, and the confusion for which she would be unable to satisfyingly account in the case of the latter. So she apologized quietly and bit her tongue as the Caprice swung into the carport (ah, yes, it wouldn't be until around maybe 2004 that some walls and a door would make a proper garage of it). Her parents hefted themselves out of the car, but Jenmarie stayed put in the back seat. Prior to this moment, the shock of what was happening had given her some distance from it. She had been a traveler on an unwelcome detour, but any second now, she was going to snap out of it and step back out of the High Tomb in 2019, no harm, no foul. This was a delusion she could only sustain by virtue of that remove at which she held herself. If she stepped out of this car though, walked into her childhood home in which her brother and sister, Harmon (holylivingfuck) and Melody, were waiting, by this point probably back from school and eager to tease their clumsy sister for her hospitalizing fall once Mom and Dad had sent them all up to bed…ah, yes, there they were, Melody and Jesus Christ, Harmon, with the dark skin and beautiful hair inherited from their father that only further distanced the pale, strawheaded Jenmarie from them, oblivious to what would one day become their painful pasts, ignorant of the younger brother yet unborn, for whom they would fail to be adequate role models, unaware of how closely knit the soon-to-be-dead brother and the older sister would become as a result of Jenmarie's self-imposed exile from the family, having no reason to so much as consider the possibility that Harmon (who leaned against the doorframe to the still semi-fresh mudroom, alive and in the flesh and *alive*, holy fucking Christ, only sixteen years old and so *young* and so *alive* and trying to look bigger than his already considerable five feet and nine inches, giggling about how Jenmarie oughta have watched that first step, it being, naturally, a doozy) would be killed by a drunk driver in 2015, which would cause Melody (now fifteen, peeking out from under Harmon's brawny arm, having the decency to favor Jenmarie with a look of concern that would snap into something pointier once Harmon, whom she still idolized at this age, no longer had his back to her) to confront her own alcoholism, which would in turn open the floodgates to their parents' confessions of substance abuse (a self-destructive pattern from which Carrie had at this point removed herself, from which Barry never truly would)...

Jenmarie had already lived through all of this. Had neither the desire, nor, she was certain, the *strength,* to live through it again. So she sat in the car, because as long as she remained here, as long as she never got out and said hello to her siblings, never stepped into the house, never suffered the past's overly gracious embrace...then she wouldn't have to. The distance would be preserved. The dream would never testify to its own horrible truth.

Barry, master of observation that he was, noticed that Jenmarie hadn't gotten out of the car. So he turned around, opened the driverside door back up, and stuck his head in. "You dizzy?"

Carrie's head sprouted from Jenmarie's right peripheral; she'd taken a more direct ingress through the rear passengerside door, which made it easier for her to reach towards Jenmarie. "Do you need a hand?" Carrie didn't wait for an answer, instead pawing at the clasp of Jenmarie's seatbelt. The hands felt like ice. They were cold, they burned her, they were real. This was real. This was her life now. Again.

So Jenmarie has a positively mythological meltdown, shrieking and wailing and gnashing and smiting and rending. Cold comfort then, that this proved sufficient to wipe the dopey grin from Harmon's face, or to deepen the feeling on Melody's. Cold, burning comfort, because Jenmarie already knew how life itself would effect both of those changes far more permanently. Sure, she could try to redirect things, use her knowledge of the dismal future to steer it down more agreeable paths. But she didn't want to. Given the choice, she'd have zapped herself right back into the future from which she'd come, back into the life she'd known, because for all of the ways in which that life was an awful little thing, for all of the ways in which it was never a life she would have wished herself to have, it was the life she'd arrived at as a result of having lived it. The fact of the life and the act of the living, these were somehow completely different things to Jenmarie. A life might be absolutely miserable, but it was nothing compared to the horror that was *living* it. So yes, without a second thought, she would consign her older brother to an early grave, her sister to a depth of depression that would break her in ways that she could tend to but never truly repair, and her younger brother to reach adulthood in a family that would grow a touch too protective of the love they still had left to give. She would happily have rerun the whole experiment just as it had been run the first time, if only it meant she could have her miserable, awful, horrible little life back the way it had been.

Between gasps and sobs, she considered the possibility that what she believed to have been her first 'run' through life was not, in fact, the first. Put the fast-fading memory of her old life (to which she would cling as driftwood) to one side; what if somebody else had found the High Tomb at some point, and reset the clock for themselves, and so everyone else? What if the 'infinite universes' theory was true simply by virtue of the fact that millions, perhaps billions of resets had been performed through the High Tomb, each one generating a new divergent timeline? Good Jesus, it only made sense that Jenmarie had reset the entire universe back to Earth's 1999 when she went through the High Tomb, right? It wasn't as though it made sense to imagine that *only* Earth had been wound back, did it? So what did that mean? Where there more High Tombs out there, setting and resetting the universe? For how long? Were there an infinite number of Jenmaries out there...or were there a *finite* number, and yet an infinite number of universes in which she, her parents, her entire lineage, the human race, never made an appearance? And however many other Jenmaries there were out there, how many of *them* had stumbled upon the High Tomb, and gone on resetting, creating new timelines, new universes?

It was a lot to think about, so Jenmarie focused on the skeleton touch of her mother and screamed and screamed and screamed, no longer crying, just screaming.

F
A
C
E

This was her life now.

What drove this fact home wasn't sitting at the dinner table, the glasstop monstrosity that Jenmarie realized with a chill reminded her of the one she'd had in the apartment she'd shared with Eddie – who was surely a child again too, somewhere out there, innocent of all the hurt he would visit upon Jenmarie, but in a certain sense, already guilty…anyway, she was sitting at the glasstop table here and now, the one that Barry (she struggled to think of him as *Dad* again, as reverting to the formality of the first name had been such an essential step of her freeing herself from their smothering orbit) had bought in a paroxysm of pre-tention, foreshadowing the gestures he would make towards the concept of landscaping once the big spenders came to claim the top of the hill (as was their wont), the purchase of the table being a self-defeating gesture, a perpetual reminder of the Bells' earthy origins, as the circular pane of glass was impossible to keep clean, the ornate wrought-iron laurels upon which it rested (and what a fun own-goal *that* could be read as) being perfectly designed and placed to slice one's thighs into ribbons. But that wasn't what drove the fact, *the* fact, home. Nor was it eating the meal that, at thirteen, had been her very favorite, mom's homemade spaghetti alfredo (the secret ingredient was cream cheese, which explained why it was kept a secret), a dish that in her older years she had decried as being far too unhealthy, and dairy didn't agree with her anyway, and frankly she could get that at any restaurant, and she didn't even like spaghetti, and anyway it was supposed to be fettuccini, *Mom*, but all the same a dish that was today, right now, sitting before her, where all of these eventual criticisms lay, that being *before her*, but so then Jenmarie ate her youthful favorite and found it better than she'd remembered, a fact (but not *the* fact) which she chalked up to her being once more possessed of youthful taste buds. Nor was it returning to her adolescent bedroom that cemented the hopelessness of her situation, seeing the gargantuan cardboard theater standee from *Titanic* that she'd begged, *begged* her father to pester the manager of the single-screen Terrific Theater (long-since closed, except scratch that, still open for another two years) to give to her because she had simply *adored* the film, it had nothing to do with Leonardo DiCaprio, really, nobody believed her but it was true, well it was *mostly* true, no, her favorite part was when the boat was pointing straight up and people kept falling off and hitting tables and propellers on the way down, the romance story was great and she really did adore the rest of the film like she said, just adored it, simply, but it was the people-falling-down bits that really put *Titanic*, ha, over the edge, because how often do you get a romance film with a body count, huh? It was all of thirteen-year-old Jenmarie's favorite things! And so Barry had gotten it for her, the standee, and there it was, taking up a good third of her room, a giant cardboard Titanic to remind her of the people pinballing their way to oblivion, a reminder that would become redundant once she'd bumbled into a romantic life of her own (which, come to think of it, had less in common with Jack and Rose than the poor pinball-people). And the other two-thirds of the room; here was the four-poster bed that was a family heirloom but she'd always hated because when she shifted around at night, and she was a restless sleeper so that happened quite a lot, the bedframe would creak and complain even though it only had one fucking job to do, well technically two because it had been retrofitted to be a bunk bed, as Jenmarie and Melody shared the room, and come to think of it maybe that was why it was always moaning; there was the hand-me-down faux-mahogany dresser that had been Melody's but was now Jenmarie's, a changing of the guard that had been carried out with such little ceremony ("Mom wants you to use this") that six-year-old Jenmarie had always wrestled with the feeling that she was doing something wrong by using it, as though it weren't really *hers*, until she was eight-year-old Jenmarie; here were Melody's N*Sync posters, because of course Melody had N*Sync posters, she was so fucking basic, although to be fair N*Sync hadn't hit their astronomically successful stride just yet so technically Melody was ahead of the curve, driving the bandwagon if you will; there, holy shit, there was Jenmarie's Glow Moon, she didn't know what else to call it, it was this little glass ball with a fake moon inside that glowed in the dark (allegedly; its luminescence had more to do with wishful thinking on the part of the observer than any properties of the tchotchke itself), one of those useless baubles from childhood with which one forms an outsize attachment as one grows older (and after one has long since lost the bauble), and in this particular instance one whose magical disappearance would be the most vexing of unsolved mysteries for Jenmarie four years hence, even though of *course* Melody had stolen it. Scattered between these were all of those familiar little details, the paint scuffs incurred when Jenmarie and Melody play-wrestled right over the boundary into real-wrestling, the hole in the ceiling left by the hook from which Melody had mischievously hung a truly terrible *papier-mâché* orrery that Jenmarie had slapped together for science class and received a failing grade on (quite literally *on* – Mrs. Bozeman had scrawled her big red F directly onto the sun), the ugly globs of paint on the southern wall that clearly indicated where Harmon's half-hearted contributions to the 1993 redecoration efforts had been centered.

All of this was, in many ways, an overwhelming refutation of Jenmarie's own memory. It was as though she'd watched *Titanic* again to discover that, yes, it was about star-crossed lovers on an ill-fated vehicle, but what separated the young hearts was not class but species, one being a frog and the other being a tomato, and also the vehicle wasn't a cruise ship but a tandem bicycle careening towards a junkyard. The broad strokes were all correct, if one was willing to accept the word *broad* in its, well, broadest sense, but so many details were wrong that it would be nearer the mark to do what Jenmarie did, which was mumble "shit, I didn't remember this right at all."

Melody laughed nervously. "What does that mean?"

Jenmarie shrugged. "Nothing."

And then Melody said the thing that, more than the kitchen

table or the spaghetti alfredo or the structurally unsound bunk-bed or the big cardboard tragedy or the scuffs or smudges or globs or anything else Jenmarie had seen today, drove home the inescapable fact of what was happening, the fact that it *was* happening. Precisely why the five words she was to utter momentarily should contain within them a world of certainty was something Jenmarie would never understand. But they did.

Melody asked Jenmarie, "what happened to your face?"

Jenmarie narrowed her eyes at her sister, who wasn't prone to playing tricks if Harmon wasn't around to see, and so give his approval, but who also wasn't completely averse to pranking for an audience of one. "What," Jenmarie demanded, "does that mean?"

Melody started to point to her own face, but Jenmarie was out the door and sprinting to the bathroom before her sister's finger had lifted past her clavicle; she knew where Melody was going to point. She knew what she meant to indicate.

There, in the mirror, was Jenmarie as she had never seen herself: young, in the flesh, but with the tragic imposition of hindsight. It was one thing to look back at old pictures and think *that kid has no idea what life has in store for them*. It's another thing entirely to look at one's own face, still soft and unlined, and think, *I know* exactly *what life has in store for me*.

About being unlined, though. That wasn't true. It was what Melody had been starting to tell her. It was what nearly broke Jenmarie, but instead hardened her to her plight.

Her chin. The scar on her chin, the one that had been a gash, earned from slamming onto the floor of a bathroom, twenty years from now.

She still had it. She *already* had it.

How? How was that possible? It wasn't as though she'd landed in her thirteen-year-old body with her iPhone and credit cards and driver's license too. Nor did she have the freckles that would develop exclusively on her left bicep around the time she was graduating high school, a speckling for which she could receive no satisfactory explanations beyond *boy, the human body is pretty crazy sometimes!* She searched her sometimes crazy body for any other markings acquired between now and 2019; the discolored flesh where she'd branded the inside of her right wrist on a cast-iron skillet, the scars on both of her big toes where she'd had to have ingrown nails removed and the nerve beds cauterized with acid, even the chipped tooth she'd suffered in the very same fall as the one that had caused the chin scar. Nothing. Her body was, save the chin scar there, precisely as it had been on the first go-around...or, she conceded, she might be on firmer metaphysical ground to rephrase that as, her body was precisely as it had been the last time she remembered being thirteen in it. Which meant she'd need to get the fucking toe surgery again. And get her wisdom teeth out. And get glasses, but that wasn't so bad. Oh, fuck, she'd have to get braces! Fucking godfucking damnit *fuck!* Her orthodontist had kept telling her parents to wait, wait, wait, so Jenmarie hadn't gotten fucking braces until she was fucking fourteen years old. *Next year.* She bared her snaggleteeth at herself. It was only with a truly courageous application of effort that she managed to not headbutt the bathroom mirror.

This wasn't tenable. She couldn't look at her future as a bloc, she wouldn't be able to function if she let dread hollow her out and fill her up with itself. Cross bridges as they came, get braces as your dipshit asshole orthodontist mother*fuck*, with the rubber bands, she'd forgotten all about those fucking little fucking rubber bands...ok, ok. *Breathe*, she told herself, and thank goodness she was receptive to her own advice. Breathe in, breathe out.

Focus on the breath. It was just like meditating. It *was* meditating, come to think of it. Which, you know, last time she took to meditating she found the High Tomb and wound up here, needing to get fucking *braces* again, wh...no. Ok. Breathe in, breathe out. Focus on the breath. Focus on the scar.

She inspected the scar on her chin, a violence committed by the future. It looked old, far older than it had even appeared on her thirty-three-year-old face when she'd slammed the crowbar into the High Tomb. The scar tissue had receded quite a bit, now resting flat against her face where before it had beveled outward. Not to mention the hue was much calmer than the flushed purple-pink it had shown as before. It made for a nearly invisible slash across her chin, blended perfectly with the surrounding flesh. No wonder nobody had noticed it, or at least nobody thought it worth mentioning to Jenmarie, until Melody had gotten right up close to her.

Was this a dangerous thought to let in, this thought she felt circling her conscious mind at a distance? Would it only complicate an already inconceivable situation? Ah, well, what was the harm? How could she possibly be further disheartened by her lot to consider that her scar looked as though it had moved twenty years into the *future,* even as Jenmarie had slipped twenty into the *past?*

What did that mean? Did it mean anything? It was just one more riddle without a solution. Leave it, then. Jenmarie would take her scar at, ha, face value, as a wound that had gaped, ached, then healed and hardened. She would do the same, then. She would stop thinking of her immediate future as a played-out past through which she was struggling, and start thinking about it as what it, in fact, now was: a future not beholden to whatever might have happened last time. She would do this because she had to, because to attempt anything else would be to lose her fucking mind, and because doing this meant that, yes, she had a chance to live life with the mixed blessing of having her hindsight out in front of her.

Which she would do, she decided. She could do that. Quite a big decision to make in the bathroom, a place where big decisions really *shouldn't* be made. But it was an easy one to make, all the same. Because that little scar told her that the future she had already lived still existed. Somehow, maybe even some*where,* it was waiting. Another floor in another bathroom, eager to split her face in two. Jenmarie could and would do her best to steer herself towards the lovely things, sure…but more to the point, she would live a life that kept her as far from that floor as possible. Among other familiar little evils.

There. That was the decision. Big. Easy.

So she returned to her room, telling Melody "huh, weird, I don't know what that line on my chin is," and then truthfully claimed exhaustion, got in to her little pajamas, and crawled into her little lower bunk (she would be promised the upper bunk "some day" by her father, and never receive it) where she got little sleep, fearful as she was of dreams about High Tombs and colossal orthodontics.

B
I
D
E

Much to her surprise, the greatest challenge turned out to be not sustaining that sense of distance from her old-new-current life, but closing it. As she ate breakfast with her family, trying vainly to reassure them that yes, she was fine, just a slip that scrambled her up a bit, well sure come to think of it the scrambling did precede and so prompt the slip, and what do you mean I'm speaking differently, uh, I ain't no certain what you mean, maw – and so on; as she made the familiar trek down Hotdog Lane with her siblings, onto the cracked and buckling pavement of the Ruritan Road, which as far as she could remember would never see the least infrastructural improvements in the next twenty years, and finally out to where the four-lane would one day stretch across the little dirt

191

path where the school bus rumbled into the shoulder to pick them up before launching, much to the chagrin of its less-than-adequate pickup, back onto the dirt road at speed, a maneuver that young Jenmarie had always taken for granted as The Way Things Were Done, and which the older-young Jenmarie now recognized, given the number of animals and openly truant kids who tended to meander along the middle of that path, as a *fucking insane* way to drive a big metal rectangle full of youngsters, though she also knew that the school bus was never involved in an accident but still, *fucking insane* all the same; as she drifted through her classes, marveling at the unsatisfactory state of the curriculum (the modules on the Civil War were, when viewed with a more comprehensively informed eye, *not great),* struggling vainly to recall where she was meant to go from one period to the next (how many kids remembered their eighth grade schedule two decades after the fact, huh?), having to obtain a printout of her day from a highly suspicious Ms. Bullshea; as all of this was happening to and around and past Jenmarie, she found it astonishingly difficult to engage with. For hopeful though she'd been that knowledge of the future would steer her towards a better revision of the same, the churlish present was quick to curb those sunny thoughts. She knew how everything turned out, yes, but she had little to no memory of the million and one little intermediary steps between her previous past and…well, she supposed the future from which she'd come now *was* her previous past, and this new past was her current present, which meant her previous past future was also her *past* future as she would be returning to a new *future* future…or, current…uh…point was, nothing good came of thinking too hard about any of this, in any sense. For the simple fact was that while she could more or less remember a few of the highlights from her youth, she couldn't recall any of the bits around them. Which made it nigh impossible to know whether she was making the same decisions as she had during her previous life or not…which made knowledge of those highlights more or less useless.

Still. It stood to reason that this little life of hers would be more chockablock with sagacious conduct, if for no other reason than *this* little life's being lived by a grown-ass woman. She had so much more life experience. What did it matter if Jenmarie couldn't recall how she'd responded to the embarrassment of asking to run back to the library to grab an especially good pencil, failing to find it, and glumly rejoining the line of classmates who'd had to wait in the hall while she finished her little errand, only for fucking Cody to shout "it's behind your ear!" and everybody laughed at her, and the teacher didn't even tell them to stop, she just chuckled too and then got them moving again, which was…whatever, it was just embarrassing was all, just as much as it had been the first time it had happened, and so what if Jenmarie couldn't remember how she'd responded to it last time? She was far more mature now. All she had to do was respond authentically, and it would be an improvement over last time. And incremental improvements of that nature would inevitably shepherd her into a better life.

It wouldn't occur to her until much, much later that the "improvement" she was actually after would have been recalling the pencil behind the ear before she'd raised her hand to announce that it had gone missing. As opposed to meeting that flush of embarrassment as a long-forgotten friend. Just as a for instance. But, of course, she had other things on her mind in those early days. Not the least of which was an even more familiar, not-at-all-forgotten friend.

Jenmarie had met Mavis in second grade, and by third the two were inseparable. With a single exception (the time in fourth grade Jenmarie had "accidentally" dropped an action figure on a massive LEGO village Mavis had built using her brother's bricks – her brother being the Lucky who would one day organize the resident's getaway at which Jenmarie would meet her future ex-husband Eddie, *Christ* it made her head spin to have so much of the future already charted! – but anyway "accidentally" was in quotes because Jenmarie had done it on purpose, because she'd wanted to see how the big Technicolor steeple would explode under the weight of a Street Shark falling at terminal velocity, the answer being *awesomely!*, but then Mavis had started crying which really brought the mood down), they'd never even fought, hardly ever even gotten on each other's nerves. Their relationship generated a kind of gravity, such that teachers who positioned them on opposite ends of the room at the beginning of the period would, forty-five minutes later, dismiss a classroom in which Jenmarie and Mavis were sitting together, dead center. It was a poorly kept secret that the two pals' names had been added to The List, a legendary collection of names whose schedules were flagged for personal review by the administrators. Generally speaking, one's name was affixed to The List as a result of bad behavior, bullying or threats or fights, that sort of thing. Jenmarie and Mavis were, as far as any of the students knew, the only two who had made it onto The List on account of friendship.

The upshot to all of this, the *point*, was that Jenmarie and Mavis were peas in a pod, potatoes in a pot, the ball to the socket, the coins in the pocket. Super fucking tight, that was the *point*.

So in fifth period, as she walked into Mr. Squibb's Science class (as one might expect from a class called *Science* in this part of the country, evolution was begrudgingly covered as a *theory*), Jenmarie felt the most exultant sort of joy upon seeing Mavis sat on her stool by the rear window, arms resting on the high, fire-retardant black desktops wide enough for two. Indifferent to the ambient energy in his room, or indeed anything that couldn't be poured into a beaker and made to explode, Mr. Squibb had allowed his class to chose their own seats, which naturally meant that Jenmarie and Mavis ran their experiments and took their tests and copied their test answers together.

Mavis looked up and saw Jenmarie, a broad smile reminding Jenmarie of just how gorgeous her friend would become (yeah, she was cute now, but this was Mavis in her pimple phase, so it was cute with a pus-dribbling asterisk). This was, Jenmarie marveled, technically the first time she had seen Mavis as anything but a collection of pixels on a screen in at least two or three years. Oh, and how incredible, how downright *Jetsons* the concept of a free video call over wireless internet seemed in this age of Instant Messenger and dial-up AOL! Suddenly the present she had taken for granted seemed the most wonderful thing in the world, now that it was a future. Jenmarie savored the feeling while she could; there was no way, no possible way this marvelous lightness of mind could survive the brutal lassitude of sand through class (ahem, glass), hands on a face, shadows on a dial. Time devoured wonder.

Whatever. Didn't matter. Here was Mavis, here was her friend. Jenmarie hustled over to her seat, plopped her backpack down by her feet, turned to her friend, and despaired.

"Oh my *God,*" Mavis began in precisely the sort of faux-valley girl patois that turned "God" into a three syllable word. Had Mavis actually spoken like this? Or had Jenmarie somehow High Tombed herself into a far darker dimension than the one she'd left? "Hell-*OOOOO,*" Mavis continued, "Earth to Jem! Paging Jem, party of hell-*OOOOO!*"

Jenmarie tried to blink away this Mavis-shaped monster before her. "What?"

"I said," the creature from the yak la-*GOOOOON* reiterated, "Oh my *God.*"

"Wh…what did you call me?"

Mavis squinted at Jenmarie. "Jem."

"But only…" she didn't finish the sentence, which concluded with *Eddie calls me that.* Had Mavis also referred to her thusly, once upon a time? Jem d…*Jenmarie* didn't think so. She was almost positive she'd never been called Jem before Eddie had entered her life. So…how the hell was the sobriquet on Mavis' lips? This was truly, truly, truly outrageous.

"Jem! Earth to Jem!"

"…why?"

"Because you're a space cadet, hell-*OOO!*"

"No, um, why did you say 'oh my god'?"

Mavis scoffed, as she'd no doubt heard somebody on TV do. "Why? *Why?* You haven't heard? How haven't you heard? Grace told me that Brooke said that she has a crush on Nick. Nick *Ayer*, not Nick *Palance*. *Nick Ayer!* So Grace told me that she told Brooke, listen, I heard – and now I'm being Grace, I should say that I, Mavis, am being Grace when I, which is me, say I, which is Grace – anyway I'm Grace, she says, and I, Grace, heard from Troy that Nick said that he has a crush on Alexandra, so you know, don't get your hopes up, you being Brooke. So Brooke said to me, who is Grace, she tells me that she, Brooke, doesn't care about Alexandra because she heard that she, Alexandra, well she's the second she but the first she is Brooke, so that doesn't matter, the point is, Brooke told Grace that Brooke doesn't care about Alexandra, if Nick has a crush on her, Alexandra, or what, because she, Brooke, heard that she, Alexandra, got the *clap* from

Dylan, and the *clap* is like when you kiss, well, not *you*, but, um, you could, but it's like when Alexandra kisses Dylan and then they have, and then their mouths itch or something, the *clap*, that's what that is. And so but then I, who am still Grace, or *is*, said that she…"

At that point Jenmarie tuned Mavis out and remembered one very important detail about her friend: Mavis had a condition. It would later be diagnosed and treated as a mild form of schizo-phrenia, and while her medications did take the edge off, Mavis would remain unconvinced that the diagnosis was sound. It was part of what would prompt her to apply to, and attend, Emory alongside Jenmarie, albeit in the Department of Human Gene-tics. When had the treatment begun, then? It must have been sometime this year or next; Jenmarie's memory of Mavis at her family's Y2K New Year's party, which Jenmarie's folks had let her attend on the condition that she take a 'go bag' full of bottled water, energy bars, and hand-cranked emergency electronics like a flashlight/radio combo, just so she'd be prepared in case soci-ety completely collapsed when all the computers switched from 1999 to 2000, anyway, Jenmarie's memory of that was that her friend had been her, gosh this sounded mean but the word fit, *rational* self at that party. Not so manic, anyway. And that was to be just eight-odd months from now. So surely this was the last gasp of the fruitcake Mavis, right? Well, maybe, but the fact that Jenmarie seemed to have completely expunged this babbling iter-ation of her friend from memory threw the timeline into ques-tion. Maybe Mavis had been like this far later than Jenmarie had realized, and she'd simply forced herself to forget, for the sake of the friendship?

Or, of course, there was always a far simpler explanation: that Jenmarie hadn't registered this behavior as divergent from the "rational Mavis" because, as far as young Jenmarie had been concerned, this *was* "rational Mavis." Perhaps Jenmarie had been just as committed to gossip as Mavis clearly was. If that were the case, then she'd done a hell of a job wiping that particular cognitive floppy too.

Either way, it came out to the same thing for this moment, right now: Jenmarie did not actually have her friend to lean on here, because this Mavis was not the Mavis she had left in 2019. Nor was this Jenmarie the Jenmarie to whom this Mavis had said 'see you tomorrow' yesterday.

This Jenmarie's vision went a bit swimmy, her head threatening to roll right off her shoulders. Christ, why did they make these stools so high? What was wrong with the seats they had in every other class, huh? What did science have against chairs with little desks mounted right onto them? Breath. No. *Breathe.* Focus on the breathe. *Breath.* Fuck.

It was too much to keep track of. Her friends were not the friends she'd known, her family had the right number of members but the lineup wasn't the same, her little scar even denied her continuity with her own past self by imposing her future over top the present (but not in any ways that might be mistaken for useful). How the fuck was she supposed to…what? What was she even supposed to *not* supposed to be able to do?

The ground rushed away from her. She gripped the desk as tightly as she could, but the desk was a table and it was too high off the ground, the ground was too far beneath her feet, the walls were closing in and Mavis was still talking, still nattering on about Chris and Brooke and Troy and Grace and people Jenmarie didn't even fucking remember, she couldn't put faces to the names, this was her past and she was lost in it, so how could it even be considered hers, it was somebody else's, it belonged to the version of herself that, in turn, belonged to the past. She didn't belong here, this Jenmarie, the Jenmarie of 2019, the doctor, the divorcee, the depressive, the obsessive, the maybe-problem drinker, the definitely-unhealthy eater, the coauthor of a Scientific American article, the bargain-hunter, the bad dancer who loved to dance, the poor decision-maker who couldn't stop making decisions, the woman, the adult woman who had nothing in common with her own best friend anymore, and who therefore couldn't imagine a future in which she was without her best friend, and yet *had to*, because it was precisely these years, the arm-in-arm dash through the gauntlets of puberty and prom and standardized testing and yes alright gossip and rumors but also academics and families, these shared struggles were what strengthened a friendship, and to be unable to fully engage with Mavis now meant that their relationship would wither and die, and without Mavis how could Jenmarie find the strength to leave her family as she had, how could she feel confident about going to Emory, even if she'd been the one to apply first, it was only once she knew Mavis was going too that she'd thought, ok, I can do this, I won't be alone. But as Mavis had only applied (or so Jenmarie suspected) because she'd drawn a similar inspiration from *her* friend, i.e. Jenmarie, this meant an Emory career without Mavis. Which, incidentally, meant no Lucky getting Jenmarie to the house at which she met Eddie Mark on the porch, shoeless and embarrassed but also glad of the convenient icebreaker…but if she couldn't stay friends with Mavis now – not just stay friends but become even closer, even tighter, the bestest of best friends who ever friended bestly – then her second chance would be blown, not just with Eddie but with life, *her* life, and then, really, what was the silver lining on this big, black cloud that had *become* her life, a cloud shaped like the High Tomb and which stank of rot? "Oh," Jenmarie heard herself say, and then she heard the crack of somebody's head hitting the floor from a great height, poor sucker, whoever it was, she couldn't be sure because she couldn't see anything through the big black cloud.

Soft success there; at least she'd avoided the bathroom floor that had split her face in the last life. She'd avoided that *specific* floor.

She awoke to discover that she had been pulled out of school, her parents opting for a homeschooling curriculum that they were singularly unqualified to administer. It was alright, though, because Jenmarie knew it all already. She also knew that she should have been taking two medications her parents wouldn't even deign to pronounce, and she knew that her quitting them cold turkey (due to unexpected fucking time travel), whether the withdrawal was a physical fact akin to the scar tissue on her chin or purely psychosomatic, was yet another cause for the deep, dark funk into which she had sunk. Not being in school, she lost touch with Mavis. Having no social outlet, she wallowed in her dead-end ennui. Wallowing, her parents doted on her all the more aggressively. Doting on their daughter, Barry and Carrie hardly had time for their other two extant children. Having no time, they were more careful about their contraceptive practices, or else ceased the practices which would require their being more careful (Jenmarie didn't ask for details). Through care or chastity, Tomjohn was never conceived. Never having a younger brother, Jenmarie had nobody to soak up the grating attentions of her parents, to serve as a point of contact with her old life, to help her feel connected to the person she had been, now was again, wished desperately she could stop being. The way Tomjohn had stopped being, would never be. Wasn't. Because of her.

Turned out, her depression wasn't as all-consuming as she'd

thought: Jenmarie felt that. In the wash of numbness, she felt Tomjohn's absence. Her brother. Her friend. Nowhere. Floating in nowhere. Except not. Obviously not. He wasn't floating. He wasn't anything. He was nothing.

How could one mourn a loss yet to come? How could one not, when it was a beloved brother one had lost? A brother to whom one had never had the courage – nay, the decency – to say the word *love?*

That was a question over which she had plenty of time to puzzle, for there was no end in sight to the barrage of things that should have been but weren't, things that could have been but never would be. She wasn't so much living her current life as mourning (but how) her last one, watching with horror as the steps she would need to take to get her from where she was to where she wanted to be (which was where she *had* been) compounded in both quantity and complexity, until it was so much simpler to say it was functionally impossible for her to ever achieve anything like her old life. Even if she'd felt confident enough to make it to Emory without Mavis, who had all but fallen out of Jenmarie's orbit, she just didn't have the grades to get in. Granted, it was a bit premature to say this in eighth grade, but only just. And the years would pass, her academics getting worse and worse despite the fact that she already fucking knew her multiplication tables, had a firmer grasp on history (*especially* the history that hadn't happened yet) than did her hillbilly parents who had the audacity to proctor the exam, understood the capital-S *Science* material so well she was mentally correcting the test questions even as she couldn't muster up the enthusiasm to scribble in the right bubble on the stupid little sheet. Her despondency deepened to the point where psychiatrics shouldered out academics. Barry and Carrie drove their increasingly non-verbal daughter all over town, and then the state, and then the tri-state area, and so drove themselves to exhaustion and penury. They took out personal loans, went to the closest-to-wealthy friends they had with hat firmly in hand, all to help their daughter get the care they believed she needed. This, of course, accomplished little besides make Jenmarie feel even worse about herself. Because just as her memory of Mavis had been, hm, what was a word that *didn't* sound nasty, not contaminated or poisoned or tainted but let's say *influenced* by her present-future perceptions, so too had been her recollection of her family life. Contrary to how she'd recalled them, the elder Bells were nothing but supportive, to the point of enabling her lower moods. Harmon revealed a tenderness Jenmarie hadn't known him capable of; Melody grew a spine, going so far as to stand up to Harmon on Jenmarie's behalf when their brother's hormones got the best of him, spinning him into fits of smoldering, untargeted aggression. And her parents, whom she had despised for, what, their provincialism? Their satisfaction with a small life? Whatever had driven a wedge between them, she couldn't find it now, attentively though she scoured their faces for it. What she did see, though, was the toll that her taciturnity was taking on them; what money didn't go in to supporting her went into booze for the both of them. At first they tried to hide the frequency of their consumption, but driving to the dump two or three times a week was too much work, and so the bags that went clink dingle ding when you moved them piled up by the mudroom door (there was no recycling in this part of town, nor would there be even by 2019). Oh, and Jenmarie got her wish, skipping braces entirely, the consequences of which became apparent as her cakes boasted fourteen candles, and then fifteen, and then none because there was no cake, they couldn't afford it.

By this point, though, Jenmarie didn't care. And for good reason. She didn't care that the psychiatrists and psychologists and priests and homeopaths and self-help coaches and acupuncturists and chiropractors and every stop she made along the quality-to-quack spectrum was costing her parents a fortune, wasting her time listening to the "professional opinion" of yet another person who had no concept of what she was actually going through, no framework to even begin to understand it, and at any rate no interest in listening. The first child psychologist her Mom had taken the then-eighth grade Jenmarie to, and this was so early in the process her dear mother thought it exigent to use the euphemism "talking doctor" (as though Jenmarie were even more of a child than she already was), had unknowingly set the tone for the whole circus that was to follow. Upon asking Jenmarie to describe her problem, Jenmarie did precisely that, at length and in great detail, sprinkling in hedges and professions that she didn't expect him to believe her, that she knew how she sounded, but the Tomb was the truth and every word she spoke about it and her journey through it had happened precisely as she said, and if he didn't believe her now, wait until George W. and the Florida recount, wait until 9/11, wait until the Axis of Evil, wait until Hurricane Katrina, wait until Obama, wait until the 2008 economic collapse, wait until the Marvel Cinematic Universe, wait until Taylor Swift, wait until smartphones, wait until Kony, wait until Hamilton, wait until self-driving cars, wait until Me-Too, wait wait wait for every glimpse of the future she offered to attain precisely as and when she told him it would, wait and he would know that every word she had told him was the truth, even if it would be years before he believed her, even if by that point it might not matter anymore, just wait. To all of this, the doctor had listened, stroking his scruffy chin and nodding. Then he'd asked her if she'd like to play a little game, and brought out a piece of paper and some crayons. Draw whatever comes to mind, he'd told her. So Jenmarie drew the doctor, helpfully labeled with "YOU" and an arrow, standing beneath a giant hand presenting a giant middle finger that was also a giant penis, drowning the grinning doctor in giant globules of cartoon semen. Subject matter aside, it was a terrific illustration, absolutely jam-packed with detail. Alas, Jenmarie was not prescribed the medications she requested, and she would never again be so forthcoming with a psychiatric professional.

(She would wonder whether or not the doctor, whose name she wouldn't bother committing to memory, ever thought of her, as one by one her prognostications came true. In 2002 she would get his name from her mother and look him up, only to discover that he'd drowned, which in a way rendered her flippant illustration ominous enough to make her wonder, however briefly, if she were perhaps more able to shape events in this new time-line/universe/whatever than she suspected. It took only a single frustrating visit to an online poker site to realize that, no, she wasn't.)

But she didn't care about any of this, and the reason for that indifference was precisely the same reason that kept her from unburdening herself to the so-called help her family sought for her. A child going on and on about something that was less reincarnation than a soft reboot was a 'problem child.' Someone of more advanced years – nearing the boundary of adulthood, in fact – banging on about the very same stuff was just a problem. And what, particularly in this less-than-enlightened corner of the country, in this less-than-propitious time for mental health awareness, did one do with problems? Why, one tucked them in a closet and never spoke of them again. The prospect of being locked away in a psychiatric hospital was mortifying to Jenmarie, for reasons beyond the obvious. Well, not so much reasons plural. More the one reason.

She'd tried, tried, and failed to get her parents to take her to a doctor in New York City. For if she could get to New York, she could get to the High Tomb. And if she could get to the High Tomb…none of what was happening now would matter. Because she would find her way back. Back to her horrible little life, back to her aimless isolation. Back to the problems that were *hers,* goddamnit.

How did she know this was possible? Simple. Simple, stupid. It was the scar. The scar on her chin, a sign from the future that she'd read all wrong. Or, at least, she'd read it in the wrong tone of voice. *Your old life is still out there,* that was how she'd taken it, and at first blush that had struck her as a threat. Back when she'd believed herself capable of doing better. Of steering clear of that old life in favor of something better. Now, though? *Your old life is still out there* was a glorious promise. It was hope. The only hope she had left.

And as that hope had bloomed within her, so too did that creeping indifference to this life. For the pitfalls of this particular life were not hers. Not her pitfalls, not her life. Not hers. No thank you. She'd learned her lesson. That was what these little time loops were always about, right? In movies, someone had a lesson to learn, and they were stuck until they learned it. Well, Jenmarie had learned hers. There. She would call everyone and tell them how wrong she had been, call Mavis and be more enthusiastic about her kid, call Tomjohn and articulate how deeply important he was to her without couching it in schoolyard taunting, call Eddie and, uh, well, just hear his voice again, that'd be nice, she could take it from there depending on what his tone was, uh, anyway, call her parents and…oh, hell, go *visit* them, to apologize in person. She would do all of that, because she had learned her lesson.

She just needed to get back home. For the love of any and all gods, she just wanted to go *home.*

This, after all these years, had been the foundation of her app-arent depression; she was biding her time, exaggerating her des-pondency, to get her parents to look further and further afield for care. Well, alright, maybe that was a bit of *post-hoc* fluffing to make herself feel better. Her depression hadn't been *apparent,* her despondency had required no *exaggeration.* Still and all, she'd felt satisfaction each time her parents sought professional help fur-ther and further into Yankeeland. Horrible to say, given the hair-tearing frenzy with which her folks did that searching…but, well, that too would be undone, if they would only take her to New York. For Jenmarie understood the Big Apple's subway system perfectly well, so going *anywhere* with MTA access was as good as delivering her directly to the High Tomb. And if she could get to the High Tomb, she was as good as home. 2019, baby. Not a great year, sure, but it was the only one she wanted to be in right now.

This was her plan, but a plan it would remain unless and until she could get her ass to the High Tomb. Which meant *not* getting said ass locked up in an asylum. So she pretended to rise out of the funk she'd, ahem, pretended to fall into, only to discover that the mask had, as they say, eaten in to the face. So effective had her performance been that, even at curtain call, she found it hard to break character. Wasn't there that study, that demonstrated that if you frowned, you were more likely to have negative reactions to things than if you smiled? Well, that seemed to track: between 1999 and 2004, Jenmarie estimated that she'd smiled perhaps thirty times, lest she demonstrate to the world the importance of, ha, biting the bullet re: braces. "I'm fine," she would protest through pursed lips, which would only concern her family even more, because much like "I'm not crazy" or "it's not a cult," if one feels the need to say "I'm fine," it's already too late. And so the quack convoy continued, at one point taking Jenmarie as far as Albany. She considered attempting to sneak out of the motel in which they were holed up, to try her luck getting to Manhattan, but running away now would make running away in the City proper that much harder. So she bit her tongue and fumed, and the sands plop plop plopped through the glass, and the years passed, and there was George W. and the Florida recount and 9/11 and the Axis of Evil and Hurricane Katrina, and then it was 2006 and Jenmarie was friendless and jobless and a burden on her family but it was fine because nothing mattered, she'd suffered through seven fucking years in this worthless fucking timeline where her family lost their home and had moved nearer the Appalachians with what Dad at first contemptuously referred to as the 'mountain people' but eventually just called neighbors because now the Bells were mountain people too because they couldn't afford anything else because they'd spent it all on failed treatments for their daughter, but so and now, finally, when her parents asked her what she wanted for her twenty-first birthday, not that they had much to give but they asked anyway, and she told them she wanted to go to New York City, and they said we can't afford it, so Jenmarie remembered that holy shit she was an adult now, so she went out and got herself a credit card because it wasn't like she was going to have to pay that sucker off or anything, fuck it, who gave a shit, nothing mattered here, and she used that credit card to get her ass to Manhattan, first fucking class all the way, charge it baby, put it on my tab, and then she landed at JFK and rented the biggest fucking car at Hertz, a Hummer H3, it would be a pain in the ass to drive through Manhattan but she could just put it in neutral and step out any time she wanted, park it in front of a fire hydrant, there were no consequences, all of this would be wiped away soon enough.

In short, not that it needed repeating, but the nightmare was almost over, and it felt good to say it, so say it: Fuck. It.

She cruised right on up to Fourth and 57th, mounting the curb, upsetting a guy who was walking his or somebody else's dogs but again, was this her problem, no it was not, and she left the car running and got out and looked up and there it was, The High Tomb, maybe not as high as it would soon be but just as tomb, the marble was still swirling and the doors were still fake and as she focused on them people started bumping into her so all was as all was to be, ought to have been, and so it was, and would be. Weaving between pedestrians, she worked her way to the doors and remembered she really probably definitely should have brought a crowbar or maybe just something priapic to jab at the frame, it probably wasn't as though a crowbar was the only thing that would work to get her inside but her fingers weren't working, she was trying hard to stuff them in the crack between the door and its setting but no dice, not deep enough or what, who knew, but she felt a mounting terror that perhaps maybe what if the tomb wasn't ready for her yet, and she were stuck here, now, in this life, with these choices she had made, with the destitute family and the impossible credit card debt and an illegally parked gas-guzzler and no prospects and no friends, what if the High Tomb only gave you one do-over and this was how she'd used hers and she'd squandered it assuming she'd get to go back to her old life and now this *was* her life, this was the way of her days unto the end, and the nights why they would be long and sleepless and she would get to know every inch of the ceiling above her head, hello old friend, spreading stain and peeling paint, hello but never goodnight, and now not then not in the possible future but in the definite present she felt herself growing dizzy, her world closing in, any second now the pavement would rush up to break her fall and maybe her nose too but no she shook her head to clear it for just a little longer because she was so close, so close to wiping all of this off the board, scrubbing the slate, scribbling her old mistakes back into being, her old life, her *real* life. So she got back in her car and drove to the nearest hardware store which was more like a hard*where* store ha because it was *hard* to find *where* it was because she couldn't remember where that little store with the stupid name she'd gone to last time was and she didn't have a smartphone to help her out there because the iPhone wouldn't come out for another year and that was just the first one and so how the fuck was she supposed to know where anything was well she asked a guy manning a food cart and he told her about a hardware store that was like fifteen blocks away and she said thanks and drove there even though she knew damn well there was one closer that the guy didn't know about but also she didn't know about it either she supp-osed because even if she knew it existed she couldn't remember where it was in which case was that knowing did that even count as *knowing* but whatever fifteen blocks would do she just didn't like driving this big fucking car but she'd picked it so she didn't really have anybody to blame but herself and maybe the guy at the food cart who made her drive fifteen blocks well thirty if you counted the return trip and it wasn't like buying the crowbar was much of a break because it was crowded in the hardware store and Jenmarie was frankly sick of people right now and feeling like holy shit she might not even be able to keep conscious for

209

the trip back to Fourth and 57th and what if she passed out en route and crashed and died or hurt herself and had to be taken to the hospital and got sent back to Tennessee and then what it was back to square one, so she got back in the Hummer and just sat in the parking spot she'd found three blocks from the hardware store because it was just a little neighborhood hole in the wall not a megastore with its own parking lot, and can you even appreciate how hard it is to find a Hummer-sized parking spot in Manhattan in the middle of the day, very hard, though she'd found this one fairly quickly which was lucky, holy hell, so she felt better and drove back and got out of the car and slammed the crowbar into the door of the High Tomb and

N
O
W

She smiles. The world is once again silence. A medusozoac hush.

Breathe in. Squish. Breathe out.

Taking another deep, lung-loving breath through her nose, Jenmarie opens her eyes. The jellyfish innards are just as she remembers them; suffused with a lightless glow, stretching between voids, opening and closing on glimpses of impossible worlds. Her first visit here had been unexpected, horrifying, disorienting. Not great. But now, having had the chance to prepare for, even *anticipate* her return, she finds what beauty there is to be found, in this place. This terrible place. The silence. Ah, how soothing its stillness! Even the peristaltic pumping of the walls, at first blush so evocative of a titan's innards, now call to mind the gentle sway of a hammock. This is something she can get used to. This is a place she'd be happy to remain, were it in the nature of the place to permit extended stays. But it's not; how she knows this, she knows not, but know it she does all the same. The place does nothing to gainsay this knowledge.

Now, here she is again. What she would consider to be the High Tomb proper. Darkless light, syrup sky. The usual. She reaches up and withdraws another goopy finger. This time with a smile on her face. Hello, Tomb. Take me home.

She calls to mind a scene from her past life: the moment on the porch in Athens (Georgia, not Greece), she barefoot and he on the porch.

Above her, the syrup stirs, but does not yield. No luminescence stakes its claim to the shadowless heights.

At this, Jenmarie frowns, or at the very least, embodies the feeling of doing so. Perhaps she has misunderstood the function of this place. The, ah, the *rules* of it. Does it not plunge one into the icy deep of memory? Does it not...ah, but another memory occurs to Jenmarie. That of the birthday party (she recalls it as having been for her fifteenth birthday, but who can be sure) when her parents had decided it would be fun to fill a bucket with water and have Jenmarie and her guests go bobbing for fresh apples they'd bought from Ralph Gary's homestead down by where the train tracks swung unnervingly near the creek, or "at the corner of creek and crick" as Ralph was inexplicably fond of saying. Splish splash sploosh, the apples had been tossed into the bucket, and one by one the girls had plunged their faces in, mouths agape, inevitably swallowing a bit of water, but that was to be expected in apple bobbing. Less expected was the violent vomiting that soon enough laid out the entire party; whether the cause was something wrong with the apples or the water in which they floated was never determined, but the effect was something quite dramatically wrong with the carpets throughout the Bell household and, as a result of one downright acrobatic heave from Suzie, a stain on the wallpaper that launched Carrie Bell into a three-week redecorative fugue state. Barry, for his part, would blame Ralph and his damned apples for the upchuck fiasco, though it would be a matter of debate between Jenmarie and her siblings, for years to come, whether this was because Barry genuinely believed Ralph's apples had been to blame, or he'd just wanted an excuse to quip that "Ralph's yield's as good as his name," which he did at every opportunity, despite, or perhaps because of, the unlaughing silence with which the quip was reliably received.

Ah, but this is a different time, a different place, if indeed it is either at all. So Jenmarie finally giggles at the quip, which is to say, at the memory of it. Until a bloom of unbodied sight captures her attention. From below. She glances down past her feet to find it shimmering in the shadowless down. It? Her memory. The Tomb approves of this one, it seems. The Tomb enjoys the quip. The Tomb laughs.

Jenmarie descends, not quite floating, not quite stepping. She descends. The how is irrelevant. She descends. And having descended, comes level to the memory now in front of her, open, perhaps beckoning, at least inviting. Come, it coos. Step, or float, approach as you wish, approach as you will. Jenmarie nearly does, but pauses at a realization. This hadn't been her fifteenth birthday party. It had been her *ninth* birthday.

Half a decade off. It's remarkable, how living one's adolescence twice over can turn one around in one's own memory palace.

Ah. The uncontained space that is Jenmarie glimmers with understanding. With knowledge. The Tomb approves of the apple-bobbing but not the porch-approaching, for Ralph's yields were as good as their name in *both* of the lives Jenmarie has lived. Her ninth birthday exists in both timelines, the division between the two lives having come at age thirteen. Whereas she had only met Ralph in the first. No, wait. *Eddie.* Oh, these things do have a way of bleeding into one another. Memories.

Yet here is a division between the two, unmistakable, unappealable. The Tomb will suffer one's return to a point earlier in one's current timeline, it seems. But travel between lives, between universes, will not be tolerated.

Were this a place for human hearts, Jenmarie knows hers would have begun to beat faster. Were this a place for flesh, hers would have puckered with goosebumps. Were this a place for tears...oh, but it isn't. There is much she would have done, but can not do, for this is not a place for it. Yet devastation remains, and it is what she feels, *becomes,* in the face of the knowledge which has now touched her. The knowledge that she will never again return to her life. To the life she had lived. That first life is gone. Forever. Lost to the Tomb.

For a time she floats, but this is no more a place for time than tears. So she floats, her mind a blank, until memory once more asserts its dominance. Unbidden, unwanted, the memory of Jenmarie's getting the wind knocked out of her in gymnastics drowns her from within. First time in her life, that had been. For the wind-knocking, not the gymnastics. She'd been in at *least* ninth grade, as it hadn't been until high school that her parents had pushed her to find an extracurricular. Good grades were one thing, they'd reminded her, not that she'd had them, but they'd often pretended she did in the course of reminding her that the sorts of colleges in which she'd been expressing interest looked for things other than good grades. In addition to them, rather. And besides, Carrie had been pregnant with Tomjohn by this point, and so the prospect of finding something that would get her out of the house was…a…

Losing one's wind for the very first time is an unforgettable experience. One Jenmarie can confidently place in her first life, and only her first life. Along with her mother's pregnancy, with Tomjohn. Yet unborn in 1999. Which is as far into that first life as she can ever return.

Jenmarie thinks of Tomjohn, conjures his face in the darkness before her, turns her mind to the tree in front of their friend Marley's house that Jenmarie and Tomjohn would scale together when Jenmarie had tired of being the older sibling and wanted nothing more than to climb a tree with her kid brother, despite Marley's mom having declared that tree off-limits after Marley's dipshit brother had fallen from it and broken his arm, though which Jenmarie and Tomjohn would nonetheless continue to scale, giggling at their insolence, whenever Marley's mom was futzing around in the rear-facing kitchen. No hueless flush, up or down the Tomb. From this sprang the memory of Tomjohn coming home from fourth grade one day to inform Jenmarie that his friend Ben had come running up to him during recess, having just left a snickering clutch of buddies, which Tomjohn had known meant trouble right away, but then Ben had told him that Mike had had a wet dream about his sister, Tomjohn's sister, which was to say Jenmarie, last night. Tomjohn hadn't known what a wet dream was, but from the way Ben's friends all exploded in laughter, and the long, sheepish grin Mike had fixed on his feet from the center of the group, he'd gotten a pretty good idea that it was something gross. Yet it was Jenmarie whom he asked to explain the term *wet dream*, a call she answered not with a definition but with a deflection, a redirection to *go ask Mom,* which Tomjohn knew enough not to do. No lights, no blooms, no approval from the Tomb. Ah, but now Jenmarie was fully in thrall to a dead universe: she was helpless but to think of the brief stretch when, after Barry had brought home a baseball cap from the little league games he coached – the ones down at the Ruritan field nestled at the base of the hill upon which their house sat, the ones Jenmarie had never attended but nonetheless loved because on still evenings she could open her bedroom window and hear the distant crack of bats against big yellow softballs – six-year-old Tomjohn had taken that hat and insisted that he was now a professional hat collector, a calling at which he threw himself for all of three hours, time enough to assemble every chapeau in the chateau on his bed, but not enough to return them whence he'd snatched them.

No deadlights, up or down the High Tomb. No path back to Tomjohn. Yet a revue of recollections from her latest miserable life, or her pre-1999 years, rip holes in the veil of presence and let the past peer through.

And, at the same time, up above. *Way* up, beyond the sorghum sky.

Jenmarie squints at the memory that can't possibly be a memory. There's no sense of perspective here, no reference points by which to chart distance…but all the same, she's fairly certain that memory, or at least that gleam of the past, is further above her head than the most distant recollections she can summon appear below her feet. And if Down leads her deeper into the past…

Is that a door to her future? How? And what did she think of, to cleft that particular bolt of twilight in twain? A baseball hat?

She walks floats whatevers upwards, but as before finds the molasses ceiling to be impassable. Yet there above her is the future memory, Polaris taunting her from the far side of the galaxy. Unless it isn't a guide, but a destination unto itself?

She puzzles and wonders and ruminates and gives up and then

something occurs to her, a deductive chain with a slightly disturbing conclusion. The three Tomjohn memories with which her mind had seen fit to torment her were: tree-climbing, wet dream, baseball caps. Distilled to their essence, they were: tree, dream, baseball. And having grown up so near a baseball diamond, as the daughter of a man who spent so much time volunteering there, Jenmarie happened to know that most modern bats are made of ash. So swap that in, and her mind had generated: tree, dream, ash.

Her dream. The one from her first timeline. That of the ash tree, and the vine.

To recall the dream is to stoke the little ember above her head.

Is…is she seeing a dream up there? How is that possible? The dream is in her future? A premonition? Is it something she herself had dreamt, or had it been, ha, *planted* by the High Tomb? If memory serves her (though she's beginning to suspect the inverse is more accurate), she'd only had the dream *after* she was on the High Tomb's scent. Though, of course…that wasn't true. The dream had preceded the Tomb. Though that was not to say it hadn't been planted all the same.

So what does that tell her? Anything?

Almost certainly not. Yet the dream speaks for itself. Its words are warm. She is close enough to feel them, yet too far to understand them. They resemble answers, Jenmarie can tell. Not answers to questions. Just answers.

She must reach it, she realizes. She's never longed for something, *craved* something so desperately. That light up there is an end to confusion. To uncertainty. How does she know this? Well, she isn't sure. But she'll know once she gets there. This is the first thing it will show her. That light up there.

A way to reach it occurs to her. Down is past and up is the

opposite, that's the way things seem to be, and if up is opposite, er, forward, no, *future,* and the dream is up…then there is a way to reach it, and the way, as mentioned, occurs. It's a rather horrible way, the mere contemplation of which exhausts and terrifies Jenmarie in equal measure. Because it's also the only way that anybody ever reaches *anything:*

She can live her life.

She can leave the Tomb, return to the world far back enough to undo the damage her own apathy had done to…oh, alright, no sense phrasing it passively. She must go back far enough to erase the poor choices that *she* had made (apathy is but an excuse), and keep living and living and living for as long as she can. Which necessarily means never returning to the High Tomb, lest she prolong the endeavor by looping back into memory. Only once she believes herself to be on the precipice of death may she return here, to think of the dream once more, to see if she hasn't reached it. And if she hasn't, well, she can try again, try to live even longer the next time.

She reminds herself that she really must be careful to not die, for if she dies, she won't be able to get back to the High Tomb. *No shit,* she tries to say, but no words come out, and that's ok. It would be a shame to spoil the consummate quiet of this place with human speech, let alone profanity (but what, in a place like this, is the difference). Still, she can laugh inside of herself, which she does. With one final glance up at the dream, flexing it by bringing her focus nearer and further, nearer and further from the vine with the ash-shaped hole in its heart, Jenmarie sighs and plumbs the depths of retrospection for a suitable point of entry. No braces in the life; she'll just have to get them again, then. Among other necessary discomforts. But if she can only live her best possible life on this third pass, taking all the tests, making all the friends, getting all the braces, then she'll have a best-of-all-possible-timelines life to which she can return…should returning prove necessary for another run at the dream, of course. Only for that.

Oh, she is already tired. So tired. But this is the way forward. This is the only way.

Ok then, well, if she's committing to the life well-lived, then there's no sense starting on the wrong foot, is there? No sir, no ma'am. What's her earliest memory then, the cleanest slate she can possibly give herself? Probably the one about the baby robin that had fallen from a tree in their backyard, that she'd convinced Mom, er, Carrie, to let her bring into the house and nurse back to health. Jenmarie had barely been verbal at that point, but she'd had brain enough to record quite a vivid memory of her spindly little fingers gently stroking the dark feathers atop the chick's trembling noggin.

There, beneath Jenmarie's shoes, which are no longer shoes, they are simply feet, if they are even that…beneath whatever she is now, then: the incendiary past.

Except…is that what it is? For clear in her mind though the baby robin in the straw-filled shoebox is, another memory winks from just a short distance above that one, a memory of Jenmarie asking her mother if she remembers what had happened to that little baby robin, only for Carrie to look askance (yes, askance!) at her daughter and ask her what she was talking about, and no matter how vehemently Jenmarie insisted that she remembered cradling the bird in her palms, placing it tenderly into the shoe-box, watching its little chest rise and fall as she ferried it into the living room, Carrie just smiled and shook her head and assured her daughter that, no, nothing like that had ever happened, not unless it was a secret between Jenmarie and her father, and Barry, when he got home, professed the same ignorance, and the final nail in the coffin came when Harmon, smack in the middle of his cruel adolescence, insisted that, oh, yeah, he remembered that, he remembered jumping on the bird so hard that its *head* popped off and flew straight into Melody's *mouth!* He'd growled this at dinner, just as Melody had a mouthful of meatball, which nearly occasioned a repeat performance of Jenmarie's ninth birthday, albeit with a different spherical comestible. But what echo has ever perfectly captured its genesis?

Naturally, if young-teen Harmon had said it was true, then it absolutely wasn't, and if Jenmarie doubted this, any number of memories leapt at the chance to set her straight.

But, of course, then again, yet also, there below these indisputable truths glitters the memory of the robin in the shoebox, an equally insistent come-hither. Jenmarie toggles between the two memories, the nearer one perfectly invalidating the further.

A dream above, a lie below. Maybe. Perhaps. And Jenmarie in the middle, weighing her options, considering the outcomes, reaching the conclusion that perhaps the best way to a dream is through a lie. Definitely. They are, after all, the same cognitive geegaw seen from different angles. And more pragmatically, she's been through her regular life twice now. It wasn't so great a life that it couldn't be improved with a bit of creative license. Therefore, then, and so, she makes fiction (for the more she thinks on it, the less real it seems) the object of her focus, remembering each of the poor robin's pitiful cheeps and squeaks, recalling the care with which she poured water into the overturned plastic cap of a Sprite bottle and placed it in the box, swaddling herself in a memory she is almost certain is a whole-cloth fabrication, all that she might live well in it, live a life of pure will in her new shoebox universe.

F
L
I
G
H
T

The bird was lying on its belly, head dangling from its fat neck like the bulb of a dying lily. It was small enough to be nearly lost in the grass, just a dollop of darkness in a breeze-tickled yard.

Jenmarie stared down at the poor creature, wondering how she had come upon it. If, indeed, she had. Which was a ridiculous thought, of course. Clearly she had come upon the bird, because that was where she now was. Upon it. Standing over it. Looking down at it.

She lifted her eyes to the sky, blue with bits of grey, no surprises there, no curveballs. Just a sky. As the yard was just a yard. As the bird was just a bird. All was as all should be, in the universe.

Jenmarie knelt down, scooped up the sickly chick, and took it inside. Where she expected to find, and found, her mother, younger than last she'd left her for the second time.

Mom tutted just the right amount, then asked Jenmarie what she wanted to name it, and Jenmarie said "Cherry Chirpworth" because that seemed like something a cute little girl who was definitely three or four years old, instead of nearer to fifty, would come up with. She fetched a shoebox from Mom's closet (hers, being boxes for children's shoes, were all too small), grabbed some straw from the small empty coop that had once held, and would again hold, chickens, and made Cherry a bed. The little robin chick chirruped as Jenmarie scooped it up, gently as she could, and placed it in the shoebox, which she placed on the sill of her window. It was a precarious placement, one with which Jenmarie was only halfway comfortable once she'd extracted a promise from Melody, with Mom's help, that big sister wouldn't disturb Cherry's convalescence. That was the word Jenmarie used – convalescence – which got her one hell of a look from Mom, but the suspicion was quickly diverted by insisting that she had peed herself when, in fact, she had not. So effective had the ruse proven, that Jenmarie wondered how many other crises in her life could have been similarly averted.

The first few weeks of transition back into adolescence (again) were stressful, to be sure – Jenmarie, for whom independence was something more urgent than even the words *natural right* could convey, chafed under her parents' infantilizing aegis (and hey, how did *they* get an aegis, huh?). She couldn't well blame them though, could she? Jenmarie was, after all, an infant again. Well, an adolescent to be sure. She discovered that she was four years old by asking Carrie "how old am I?", and being told. Yeah, it wasn't all bad being four again, particularly when one had been zapped back into their youthful body and needed a hell of a lot of exposition to reorient themselves; four year olds were *expected* to ask dumb questions with obvious answers (the chilling thought that all children were veterans of the Tomb certainly occurred, and was forcefully dislodged), so at no point did Jenmarie need to pretend to remember a long-forgotten neighbor who would move away before her eighth birthday, or last year's Christmas present she'd been so happy to receive, nor was it considered unusual that she needed a friendly reminder which of the one two count 'em *two* rooms at the preschool she was expected to be in.

Because, yes, she was in preschool. And, yes, she felt pretty fucking weird about taking her decades of life experience and telling it to take the afternoon off, she needed to crash to her hands and knees and play Three Large Blocks and What Color Shape and Car Goes Moo (she was worried about that kid) with the toddlers. Furthermore, on the topic of the Pretty Fucking Weird, it was a headtrip to be playing these games with toddlers who were the same size as her, sometimes even larger. Because, important to remember, she wasn't playing with the toddlers; she was playing with the *other* toddlers. The word *surreal* might have covered this once upon a time, but her seven years in a second life, not to mention the atemporal *intermezzos* in the High Tomb, had so expanded Jenmarie's definition of reality to include watching children who would become adults whose unhappy futures she had seen first-hand gamboling around a bright indoor playset. Case in point: she could only stare after receiving a bright smile and a wave from little Anthony, who would go by Ant by the time he would be called on to read aloud from *Great Expectations* some years hence, specifically the part where Pip first enters, gosh, it was some sort of castle, maybe Miss Havisham's house?

Or where he discovers the identity of his benefactor? Anyway, Pip goes in and calls out something to the effect of "is there anybody here?", only when Anthony, who would by this point go by Ant, read it, his voice cracked, *will* crack, on the word *here*, and when Pip calls out his question a second time, Ant's voice will crack on the exact same word, in the exact same way, and the entire class will laugh. And then later, Ant will insist he be called Tony as he takes Simone to the prom and they both staggered (will stagger) out of their limo, having pregamed a bit *too* hard, and will later vanish into a stall in the men's bathroom only to emerge partially covered in vomit, the provenance of which neither could recall, but as it was more on Simone it was assumed to be Tony's, and unfortunately for both this story will quickly be relegated to a footnote as the headline of the evening will come to be Simone's pregnancy, which will prompt a proposal from Tony that Simone will wisely turn down, and Jenmarie would never find out what happened to Simone or the kid but last she'd heard Tony moved (and so will move) to Elko, Nevada and became (and so will become) some kind of middle manager at a Firestone or something. But that will be Tony, who had been Ant, who began as Anthony, who was now just a grubby-kneed child without the attention span to wait for a wave in return, running a wooden bead along one of those little doctor's-office-waiting-room tabletop rollercoasters, oblivious to all of the hurt that life will visit upon him, in time. So what was surreal about this, to an ex-lady baby on her third crack at the Things To Come? Nothing. The Real was ample enough to take this, and things far stranger, on board without breaking stride.

So Jenmarie crawled over to the tic-tac-toe board, comprised of nine big rotatable blocks skewered three to a spit, and tried to explain the game to a girl named Annie, who must have moved out of the district not too long after this, because Jenmarie had no recollection of her at all. Then again, young Annie hardly seemed a luminary; after Jenmarie devoted five minutes to trying and failing to communicate to her the fun that could be had from lining up three of *your* shape, the X or the O, in a row, no, *I* picked the X so you can't just change my X to an O, Annie cut it out, fuc…er…*stop* – five minutes of *that* was all Jenmarie needed to decide that Annie wasn't worth remembering, eventual emigrant or not.

Nor was much of what Jenmarie encountered in the pre-school. Or kindergarten. Or first grade. But year after year, she kept her shoulder to the wheel, her nose to the grindstone, only using her knowledge of the future to her advantage in surreptitious ways. She'd had a real go at slightly more overt advantage-wrangling, recommending a few investments to her parents that she knew would pay dividends in time, but as it turned out the elder Bells weren't prepared to take financial advice from a daughter who was closer to being a fetus than a teenager. So Jenmarie contented herself with angling friends into her orbit (hello, Mavis, why wait until third grade?) and gracefully pirouetting around the social faux-pas that, even obviated in this timeline, would periodically humiliate her from their original dimension. On the other hand…that *papier-mâché* orrery she'd totally fuck up, that another universe's Melody would hang from the ceiling of their shared room? Guess what? A the fuck minus, that was what! The minus was down to her forgetting that Pluto was still a planet at this time, but future history would vindicate her. She just had to wait for it.

And much to her surprise…she was looking forward to it. The future. For unlike poor Anthony, Jenmarie knew precisely what the future had in store for her. Knew *some* of it, at any rate.

225

Enough to steer by. Enough by which to steer.

For the first year or two of this charmed third life, Cherry Chirpworth was a steadfast companion. Each morning, Jenmarie would crack her bedroom window a few inches (which, in all but the most agreeable of weather, earned an inarticulate protest from Melody), an egress of which Cherry would avail herself to see to her chirpy little chores. Open the window would remain, until each evening when Cherry would flutter back in to roost for the night, softly serenading the sisters to sleep (and about this, even Melody couldn't complain). Carrie, who really did insist on being called *Mom*, very belatedly got around to expressing concern about the whole arrangement. She must have read something in a magazine, Jenmarie imagined. Or perhaps several somethings, in several magazines.

"Birds've got diseases," *Mom* insisted on more than one occasion.

"Well, I don't feel sick," Jenmarie replied each time.

"Well," came the second objection, "how are you getting up and reaching the window if you're not climbing on the dresser? You better not be climbing on the dresser, Jenmarie Bell."

Fair play; climbing on the dresser was *precisely* how Jenmarie reached the window. But all it took was cadging a stepstool from the garage (with Dad's permission, secured via liberal application of big, plaintive, *it's-me-your-youngest-daughter* eyes) to cut that complaint off at the knees.

Here came Mom's final assault: "Jenmarie, you need to understand that one day...one day Cherry's going to find her bird family and go off with them, and she won't come back. You need to be ready for that."

That was one objection Jenmarie couldn't well address as effectively as she, well, *could*. She was (at the time this objection had been raised) four years old, after all, and shouting "hey *Mom*, I got divorced over text, I can handle a birdie flying away" didn't strike her as a quick way to close out the conversation. Besides, even making the effort would constitute lifting her nose from the grindstone, her shoulder from the wheel. Down that path lay her second timeline, a life of indigent hope waiting to fall upon her as a tire shop in Nevada was for poor Anthony. This third time was going to be the goddamned charm. She wouldn't need a fourth time.

It would be tempting, of course. To go back. To fix those new pitfalls into which she inevitably...pitfell. But the temptation was fine, wasn't it? There was nothing wrong with temptation – with *cravings*. The problem was merely in succumbing to them. So, don't succumb. That was the goal. It was that simple. Don't succumb. Easy to say now, at this age, when getting to New York City on her own, i.e. step one in the succumbing process, was all but impossible. But even so, she felt there was contentment enough within reach to make a return to the Tomb something she merely entertained, rather than indulged. If there was a difference. Which there was, goddamnit.

Thus, it was for this that she reached, unaware that her little body and brain were yet too pure to sustain the cynicism she would earn later in life. Until, near the end of first grade, the morning Cherry went out and never returned. Despite Jenmarie's having been divorced over fucking text in her first life, despite all the little humiliations of her second, Cherry's departure *hurt*. A considerable portion of the pain stemmed from the uncertainty of *why* Ms. Chirpworth left. Was it to chase a happier ending? To seek out a Mr. Chirpworth? Or had she gotten snatched out of the air by a cat, or dive-bombed by an eagle, or strafed by a fighter jet? The sad fact of this life, as with all others, was that the tragic endings were far more common, far easier to imagine, than the happy ones. And so it was that pessimism returned to Jenmarie, balling up her naivety and tossing it right back in her face. *Oh, you're angling for a long, happy life? Word? No reason to think you won't be successful, with such a unique and clear-cut objective.* Optimism rejoined, though with far less gusto, that Jenmarie had an advantage over most people, including past iterations of herself; she knew how things would turn out. She could see three, four, five steps ahead. Except, of course, for the fact that her premonitory powers failed her the moment *she* took a first step that knocked all subsequent states from the path on which she'd last met them. There were little glimpses of this here and there, most notably in her relationship with her parents. Rather than fighting their affections, or resenting their bumpkinisms, she worked hard to accept them as they were. She went out and repaired the chicken coop with Dad and Harmon, and so brought fresh eggs back into their lives five years earlier than would have been the case had she demurred *a la* her first life. She let Mom teach her how to knit hats on that knubby little ring loom, finding herself laughing with her mother as she counted off the fuck-ups in each of her attempts (she once fucked up by actually calling her fuck-ups *fuck-ups*, which made Mom gasp and then laugh, which made Jenmarie laugh and then follow that up by wondering if they oughtn't be pluralized as *fucks-up,* which didn't go over quite as well), something she couldn't remember having done in any other timeline. And as arts and crafts became a staple of the Bell household, so too did an ambition of which Jenmarie had never imagined her folks capable, which supplied Jenmarie her first dramatic *for instance* of how little use knowledge of alternative timelines was, as one traveled further and further along in a new current.

"I wanna get some livestock," Barry announced one night at dinner. Jenmarie, just shy of nine years old (and quite emphatic, apropos of seemingly nothing, that there be *no apple bobbing* at her next birthday party), and consequently pushing sixty, wasn't sure whether to be embarrassed by her enthusiasm for the idea or not. Certainly, the prospect of her family sliding further into any kind of aw-shucks, suspender-snapping Southern stereotypes wasn't one she welcomed even in her sunniest moments. But, well, it was something to try, wasn't it? She'd been getting along far better with her family than she'd thought possible, she'd been keeping her grades up, she had friends in school…it was hard to believe, but for the first time since, well…maybe for the first time full stop, life was going well. Which was to say, it was getting a little bit boring. Because a good life required discipline, which required routine, which required repetition, which was *fucking boring*. Introducing a new wrinkle, one for which she had no precedent in either of her other lives, would keep things interesting during the most arduous years, they of the periods and braces and standardized tests. And if they didn't? If things got worse instead of better? Why, it would be the simplest thing in the world to convince her family to take her to New York City for a birthday. They loved their little Jenmarie. And you know what? She loved them too. There was another new *h*-wrinkle.

So Jenmarie, even more so than either of her siblings, co-signed on her father's enthusiasm, and likewise endorsed her mother's caveats: they would raise nothing that would be eaten. Byproducts were fine, like the eggs of chickens or milk from cows, but she wouldn't have her backyard turned into an abattoir. Barry, perhaps expecting this, wondered if she might be more interested in, say, something with wool, something she could shear and spin and use in her knitting. Carrie thought that was a swell idea, and thus Barry was able to frame the decision to buy out the plot behind their house – sixty-some square acres in the valley of which their residential hill formed one side – and invest in twenty llamas, as a joint decision. In truth, though, it had been Dad's design all along. The rest of the Bells felt it best to let him believe that none of them recognized this. Over the following four years, though, a number of purchases were made in which the family took a more active role; land, llamas, and labor. The property was fenced in, a modest vegetable patch was installed in the basin of the gorge, elevated and irrigated for reasons Jenmarie couldn't understand – wouldn't the rain just sluice down and handle the irrigation for them? – until a particularly hardy rainfall flooded the valley and killed their crop, prompting a further raising of the beds. The llamas, for their part, were easier to handle. They were essentially big, poorly-proportioned cats, none-too-pleased to be approached but all-too-happy to approach *you*, essentially docile but given to fits of truculence (replacing claws with truly noxious spit). Dad claimed they were 'companion livestock', which struck Jenmarie as akin to thinking of kids as 'moody 401k's. There were far better animals for companionship, if companionship was the goal. But, speaking of retirement funds, Barry and Carrie quickly discovered that the llamas could be more than just a hobby; their popularity was increasing around the rural parts of the country, and in 2000 Carrie trekked out to an auction in Indiana and watched some guy from Nebraska sell his baby llamas for three grand a head. Three grand! Following this, the Bells became barnyard eugenicists, breeding llamas with an eye towards fiber quality and presentation (a right angle between the back and the neck was worth a good seven-to-eight hundred bucks alone…as in, that quality on a llama, not like you could sell that part of a llama's body by itself for that amount of money). In 2002, a brace-faced Jenmarie helped her Dad load four baby llamas into a trailer, to be shuttled out to the auction, where they sold – one to a family in Pennsylvania, the other three south to a Georgian couple – for a total of fourteen thousand dollars. From that moment on, the Bells were full-time llama breeders.

In the, gosh, thirteen-or-so years since she'd entered this third life, Jenmarie had been enjoying the ride too much to dwell on the long-term consequences. Yes, her knowledge of future events was zilch (at least, as pertained to her personal life – the big world-event stuff kept its schedule), but thus far she hadn't really needed it. Barring the inevitable infelicities of life as an adolescent girl, Jenmarie had been happy. Her relationship with her entire family had been sunnier than it had ever been, in *any* universe, and likewise for her academics. On her first go-around, it had taken some gnarly student loans to get her through Emory. But with these grades, almost all A's except for English because fuck the classics, just a bunch of dead dickheads who wouldn't know narrative momentum if it tackled them from behind and shouted *it's me, narrative momentum,* that was Jenmarie's position, but anyway with the rest of her report card reading like the dictation of someone falling out of a helicopter, she was sure to get a full-ride scholarship to wherever the hell she wanted to go. Which, she was pretty sure, was still Emory. *Pretty* sure. She'd liked it plenty the first time, after all. Knew all the best teachers, the easiest classes, the best parties. The very best ones. True, this life's Mavis was making noises about going to other schools this time around, but Jenmarie wasn't worried about that, wasn't worried about the fact that Mavis was her connection (give or take a brother – and not in the way the Tomb had) to some of the aforementioned best parties. No need to worry on that score, because Jenmarie and Mavis were still the best of friends in this timeline.

Jenmarie had made sure to not only tolerate, but encourage and engage with, the most tedious of Mavis' gossip trances. Really, all it took was nodding and periodically saying things like "she *didn't,*" or "No. Way." Then Mavis grew out of it and bang, Jenmarie had her best friend back, for the first time in just about twenty years. She'd been skeptical that she'd ever truly align with Mavis again, fearing that the Jenmarie who had accrued so many impossible life experiences (or, she supposed, *lives* experiences) might have as little in common with the new version of her old best friend as she'd had with older version of the young Mavis in timeline two. Even considering that possibility made her head spin, but focusing on the breath had a palliative effect in every timeline, and brought her into the present moment, which was here, with Mavis, enjoying life, trying not to compare the Mavis of timeline three and the Mavis of timeline one. Mavis-3, for example, had worse taste in music than Mavis-1. How was that possible?

It didn't matter. What mattered was that Jenmarie was effectively best friends with a high schooler, which meant being swept into all of the little dramas which plagued girls of poor Mavis' age. And much to Jenmarie's chagrin, she found herself being well and truly *swept into them.* She was no longer just indulging Mavis when she gawped at the revelation that, oh my *god,* Chloe was grinding on Sean at Joey's party, when everybody *knew* that Chloe and Will were going steady! Just because Jenmarie was a transdimensional traveler pushing one hundred years old (that was perhaps stretching the truth a bit, but who was going to call her on it) didn't mean she was immune to the sheer *juiciness* of Chloe cheating on Will, when everybody knew that Will had cheated on, well, it was a long story. Long and juicy, regardless of how many timelines one had passed through.

Similar but different: Jenmarie didn't care how infinite and omniversal one's perspective was, there was no way not to die inside when Robbie was the only one to ask you to prom. Fucking *Robbie*.

"My parents are out of town that weekend too," fucking Robbie (who aged into a life of such indistinction that all Jenmarie knew of him was his having followed Van Halen on both the first and second legs of their 2012 tour) dropped one Friday, with all the subtlty of a sandbag. "If you wanna, you know…we're, you know, I'm doin' a party. After the uh, prom. If you wanna."

Jenmarie couldn't remember if Robbie'd had a crush on her in either of her other lives, but it was clear enough that he did now. And sweet though the kid was, he was still a kid, and 'willingness to follow a thing he liked all around the continent' wasn't exactly an attractive quality in a mate, at least not to Jenmarie. Maybe it would have been, had there been any chance of the two of them working out long-term…but she knew they wouldn't. She knew this as innately as she did that no matter how hard she jumped, she'd be back on solid ground in the very next second. It was gravity. It was pull.

It was having her hindsight out in front of her.

That said: her ancient mind was currently riding around in the body and brain of a teenager. And she hadn't so much as kissed anybody in, oh, about the entire length of her first life. Or thereabouts.

So she said yes. Because Robbie was Robbie, yeah, but beggars couldn't be choosers. Important to note: she said yes to the prom, not the party. She drew the line somewhere just beyond first base (Robbie was, as mentioned, Robbie), and at least at the prom she'd have a few eager umps to back up her call.

So they got dressed up and rented a limo (not a proper stretch, but a halfway decent Town Car) and went, which was another key divergence from Jenmarie's original life. She hadn't gone to prom the first time through. Hadn't wanted to, and not just because she hadn't been invited (though that was certainly a factor). Back then, when her world had been nothing but Chuckey, prom had seemed pretty stupid, and therefore not worth going to. Now that she knew her world to be but one of many, she recognized the truth: *everything* was pretty stupid, once you got far enough away from it. It was really just a question of not getting far away from it, then.

Jenmarie made a point of not defining either of the two *its* in that thought.

Alas, no great distances emerged between Jenmarie and Robbie that night, though there was still an arm's length remove. For Jenmarie was showing everyone else on the floor that night how the fuck it was done, assuming that particular *it* was in reference to pure enthusiasm. She didn't break out anything recognizable as a distinct move; it had been *decades* since she'd last had a proper dance, and what few moves she had known were naught but more casualties of the Tomb. Which was fine by her. She moved according to whim and nothing more, stomping and snapping and spinning as though she had constructive criticism for the rhythm of the music. Had she ever appreciated just what an outlet dancing – just *moving* – could be? She wondered what she would have done in New York without it. What she might have done to herself, without that pure animal release. What would have happened with Eddie if he hadn't grown too dour and self-involved to get out the way he used to…

The thought of Eddie Mark knocked her out of the pocket.

She didn't know how long she'd been dancing on her own, but it wasn't long enough to tucker Robbie out. He was still jerking and hopping beside her, grinning in anticipation of the couple's dance he clearly expected Jenmarie to pull him into, any second now.

Jenmarie tried to get back into her own flow, but found it a challenge now that the spectre of Eddie had entered her peripheral vision. So she had a go at dancing with Robbie (making a point to lift his seeking hand to a *very precise and non-erotic* point on the center of her torso), but smack in the middle of the next song he decided to offer her a little spin, which Jenmarie reluctantly took. Which immediately sent her mind back to that night at the House of YES with K.J. all those lives ago. Which naturally called to mind the way he had struck her, as she spun, as looking almost like Eddie...

Even after prom was over (goodnight Robbie, no kiss for you, and let us never speak of this again), that horrible little splinter from the past stuck with Jenmarie, drawing blood in the very back of her mind. Eddie. Fucking Eddie. Why the *fuck* was she thinking about Eddie? Why was she having such a hard time *not* thinking about him? It was, to be perfectly precise, really fucking annoying. Even from two dimensions over, he was getting the last laugh. He was getting to *win*. Again.

On one especially long and red night, Jenmarie charted a mental course for Eddie. Sure, he wouldn't know her from Adam, but she could tell him off just the same. Cast him out of her mind, once and for all. It wouldn't be hard. True, Mavis was veering away from Emory now, but unless the llamas stomping around the Bell property were casting some truly monstrous ripples through time and space, the resident's getaway in Athens at which Eddie would be out on the porch for at least part of

(Jenmarie couldn't remember precisely what time she'd gotten there, and so almost certainly wouldn't be able to recreate the same shoeless conditions as their first meeting, but hey, Eddie would be there) would still be happening, and Mavis' brother Lucky would know about it (he still seemed firmly Georgia-bound in this timeline), and so it would be a simple matter of calling up Mavis and asking her to ask her brother to...um, to invite her to a...ok, that was going to be a weird ask. But! Hey! Mavis had only looked at, and ultimately gone to, Emory *because* of Jenmarie's doing so. So once she applied to Emory, maybe Mavis would too. And then maybe Mavis would get in, and attend, and then Jenmarie could go somewhere else? Have her Eddie-exorcism-cake and...not eat it too. Or at all...? Point was, the *point* was, with these grades she could go anywhere. Why not try Columbia, or Harvard, see what the experience was like somewhere else? Well, then she wouldn't know about all the best teachers, the easiest classes, the most interesting parties...

Thinking about parties, thinking about ripples, thinking about gravity, finally thinking about things that weren't Eddie (or her hare-brained plan to give him a piece of a different Jenmarie's mind), thinking about, well, *llamas,* Jenmarie was forced to concede that the humming, spitting companion animals out back had indeed stamped their splitnailed imprint onto the face of the universe, or at least onto the Bells' little corner of it. To wit: the McMansions never came to blight the top of the hill. The llamas had apparently claimed the neighborhood in the name of upscale agriculture, and so over the years the land in the area was snapped up either by fellow farmers (most notably a guy up from Texas with thirty so-called Beefmaster cattle, which was the most grimly charming nomenclature Jenmarie had ever heard) or the Bells themselves, eager to expand their acreage. And why not, with the annual windfall of Indiana? They became known (to those *in* the know) as the provider of some of the country's finest llamas, which was almost definitely not true, but it was something to put on the business card. Oh yes, Carrie and Barry had business cards in this life. That was a new one, as far as Jenmarie knew, and she was stunned to find herself feeling…gosh, it was pride, she was *proud* of her parents. Even if their calling *was* mostly just working out which llamas should fuck next.

Of course, there was to be a more troubling corollary to the selective breeding ethos that had served the Bells so well: Tomjohn Bell was never to be born. Again. Carrie and Barry were simply too busy with the farm to make time for another human, or so Jenmarie imagined. At no point did Jenmarie hear her parents articulate this, be it to each other or their children, because why would they? They had three kids already, and it wasn't as though four was the norm in Chuckey. Not having a fourth kid was a *decision* in the same way as not driving to West Virginia and grabbing take-out from a five-star restaurant was. Still, Jenmarie was forced to acknowledge that she had been holding out hope – stupid, stupid hope, even after it had served her so poorly in the last life – that she could somehow save Tomjohn, perhaps create an environment more conducive to his (shudder) conception. It certainly occurred to her that this vain (weren't they all) hope was entirely for her sake, largely because there was no Tomjohn to have a sake for which to do things. She was just so tired of her heart breaking as she absent-mindedly set an extra place at the dinner table, or as she paused in consideration of just who her parents meant when they referred to "your brother."

There were other reasons Jenmarie wanted Tomjohn back, of course, but after so many years with just the older brother, she longed most of all for a younger one to fill the absences that only she could see. Too bad, then, that Tomjohn's absence this time was a result of the family's flourishing, rather than floundering. What, Jenmarie wondered on many a midnight ceiling-study, if it had been her own flourishing, in this charmed life she had made for not only herself but her family, that had erased Tomjohn from existence? What if he had originally been born simply to compensate for the disappointment that Jenmarie had been in her first life?

Well, her next thought would remind her as it wrinkled its nose and poked at the bridge of its glasses, *actually,* the likelihood that, even if her parents had decided to have another child, ugh, this was gross to think about, but the likelihood that it would be the same load of semen Dad would shoot into Mom, *yulch, yurgh,* and the likelihood that it would be precisely the same spermatozoa that would wriggle its way into the egg, and the likelihood that it would produce exactly the same human...well, it was basically nil. Which meant...the mere act of zapping back to a time before Tomjohn had denied the boy his birth. And since Jenmarie could apparently only travel *backwards*, in her *current* timeline...her initial fears had been well-founded.

She would never again know Tomjohn. He was gone, gone like Cherry Chirpworth, another bird flown to coop. Though at least Cheery had left only an empty nest that had once been full and warm, without all of the hungry shadows lurking in the Tomjohn-shaped holes in the universe. The ones that only she could see. The ones that only she would mourn. She alone. Alone.

Goodbye, hope. No kiss for you, no. And let us never speak of this again.

Oh, speaking of that: she applied to Emory and didn't get in.

How the fuck was that even possible? She'd aced the entire concept of high school, fucking *crushed* the SATs, and knocked her essay out of the park if she did say so herself, which she *did* goddamnit. Granted, she'd gotten in to Harvard and Columbia just like she'd wanted, and more to the point *Mavis* had applied to, and been accepted to, Emory. So all things considered, everything had broken her way: she would get to try out a new school, and still have the opportunity to, you know, go to parties (and their attendant porches) in Georgia, yeah, anyway, whatever, the point was that she hadn't even *wanted* to go to Emory, she'd applied to get Mavis to apply, but all the same it was fucking bullshit that she hadn't been accepted, even though she hadn't wanted to go. She wanted to write them back, maybe even on the back of their little one-page, single-sided form rejection, that, you know, you let me in two dimensions ago when I was a *way* worse candidate, so, really, all you've done is prove that it's just a total crapshoot and you guys are rolling the dice and not even accepting the best candidates…but she didn't. Instead she had a panic attack, her very first one in this charmed little life of hers. Which was also fucking bullshit; she was so much happier now than in her first go-round, so why was she having panic attacks *earlier* than she originally had?

The good news was that getting her meds was a far simpler matter than it had been when she'd been a 'problem child' in round two. She informed her GP she'd done "a lot of research," a claim her doctor accepted with bemused frustration, but go on, let the doc smirk, as long as she writes the scripts, which she did. So Jenmarie took her meds and went to Harvard (*oh yeah,* she insisted to her astonished friends and family, *not a big deal, luck of the draw,* all the while thinking *you're goddamned right I'm going to Harvard*) and tried not to compare it to Emory, tried not to hold the friends she made and the classes she took and the parties she dragged herself to against those of Life One. This, as she left behind the unprecedented novelty of the llamas and reentered academia, was the greatest challenge to her happiness, the heaviest weight upon her shoulders. The comparisons. Which life was better? Was she happier *now*, or had things been better on the first crack (the second had been a wash, and hardly merited consideration)? Was that just rosy retrospection? The feat of staying present, of bringing her focus to what was in front of her rather than behind (or, in the Tomb's terms, beneath) her, grew ever more challenging. Especially as time ticked on, as was its wont, years stumbling blindly into the week leading up to the date of the party. *The* party. The first night of the getaway. The night with the porch. The one on which Jenmarie had met/could again meet her past-future husband. Back when he'd been just a silhouette. Human-shaped potential upon which she could imagine any face she liked.

You know. That party.

The one that it would be tremendously pointless and useless and also very dumb to go to.

The one she couldn't stop fucking thinking about as the week progressed. The way it would be a chance to get Eddie out of her head. Tell him off. Exorcise him. Be free.

The one she could go to. Because if it all went belly up, then she could get away from the getaway, hie herself to Manhattan, to the corner of Fourth and 57th, to back before the party. Like magic, she'd never have gone at all.

No risk. All reward.

The first obstacle was simple enough: she simply had to get Mavis to invite her. Uncertain of how to handle what was in point of fact a self-invitation gracefully, Jenmarie opted for a blunt force approach, calling her dearest friend up and exclaiming "I have the weekend off! I wanna come visit you!"

This was a prospect Mavis met with unfeigned enthusiasm, as well as the rather confusing advice that it might, on such short notice, be cheaper to fly into LA and just get a Greyhound up.

"...why would that be cheaper?" Jenmarie wondered.

"Short-term flights can just get screwy, I've found."

"So it'd be cheaper to fly three states over?"

"...what?"

"Alright, two I guess."

"It's a big state, but it's just one state."

"Louisiana's not that big."

At this, Mavis laughed. "Oh, no. LA as in Los Angeles. Didn't I tell you? I'm at UCSF now. I transferred."

"...you quit Emory?"

"Uh, yeah. I'm not commuting between Atlanta and San Fran twice a day."

"Why?"

"The flights would be c-"

Jenmarie forced herself to chuckle, little though she felt like it just then. "No, why did you transfer?"

"Eh, just wasn't feeling Atlanta, I guess."

"You never told me that before," she couldn't stop herself from saying. To which Mavis said something to the effect of "well I don't know when I would have," but Jenmarie wasn't listening anymore. Had Mavis-1 not liked Atlanta, but stuck with it for Jenmarie? If so, that meant she'd been an even better friend than Jenmarie had realized. Mavis-1 had, at least. But, wait, hadn't Mavis-1 met her eventual-husband Stephen at Emory? The one who had literally *jumped* for joy upon learning of Mavis' pregnancy?

And how was it ok, then, that Jenmarie had apparently denied Mavis-3 Mavis-1's happily-ever-after?

Well, she decided, fuck it, because Mavis-3 had just denied Jenmarie her…

Oh, her what? Her happily-ever-after? The one she hoped would come from pushing her ex further away, rather than pulling him back to her? The fact was, that Mavis-3, by transferring out of Emory, had unwittingly made herself a martyr of sorts, sacrificing her own joyful relationship to protect Jenmarie from even thinking about recreating the one that had ruined her life.

Not that she was doing that. Thinking about recreating it. She wasn't. Who brought that up? Why would she be thinking about that? She didn't need him for a happily-ever-etc. She was happy *now*, and that was what mattered. And so was Mavis. Happy. Yeah, things weren't perfect. They could always be happier. Sure, that was true. But…uh…well, that was true.

Also true: if she, say, *hypothetically*, bought a ticket to Athens, Georgia, and crashed a party to which she had not been invited, at which she didn't technically know anybody (or perhaps it would be more accurate to say, none of them knew *her),* just to meet a guy who had made her very happy for a bit and then quite unhappy for what was now a *lot* longer, well…she might, for whatever reason, *become* unhappy then, there, in Athens, Georgia. She might well be trading in a current happiness to re-up future unhappiness, and why? Just to tell this asshole what another version of him had done to her? Was the happiness that taking Eddie down a peg could *potentially* bring into her life so great that it would justify gambling the contentment she now felt?

That was one way of thinking about it. But that way wasn't taking into account the thing about how if at any point in the future she should become unhappy, she could just *come back to this happy moment.* Ticket to New York, crowbar to the High Tomb, remember the happy now, and reclaim it. So, it didn't really matter how things worked out with Eddie, assuming she bought that ticket to Athens, assuming she went. There wouldn't be any actual consequences.

And that was the thing, the one true and eternal *thing* of Jenmarie's life: she had kicked free from consequence. By creating an ideal life to which she could at any point return, she was no longer the plaything of her poor decisions. Hell, if things went *really* sideways with Eddie (whatever *that* meant), she could grab a bowling pin and go full Plainview on him, and it wouldn't matter! Even if she got caught by the cops before beating a trail back to the High Tomb, even if she had to serve a thirty year sentence, everything would be all kinds of fine as long as she could get back to the High Tomb at some point before dying, which like, *obviously,* 'before dying' was implied. Not that she had any plans to brain her once-and-oh-let's-hope-not-future ex, but, well, it wasn't exactly *off* the table. Two valid questions, then, one of which could well serve to answer the other. First: did the timelines continue without her? And if they did, what did it mean to be responsible for somebody's murder (or in Tomjohn's case, somebody's lack-of-existence), if one no longer inhabited the dimension in which the act had been committed?

That two-parter was quite a ways above her philosophical paygrade (though she could throw any domesticated animal she liked here in Cambridge and undoubtedly hit somebody already scratching their chin about just such a conundrum), but what really set her mind on a collision course with the funny farm was the second question: was what happened in this dimension 'real'? She'd entered it, after all, through a faulty memory, one that had either been exaggerated or wholly fabricated by crummy cognitive wiring. Carrie had, in Jenmarie's original universe, flatly denied there had ever been any bird in any shoebox, and there was no reason for her to lie. Yet it was through that fiction that Jenmarie had entered this timeline, and it was in this timeline that she had experienced more happiness and good fortune than she felt was her just portion. What did that mean? Had she merely leavened a new reality with fantasy, or was this a fantasy reality into which her mind sprinkled periodic discomforts to keep her from getting suspicious? And if the latter were the case, would it even make sense to think of this as anything other than reality? Because if it *wasn't* reality, if this was all a dream universe in which nothing was real, not even the other people, least of all personal consequences for Jenmarie herself…wouldn't that free her up to do anything she wanted, to anyone, without a single wring of the hands?

Remarkably, this tangle of ruminative noodles didn't snake its way towards syncope. If anything, it spun itself into a great big arrow, pointing enthusiastically to Athens, Georgia. Still, Jenmarie stalled in buying the ticket, cursing the cliché she'd become as she found a good flight, input her card number on the payment screen, then sat with the cursor over the *PAY* button, finger trembling over the trackpad of her MacBook, until the countdown clock on the tickets hit zero and she was booted back a few windows to start all over. Sure, it was one thing to rationalize her way to *my actions have no consequences*, but that was a hard place from which to act. Because if she was wrong about that, any and all consequences would be hers to shoulder, could well follow her back through the Tomb. Assuming she went back through. Assuming…

On one of those late-night flirtations with airfare, her finger fell. Or maybe she'd dropped it. It came out to the same thing: she was going to Georgia, to a getaway she could only hope was still happening. And why wouldn't it be? Residents would always need to get away. Some things were eternal.

   Just as her email *dinged* with the flight confirmation, Jenmarie had the good sense to whisper "you're an idiot" into the dark of her apartment.

H
A
P
P
Y

She got settled at a cheap AirBnB she'd found in Watkinsville, just south of Athens, then did her best to remember precisely when she'd arrived at the party. It had been so long, *so* long since that night, and she'd been more than a little bit swirly at the time…but nine sounded right to her. Nine or ten. Somewhere in there. So she timed her arrival out for 9:30, called a Zyp, and took her shoes off en route. Because that was how she'd arrived on the first night. And she wanted to get the beginning right. The beginning had been good. It was worth getting right. In which case, maybe she ought to have grabbed a handle and gotten absolutely wrecked beforehand. Just to close the loop. Ah, well. There was always next time.

Not that she was here for a good beginning. She wasn't. She was here to read him the riot act. Really let him have it. Still, she didn't put her shoes back on.

This time, Eddie Mark wasn't to be found on the porch, which meant Jenmarie had removed her shoes in the Zyp for nothing. Unfortunately for her, she only spotted Eddie's absence after exiting the vehicle, which promptly sped away. With her fucking shoes in the well of the backseat, once again. She massaged her quiet shame by deciding that she'd repeated this particular mistake because she'd really committed to the role, she'd gone full Day-Lewis after all, just not in the way she'd expected, and anyways, it wasn't like she'd made the *exact* same dumb mistake again, no, of course not, because if she *had* made the *exact* same dumb mistake a second time that might be in some way *ominous*, and there was no room for omens in the shoebox universe, no way, no day, save -Lewis, okay? The Zyp driver, as before, as a different Zyp driver had decades ago, needed to complete another ride before he could bring back Jenmarie's shoes. But there was no Eddie out here to keep her company, and she didn't want to get lost in the shuffle inside without her shoes – the image of her feet impaled by stilettos on the dance floor was too easily accessible. Which got her wondering something she'd never wondered before: why had Eddie been on the porch in the first place, hunched over in the little swing, alone in the dark? He didn't smoke, and he didn't seem to have been waiting for anyone. Had he been waiting for her? What if...what if Eddie had his own High Tomb, and he had been waiting for her because he'd met her there before? What if they were each creating an infinite number of universes in which they were forever searching for new versions of each other to read the riot act, only ever passing further and further apart from the original version of their once-beloved?

Or, she considered, what if he'd been on the porch because he'd wanted some fresh air. You absolute gibbon. Stick with the clarity, ride the wave, focus on the breath, join the Wi-Fi, pop the clutch, rock the vote, etc. Focus.

The Zyp came back, Jenmarie got her shoes, then winced her way up the gravel drive and sat herself down on the sagging top step of the porch to slip them on.

As she did, a familiar voice bade her "oop, just gonna squeeze by ya" over her shoulder, as a foot swung around her.

It was Eddie, trying to pass her! As she was putting on the shoes! There was still a chance to read him the riot act after all!

(Though, god, hearing his voice for the first time in decades had a curious effect on her. Not romantic – not necessarily – just…curious.)

Seizing her opportunity, Jenmarie pretended to be startled, launching up to her feet just as Eddie was straddling her shoulder, trying to sneak past. The idea, the mechanics of which Jenmarie would soon admit to herself hinged on a certain degree of Looney Tunes logic, was to trip Eddie a bit, reach out and help him catch his balance, then hey presto, touch barrier broken, faces near to each other, would you like to go get a drink, why yes I would, the rest will be history, except hopefully not history like actual history had turned out. The rest would be future history that would be better than past history. The riot act read over drinks. Sure. That was the idea. Trip Eddie a bit, that was the first step in that idea.

What happened instead was that Jenmarie launched upwards with enough force to lift Eddie bodily off the ground a few inches, shift him forwards, bring his feet down in an awkward half-on-half-off position *vis a vis* the porch steps, and send him tumbling to the pavement five steps below, which he kissed more forcefully than he ever had or (let's hope) ever would kiss Jenmarie. The noise he made as he hit the concrete was not *smooch* but *CRUNCH*, a report made all the more horrific by the perfectly-formed, deep-red kissy lips Eddie stamped on the cement. There was scant time to appreciate the comedy *or* the tragedy in this, though, as Eddie immediately slumped onto his side and convulsed, shaking and shimmying like a golden retriever having a bad dream.

"Oh, Jesus," Jenmarie mumbled to herself as she hustled down the steps, nearly tripping herself in her haste. Upon reaching the bottom, she realized that despite all the expensive medical learnin' she'd gotten, she didn't actually know how to help Eddie in this moment. Unless he'd landed hard enough to suddenly develop stage four colon cancer, which her diagnostic training led her to believe he hadn't. So she said "oh, Jesus" again, and called 911.

She rode with him to the hospital, struggling to split the difference between guilt and something like glee. Given how Eddie had hurt her, in ways far deeper than a broken nose and some headwound-induced boogie shoes could atone for, it appealed to Jenmarie's more vindictive impulses to have in some small way returned the favor. Those were bad impulses, she knew, bad impulses! Bad! And she knew the road to divorce was hardly a one-way street, as surely as she knew that metaphor didn't really work the way she'd meant it to. Point was, she bore a fair amount of responsibility, she'd done her share of hurting, yes, this was all true. Also true: it brought her no pleasure to see *anybody* broken and bleeding in the back of an ambulance. The circumstances were comedic, in a cosmic kind of way, but the consequences were anything but.

Yeah, that was right. The *consequences*. Because therein lay the beauty of cosmic comedy; it endured. It was eternal. Ephemeral tragedies could be erased. All it took was a trip to Fourth and 57th, with a quick stop at a hardware store on the way. The slate could never be wiped fully clean, though. That which was brushed away would cling to the sweeping hand. That's consequence, baby. And I don't care who you are, that's funny right there. Git-R-Done.

Eddie, poor schmuck, was hooked up to machines that went beep and boop, and after more beeps and boops than Jenmarie could count, he woke up, his speech jumbled and his eyes drifting and his nose snapped hard to the right, but otherwise fine. Jenmarie asked him if he remembered her, to which he smiled and replied "you're the doozy," which Jenmarie took to be an insult until she remembered her man's frustratingly allusive 'wit.' Watch that first step, it's a doozy. At this, she chuckled, and her heart broke along familiar faults. Harmon's voice, speaking from another universe. Things given, things taken.

Jenmarie wondered if anything could ever really change, or if it was all just variations on a theme.

Here are the paths taken, the choices made which she hadn't wanted to make, the lives lived which she hadn't meant to live, few of which are worth dwelling upon: the second first date at the wine bar with the old-timey washboard band. The second first fight over whether or not Jimmy Page deserved to be considered an all-time great guitar god (to Jenmarie, the answer was yes in terms of importance and riffs, but no in terms of chops, and if you want to be a guitar god, you've gotta have the total package, goddamnit!). The second first reconciliation. The beginning of the end, again. The attempts to make it work. The failures to do the same. The end. Again.

And so, the return to Manhattan. No fingers trembling over trackpads this time; Jenmarie made the decision quickly, and dawdled only in spending two weeks trying to convince herself that she hadn't made it. Two weeks kicking herself for falling for Eddie again, so quickly, so *easily,* when she ought to have been reading him the aforementioned riot act. Two weeks thinking about what she could say to him if (when) she went back again, how she would really give it to him with both barrels. Two weeks thinking about the ticket she hadn't bought but would. Until she did. Because self-deception was an exhaustible resource, even for Jenmarie, and so she found herself on a bus, staring out the window, staring more at her own reflection than the Manhattan skyline clawing its way over the horizon. Hoping, perhaps, that she could shame herself into turning around. Trying again. Or rather, trying again in the normal way that people try again. Without taking the whole thing from the top. Or, ha, from the bottom. With a crowbar to the very bottom, which made it the top. The curious architecture of the High Tomb. Which she was admiring before she knew it. From the inside. It wasn't that she didn't know what she was doing. She knew exactly what she was doing. It was all simply happening before she knew it. It was all simply happening.

Into the High Tomb. A descent, back to happy. Back to Athens. The porch, sans the ambulance. A connection unmade. A riot act unread. The end before the beginning, as simple as that. And so back to Manhattan. Back to the High Tomb. Back to happy. Athens. The porch. A pushier proposition. The third first date at a local microbrewery. The stilted conversation; Jenmarie unable to remember what she'd talked about with *this* Eddie as opposed to the others. Knowing that she'd never brought up the riot act with him, even in passing. No third second date. Fourth and 57th. In. Down. Back. Athens. Porch. Fourth first date. Third first fight. A riot act nearly read, but not quite. No reconciliation. Tomb. In. Down. Back. Athens. Tomb. In. Down. Back. Athens. Tomb. Again. Again. Again.

Again.

What a mistake this had been, continued to be, she realized as she looked into the eyes of someone who couldn't possibly have realized how profoundly he had hurt her, would always hurt her, who hadn't yet hurt her, who wasn't even the person who *would* hurt her.

Boy, wasn't *that* the ultimate, omniversal punchline? Here was the Eddie who wasn't the Eddie who *would* hurt her. And here she was, the Jenmarie who would be hurt, who actively *sought* the agent of her agony, endlessly sought and found only a facsimile. And, of course, it wasn't only Eddie she was recreating *ad infinitum*. She'd long since lost count of the number of conversations she had which proceeded along these lines:

"You are *so* fired," Jenmarie would say to Mavis mid-conversation, a callback to one of their deeply-embedded inside jokes.

"What?" Mavis would reply.

"...nevermind," Jenmarie would conclude, upon recalling that this was an inside joke from another universe, with another Mavis. And it probably wasn't all that funny in that other one, either. Yet Mavis might have laughed, in that one which Jenmarie had left behind without a second thought (like all the others). To chase one in which she herself could be someone she didn't recognize.

This was past. This was backwards. This was beneath. Even if each was a new timeline, even if this was a universe of her creation, revisiting this old haunt would scare up the same ghosts, every damn time. Because each new Eddie would always be someone *like*, but not *quite*, the Eddie that would hurt her, while she would always be *precisely* the Jenmarie who would be hurt. And so she would reset the stage of her suffering. Always. Not because she was a masochist, or not *entirely*, but because this was her nature. Those were not the same thing. Masochism implied some sense of pleasure drawn from pain. Whereas nature was something by which one could be mortified, even as one was unable to change, even as one repeated the same mistakes over and over and over, reconstructing oneself with an eye towards a more spectacular implosion. Someone quite like, but not identical to, Eddie Mark would always hurt her, and Jenmarie would always be hurt. Always always always. The only way to escape these roles was to cancel the whole damn production. Live out the charmed life. And why not? What awaited her was happiness, joy she had known to be true, however illusory it may have been, however many shoebox universes within shoebox universes she had created for herself, the constant among them was a depth of solitude and peace, peace even with her own tooth-grinding ambition. She had known it, felt it, and so it was real, and it was *hers*. All she had to do was go to the High Tomb and go back to her happy place, her happy time, and play out that string. There was a dream awaiting her, was there not? There was something shiny and mysterious high above her, and didn't she want to see that? Of course she did. Yes, obviously. But there was no rush, because she could always return to the High Tomb, always go around once more, try to make it work with Eddie once again, even though there was no reason to, even though there were more reasons *not* to than she could hold in her head at once, even if each time her heart broke the cracks seemed to set just a little bit deeper, even if some wounds carried through time. She would go back to her happy and then back to Athens, back to Eddie, back to unhappy, back to sad, back to the Tomb, back to happy, back to Athens. Again. Again. Again. The paths differed but the destination remained the same. How many times? Again. For how many years? Again. How many lives' worth of suffering? Again. And why? Again. Again? Again. Again? Why not? Why stop? She had all the time in this, and any other, world. There were no deadlines, no due dates. There was no fucking reason, in other words, she shouldn't be able to get this right, take this single most catastrophic personal failure in her life and spin it into a victory. It had no right being this fucking intractable. She was trying everything, *everything* to tweak the variables, going so far as to stalk Eddie for days on end after the getaway, contriving to meet him at Whole Foods, at CVS, whatever other basic-ass establishments he patronized, Jenmarie would happen to meet him there, strike up conversation with him there, take it from there. But no matter the *there* from which she took it, the *there* into which it inevitably slammed her was a brick wall. She tried changing herself. She tried changing him. She tried changing their situation. She tried to keep either of them from changing at all. She tried and tried and tried, and every single time, every fucking single fucking time, she would cry so hard she would scream, as she had the first time she'd gone back through the High Tomb, only this time she wouldn't stop crying until she was back *inside* the Tomb, seeing the dream above her but thinking *later*, she would live her way to the dream *eventually*, she had all the time in the world, she had new worlds in which to make time, she had time. So again, she would try to make this shit work with the guy – and that was precisely how she had come to think of him, as *the guy*. He was his rejection, he was her failure, he was a mockery of every good quality she felt she possessed, which she felt were quite a few, a solid armful of good fucking qualities, and he didn't see any of them, none of him saw any of them, and that was too much, that was just too much, who the fuck did he think he was, this guy, to grind her down, to drive her away and call her back to him, push and pull, again and again and again, huh, who, just who, just a guy, just *the guy*, just Eddie, fucking Eddie Mark.

That the Eddie dilemma could never be solved, that the case could never be cracked, that the square could never be circled, never became clear to Jenmarie Bell. With the gift of hindsight, sweet and sour hindsight, she could well have imagined herself locked in this downward spiral without end for the rest of eternity. Well, no, not locked, unless it was she herself who had thrown the deadbolt, it would have been more accurate to say that her nature had wed her to her own self-abnegation, not the good sort of self-transcendence she'd once sought, no, this was something else entirely, a scorpion forever hitching rides from toads, forever drowning, again again again, this would have been Jenmarie, she knew it would have been…had she not been rattled from the path by the tyrant called chance, the villain called luck, the dipshit called happenstance.

R
O
L
L

The first time Eddie died marked the last time Jenmarie slept until she got back into the High Tomb, where she lingered for far longer than usual. However much she may have longed to crush his fragile bits with a heavy thing, the actual image of him lying in the street, limbs shattered and splayed, eyes fixed upon something terrible closing in from an impossible distance…it was a sight she found nearly unshakable. One she knew she would never shake. The triumph of consequence. She remained in the timeline long enough to give the license of the truck that had done the hitting and running to the police (fingers crossed there was consequence enough for the driver)…then in, Down, and back she went. Not even entertaining a reading of the riot act; now she was just relieved to see him alive, in one piece. Not because he was Eddie, but because he was a goddamned human being, and so was Jenmarie. That didn't explain falling into yet another relationship with him, of course. But what did.

The second time Eddie died, maybe, gosh, about thirty or forty timelines later (if *later* meant anything in this context), was far less grisly but no less traumatic. The powerlessness that Jenmarie felt watching him choke, on a fucking Coney Island of all things, not that there was a hierarchy of foods to choke on and Coney Islands were near the bottom, just that, well, no sweeping eulogies could lend dignity to the man done asunder by a meat-smothered weenie. Fortunately, over the next ~~twenty~~ thirty a hundred who knew how many timelines, Eddie died only once more, plummeting through an open bulkhead outside a bodega of all things. Death wasn't what brought about the end in so many of these lives, of course, wasn't what sent Jenmarie back. But the fourth time she'd watched him bite the big one, this time from dancing (after the requisite prodding from Jenmarie, albeit not as much as he would require as a married man, Eddie hit the floor with a glass of wine in his hand, spilled some, slipped on the spill, slammed his head on the counter at a terminally funny angle, and then *really* hit the floor), the spectacle had lost its ability to shock, frequency reducing it to just another one of those small frustrations that plagued the ambitious. She would roll her eyes, sigh, and book it back to the High Tomb.

Given the number of times she was rerunning the Eddie period of her life, it was inevitable that rotten things of an unpredictable nature would happen. Call it existential snake eyes; given enough rolls of the die, it was guaranteed that, well, Eddie would die. That was just probability, numbers, necessity. Sure, it was harder to explain why she should have been present for every single one of these accidents, but Jenmarie was happy to chalk that up to her being just about the only thing that got Eddie out of the house, even if that wasn't strictly, or even broadly, accurate. What was more concerning to Jenmarie – or at least, it was more concerning when it finally occurred to her, which took far longer than she'd have liked to admit – was that nothing of the struck-by-lightning and/or flattened-by-an-anvil variety had happened to her. *Ever.* Even as everyone around her suffered some fatal whoopsie-doo or another (everyone in her family had been sent to a farm upstate at least once, most remarkably when her father had been trampled by llamas eager for their feed, and though happenstance had only brained Mavis the one time, she did seem metaphysically inclined towards breaking her legs), Jenmarie remained perfectly unscathed. Save the scar on her chin, which had by now faded such that Jenmarie had to tug and bunch the flesh of her face in the mirror just to find it, she'd never sustained any other disfiguring misfortunes, nor tragedies of a more terminal sort. Fun though it was to imagine herself a demigod of each new shoebox universe she created, benign and undying, her good fortune came to seem somehow sinister, the ever-growing pile of discarded timelines beneath her lifting mere improbability into statistical impossibility. There was, quite simply, *no way* she could have existed for this long (however long that was, and she'd spent more than a few years with more than a few of the Eddies, so, you know, it had to have been a pretty long time) and avoided each and every one of the innumerable snakes coiled and waiting inside the world's many peanut jars. There was *no way*, that was, unless there was something shepherding her, ensuring her safety. Or a some*one?* Some*how*, some*one* didn't feel right to Jenmarie. The loneliness of her unending, self-inflicted recursions was too deep to permit some deistic entity that had been with her all along (*awww*). But there had to be some*thing*, not of the dun dun dun variety, but maybe some privilege granted to the creator of a new timeline, keeping her from fully popping her clogs. Because if there *weren't*…well, it was inconceivable that she hadn't died yet. Which meant it was conceivable that she *had*, and that was a whole jar of peanuts she couldn't even imagine cracking before anxiety started using her skull as a speedbag.

As if to prove her right, the some*thing* that may or may not have actually been a *real* thing offered Jenmarie a slapstick masterclass in the vagaries of impersonal cruelty. First, a dachshund, aka the canine equivalent of a Coney Island, barked loudly at Eddie as he and Jenmarie were strolling along Ludlow Street in Cincinnati, startling Eddie enough to send him backwards onto a yum-yum yellow fire hydrant, which he tumbled over, landing on the very same patch of street a moving truck that was moving a bit too fast for its own good (and certainly for Eddie's) had been hoping to occupy, and did occupy in very short order. This was, Jenmarie had to concede, perhaps a just punishment for a man who had insisted on using his precious vacation days to take his sweetheart to Ohio. Then, in the very next timeline, Eddie vanished. He and Jenmarie had made plans to go to the park and play cards, but he never showed, and failed to answer Jenmarie's increasingly frantic calls or texts. Not that he could have known, but her horror was less at the awful fate that may have befallen him, and more at the fact that the befalling wasn't happening in her presence. It was her due, was it not, her *right*, to witness Eddie's undoing? Apparently not: Eddie's buddy Hal rather courteously texted Jenmarie (though how he had her number was a matter Jenmarie would raise with Eddie on the next go-around) to inform her that Eddie had hanged himself from the pull-up bar he'd hung in his closet doorframe. Jenmarie couldn't be certain what about that horrified her most, but it was probably Eddie's having a pull-up bar. Why, she asked Hal, had Eddie done it? Not talking about the pull-up bar now. Had he left a note? Negative, Hal informed her. Were the police investigating? Also negative, no reason to suspect foul play.

"Somebody should be looking into this!" Jenmarie huffed. "Eddie's never done a suicide before!"

"Well," Hal replied, "yeah."

That was the most illuminating thing anybody could tell Jenmarie about Eddie's self-annihilation, which she found unacceptable. So for a few weeks she gainsaid common sense and stuck around, slipping comfortably into the role of lover-demanding-answers, vainly hectoring the police to *do something*, and failing that, taking a stab at solving the riddle of Eddie's truly inexplicable suicide herself. Because if there *hadn't* been foul play, and Eddie really *had* offed himself, that was important to know, wasn't it? Had there always been pain enough to do such a thing sloshing around his noggin, the noggins of his every iteration, from the beginning? Turned out detective work was hard – not the same as just Googling factoids about skyscrapers – particularly when one had no badge-shaped authority to wave at people and slam onto car windows. What was more, Jenmarie quickly came to appreciate that, for as many times as she'd known Eddie, known innumerable variations on the theme of Mr. Mark, she didn't really know who his friends were. She knew *of* Hal, but she met him maybe once every ten timelines. She also knew *of* an old college buddy of Eddie's named…what was her name? She had a name, and it was super boring, and there was no face to which Jenmarie could affix the super boring name because Jenmarie had never met this person. She tended to live in DC in most timelines, and was little more than a pen pal to most Eddies. Not knowing her name, Jenmarie couldn't exactly call her up, and Hal's contribution had ended where it began, with his alerting Jenmarie to Eddie's beating a Coney Island to the punch. So back to the High Tomb Jenmarie went, vowing to keep a closer eye on Eddie's mental state, which she did right up until his mental state went flying, along with the rest of his head, from his body state. He'd crashed the car without his seatbelt on (Jenmarie was wearing hers, of course), soaring into the windshield with enough force to punch his head through…but not enough to liberate his shoulders. So he mounted his head through the thick glass like a prize buck at a hunter's lodge, for all of three tenths of a second. Then the force that was enough for the head but not for the shoulders found a final point of compromise: the neck, which had been perforated by the jagged glass, a helpful 'tear here to open' of which inertia availed itself. Zip, rip, off with his head! It was by far the most hideous dispatch Eddie had yet suffered, but Jenmarie was too cheesed off by it to scream anything at her headless forever-ex except "fucking seriously, dude?!" The *dude* being Eddie, for not wearing his seatbelt, for driving like an asshole. The *dude* being lady luck, for killing Eddie in a *third* consecutive timeline, for indulging itself in increasingly preposterous *autos-da-fé*, in this case an *automobile-da-fé*, ha, ha. The *dude* being whatever that some*thing* that protected her was, because she climbed out of the car on two steady feet, brushing broken glass from her clothes and hair, finding nothing more on herself than a handful of superficial cuts and scrapes. No new scars to carry with her, on her next trip Down.

The *dude*s thus established: *fucking seriously* for a fourth time in a row when Eddie tried to open a window at an AirBnB in Asheville (an old building this was, with heavy windows), only to have it guillotine down and cut off the tips of two of his fingers, apparently severing an artery or else just generally channeling Verhoeven as his little stumps geysered blood all over the walls, redecorating the inside of the bedroom to look more like the inside of Eddie by emptying the latter into the former. *Fucking seriously* for the *fifth* time when, on the *very next go-around*, she and Eddie went to see *The Conjuring 2* at a Cinemark, one of those faux-fancy theaters with the assigned seating and the electric recliners, which recliners were perfectly designed for losing one's wallet in, and then malfunctioning as you (assuming you were Eddie Mark) crawled underneath to grab the fallen wallet; somehow, some fucking how, the leg extension bit pincered down and crushed him to death. *Fucking seriously* a sixth time when Eddie, for the first time in *any* dimension Jenmarie knew about, decided he wanted to try cocaine, which he purchased and used without incident, only precipitating a *fucking seriously* when, presumably in an attempt to be funny (comedy, one must remember, being subjective), he took a running dive at a solid, unopening fifth-story window. Jenmarie wondered, as he sailed straight through the shattering glass and plummeted silently to the ground (though was it just her imagination, or did she hear a slide whistle accompanying the fall?), if his apparent equanimity in the face of oncoming pavement wasn't borne of the satisfaction of, *this* time, having made it all the way through a pane of glass. The seventh consecutive *fucking seriously* would be the final one, the *fucking seriously* that inducted Jenmarie herself into *dude*hood: she and Eddie were walking down Newbury Street (Jenmarie having in this timeline convinced him to come to Boston for vacation, having herself transferred out of Harvard to join him, yes, in New York again, and how pleased she was to eventually undo *that* phenomenal backslide), hand in hand, happy as could be, not a cloud in sight, and so on. Strolling happy sunshine yippie, and then some-body to their left shouted something, and then Eddie turned to look towards the source of the shout, and then Eddie just fucking died. Dropped dead where he stood, as though an angel had snapped his neck.

It was this wackiest-of-all-demises that finally revealed Jenma-rie's role as a *dude*, as deserving of a *fucking seriously* as any of the other *dudes*. She was, after all, the one causing all of these increa-singly ludicrous deaths, for it was she who kept rolling the die. Yes, it was almost surely inevitable that, given enough rolls, sev-en snake-eyes in a row, pip pip pip pip pip pip pip, was not only possible but probable, inevitable. But it was hard for Jenmarie to consider the phenomenon as a pure quirk of large numbers, and she felt the some*thing* smirk at each of her stabs at sober contem-plation. The some*thing's* amusement was, indeed, the only satisfy-ing way to explain the escalating zaniness of Eddie's deaths. It was the only satisfying way to explain why Jenmarie should have been present for all but one of Eddie's annihilations (whereas she had *never* had the front-row seat when tragedy struck friends or members of her family). It was, come to think of it, not satisfy-ing at all. And yet, that was what made it so satisfying. Such was the logic of the High Tomb, to which Jenmarie returned, which she used to return to Eddie, whom she had watched die so many times, whom she had watched crack his own goddamned neck. She returned to the moment they were sitting across a small table from each other, grabbing a late brunch at a café called Sun In My Belly. The food hadn't arrived yet, here at the moment she'd dropped back into, but it appeared they'd ordered; this she dedu-ced from the contentment she saw in Eddie's smile.

Jenmarie tried to smile back. But still, that first, unshakable death mask, with the eyes fixed upon the distance, the one she'd seen from so many angles after so many demises, the one that proved the hardest to shake…that mask nearly overwrote the man's living visage even as Jenmarie stared across the table and studied his smile, because he didn't know yet. He'd never know until it was too late.

In an instant, before she knew it…she knew that she was done with Eddie. She *had* to be. Just like that. Simple as letting go, but not the same. It was simply not minding the thing slipping one's grasp. But not the same.

Let him live, let him die, let him do whatever he wanted, just let him do it on his own. Because were she to involve herself with him again, it wouldn't matter *what* he did. If he died, she would return to the High Tomb. If he lived and hurt her (as the one necessarily begat the other), she would return to the High Tomb. There was no scenario in which she brought Eddie into her orbit that did not end with her being knocked loose from it, fully ceding it to him as she careened through the void, towards that shadowless glow from below. It felt like finally getting a joke she'd been too young to understand the first time she'd heard it: to fixate on Eddie was to be bound by chains she herself forged, link by link, into a perfect circle. There would be no escape. No space from which to touch the bitter wisdom of hindsight. The font of all wisdom. Hindsight.

It was time to leave Eddie in the past, gift him to the High Tomb as a dim light in the Down. The best thing for her to do now, for *her*, would be to return to her Happy and build herself an Up, an Up that could live up to the Down for which she'd worked so hard, an Up that would carry her to that strange, impossible dream-memory at the top. All she had to do was let go.

And to her credit, she really would try.

M
E
L
T

Going back to the happy
with the intention of staying there was a disorienting experience.
No longer was she simply reacting to her most recent mistakes –
now she was attempting to rejoin a flow of events whose intrica-
cies she had largely forgotten, having scarcely given them a second thought since taking her leave of them to stir up more
Eddies in her wake. It was like putting a book down part way
through, and picking it back up... *how* much later, precisely? How
long had it been, since she'd busied herself with the affairs that
were hers alone? Impossible to say – she hadn't been keeping
track, and there wasn't exactly a High Tomb Log for her to consult. A little back-of-the-napkin math gave her some truly gobs-
macking numbers, though; the most conservative estimates still

ran into the hundreds. Of years. So, hundreds of years. It had been at *least* hundreds of years since she'd last regularly attended Harvard, swiped right or left on Tinder (more often the former than the latter), or maxed out her credit cards because not-so-deep down she knew shit was going to go sideways with Eddie, so why not live it up now and use the High Tomb to declare mystical bankruptcy?

"Picking up from yesterday," was how her Pathology of Cancer professor introduced the first lecture Jenmarie had sat for in centuries.

"Ah, fuck," Jenmarie mumbled to herself. She considered asking the guy next to her to email her a copy of his notes, being unable to find hers, but opted against it. She'd get the groove quickly enough, she determined.

Before the lecture was out, her new determination was that she needed to hit the Tomb one last time to start the semester over.

But that was the last time! Because after that, she was going to be responsible. Or, at least, she was going to try very hard to relearn responsibility, relearn living with the consequences of one's decisions, relearn how to make choices with an eye towards a future that she would just *pretend* was a one-way street. What she would do when she aged up to death's doorstep (or even just death's front garden) was something she'd yet to consider, something she'd have plenty of time to consider. Though, framed another way, not *all* that much – the furthest reaches of a natural human lifespan or even beyond left her with only a fraction of the length of time she'd spent hopping dimensions. Subjectively, her life was already *well* beyond halfway over. Assuming, that was, she never returned to the High Tomb…for now, all she had to do was live her very best life, as she'd successfully done for the first, gosh, how long had it been "in-universe" since she'd dropped back to find Cherry Chirpworth in the yard, twenty-odd years? Sure. The *odd* was doing quite a lot of work there, but sure. Jenmarie just needed to live as well as she had during those first twenty-odd years of this charmed life, and then…be happy? Smile and laugh a lot? Make friends? Just…live?

Worth a shot. So Jenmarie gave *just…living?* her very best shot, only periodically going back to rectify a few unfortunate decisions – and those backward steps were only offsetting her two or three days a pop. The years-long leaps were behind her, which, to be fair, perhaps didn't mean all that much to someone for whom *behind her* was more accessible to amendment than *before her* was. Example: the oral portion of her dissertation went poorly, beset by countless flubs and stutters; back to the High Tomb, back a few days, to redo the presentation with far greater success. It was only upon completing her doctorate that she deigned to question her fixation on the academic; she'd never had a real run at a life without a university track in it. Having graduated fucking Harvard, though, it seemed a waste to go back before that. So she didn't. Example: trying to to memorize what the stock market did for a week and going back to game it with her advanced knowledge (no disbelieving adults between her and fabulous wealth this time), and *still* losing money because she didn't understand the damn markets, nobody did because it was just guys in suits screaming acronyms at each other, it wasn't a real market, it was a dumb fake market, what was that saying, it was just a graph of rich people's feelings yeah that was right, and anyway money wasn't everything you know whatever who wanted money. Example: accidentally snapping at a well-meaning but horribly doltish friend of a friend, after said friend twice removed made a crack about people from the South that wasn't even that bad, more of a broad stereotype (something she herself might have said, once upon a time), but Jenmarie had come back at him much harder than she'd needed to, and the embarrassment of that sent her back to New York, back to the High Tomb, back Down, and back to the party to keep her big mouth shut.

(The friend of a friend's name had been Freddie, which, she reflected, was close enough to get her hackles up. She fucking hated that her hackles were still snapping to attention at anything resembling Eddie's name, even after she'd decided to let him go. So she focused on that hatred, and waited for it to pass. And waited. And waited. And wondered why it wasn't passing, why she couldn't just let it *go*…)

Ok, so maybe she had a problem committing to her present reality. She was a big enough woman to admit that. What she considered a Tomb-able offense amongst the countless inconveniences of everyday life was becoming a larger and larger category. The backward steps were small enough that she was still technically inching forwards in time, rather than sweeping forwards and back around in multi-year roundabouts, but six subjective years after begging off her monomaniacal quest to bring Eddie to heel, she had moved forward only one and a half diegetic years. The majority of the difference had been sacrificed to bussing from Beantown to the Big Apple, a trip that took up the better part of an entire day. So often did she run that route that she came to know precisely which driver would be working which bus, going so far as to delay a trip if she knew that the chatty driver who yelled into the intercom was going to be on the 4:00, but the 5:00 would be the mumbly guy who knew that nobody actually rode Greyhound out of brand loyalty. She reached a point of being able to sit through the entire ride with her eyes closed and knowing precisely where on the journey they were, based on a few key potholes en route that bucked or jerked the bus in unique ways. She even came to have a distressingly accurate grasp of minute-by-minute traffic patterns between the two cities. It was this last acquisition that forced her, High Priestess of the Honk-honk, to admit to herself that, once again, once the fuck again, she had a problem. Loath though she still was to cop to any kind of addictive personality, it was an ever-mounting body of evidence into whose face she was forced to hurl her denials. Did it even count as an addiction, as an impulse, to avail oneself of something so self-evidently beneficial, something that exacted no toll, imposed no burdens? She had a means of rectifying every single mistake she made in the course of living her best possible life (and she made so very, very many), of going back and putting right every wrong that befell her! And what did it cost her? Nothing! Absolutely nothing! So how could it be anything less than the most common of all sense to make as many treks to the High Tomb as necessary to keep her life charmed? It couldn't be, which was to say, it *had* to be, common sense. Which could hardly be a vice, could it? "Addicted to common sense," that didn't make *any* sense. So no, she would not allow herself to be shamed, by *herself,* for utilizing the tools and Tombs the world had put at her disposal. She *would* acknowledge, in a non-judgmental way, that she had perhaps settled into a less-than-committed relationship with consequence and misfortune, that she had become so attached to the idea of a perfect life that anything less, which was to say a *real* life, was unsatisfactory and in need of correction. She would grant that, ok, maybe part of the reason for her perpetually returning to the recent past was to put ever more distance between herself and the only real decision, the only unappealable sentence she would need to hand down to herself, sooner or (much, much) later. What *would* she do at the end? Would she allow herself to *reach* the end? She would live as long as she could, and she would see what the fuck was up with that dreamlight high, high up the tower, at the very top. But what if it wasn't anything especially interesting? What if it was a trick of the not-so-light, or a MADE IN USA sticker? That would leave her with two choices: go back down the Tomb and take up her life again, at whatever point she chose…or return to the nearer past, live out her remaining years, and then die.

Ok, ok, yes, she would further grant with midnight candor, *this* was the Tomb's tax, the cost of doing business: it had seduced her into immortality by appealing to her, yes, ok, *maybe-slightly-sometimes-addictive* personality, and so forced her into a cycle of endless existence, the only escape from which would be *choosing* to die. Suicide, in other words, by way of actively selecting passivity. The Tomb, after all, had become her default. It increasingly felt like it required an exertion of willpower *not* to buy a one-way ticket to Manhattan. Inertia spun her in wide circles, through time and along the eastern seaboard, and it would only be through sustained effort that she broke free of that. Choosing freedom from the cycle would mean choosing not to return to the High Tomb, which would mean choosing to die by choosing *not* to live, by choosing *not* to go to the corner of Fourth and 57th. Choosing death.

Not the sort of thought that facilitates a charmed life, that. Yet a charmed life was one that needed to be lived in full, and living it thusly meant dying, in time. This was a riddle Jenmarie did her level best to avoid thinking about – so imagine her surprise when she brought it up on one of her semi-regular visits to her parents back to Chuckey.

"I can't think of a nice way to ask this," she began, pausing to adjust herself in her seat and clear her throat, "but um, do you guys think about dying differently now that you're, um, closer to it?"

Unfortunately, her extant siblings were also visiting at that time, which made for a vocal peanut gallery; Harmon scoffed, and Melody laughed.

From across the porch on which all five sat, Carrie shrugged and looked thoughtfully to Barry. "Oh, I'm sure we do," she replied matter-of-factly. "Don't we, Barry?"

Barry shrugged. "No point thinkin' about it. Not like I gotta make an appointment with it."

Jenmarie sighed very loudly indeed.

"For all we know," Harmon interjected with a contrarian's giggle, "one of us could be closer to dead than they are."

Carrie jerked in her seat. "Don't say that, Harmon."

"Why not?" He leaned back in his creaking wicker throne and gestured lazily towards Jenmarie. "She brought it up."

"She brought up *us* passing," Carrie explained patiently. "The parents are meant to pass on before the children. That's the natural order."

"Well, maybe *I* don't want to think about *that.*"

"Too bad," Barry chuckled. "It's the natural order, just like your mother said."

There ensued a bit of grim ribbing, but Jenmarie kept her eyes bouncing between her parents, waiting patiently for the back-and-forth to settle. "I'm serious," she reiterated.

"Ayuh," Barry allowed, sniffing at the floorboards. "I'll say this much, I'm not so close to dyin' I think on it as how's it gonna land on me. Knock wood," he added, thumping the banister of the porch as he did. "I'm mostly thinkin', you know. Stuff. Puttin' my affairs someplace close to bein' in order."

"We don't want you kids to have to worry about all those

affairs," Carrie said.

Barry nodded. "And I don't want your mother to have to worry on it either."

"Your father is planning on dying first," Carrie explained with a wry twist of the lips.

Barry's sigh implied a great many conversations on this topic, each followed into blind alleys. "Talkin' about the natural order, *that's* the natural order. Husband goes first."

"Well...we won't get into it now."

"Natural order."

"Barry."

"You really want to leave Mom alone?" Melody marveled.

Barry cocked his head at that. "*Want* doesn't enter into it. It's the natural order." He ticked fingers off on his hand. "Man, woman, kids in the order they was born. That's how a family's meant to go."

Harmon laughed, the nervous edge in his giggling unmissable.

Jenmarie just shook her head. "I'm not asking about your estate, or the, the natural order. I'm asking...the...I'm asking about the end of you as a person. As a conscious person. You're alive, and you've got a consciousness and you want things and there's all this unspeakable pain from living and then it's over, you're not alive anymore. It's h-"

"Unspeakable pain," Carrie repeated with deep concern. "What do you mean by that?"

"I'm not..." Jenmarie sighed. "I'm just saying, it's hard to be alive. And the longer...I *imagine,* the longer you're alive, you're getting more and more of what makes it hard."

"You're getting more of what makes it good, too."

Jenmarie was primed and ready to contradict her mother, but opted not to. All at once, she realized both the answer she sought from her parents, and the absurdity of the seeking. What she wanted to hear was that there was some measure of peace to be found in drawing near an unappealable end. That, yes, one might be sad to know that the ride was over, but all the same the ride was quite an unpleasant one overall, and so it would be nice to be done with it.

She wanted simple consolation, then, a few words of encouragement to help her steer clear of the Tomb for just a few more decades, until she met oblivion on its own terms. Absurd for a host of reasons, chief among them being that she'd sought this wisdom from her elders, imagining that their age must confer some wisdom, failing to appreciate that they were no longer her elders. *She* was the elder, to her siblings and her parents and everyone else on the planet to boot. She'd been around the block more times than anybody. And a long life – *many* long lives – had conferred nothing. No wisdom, unless she'd been granted so much wisdom that she'd punched through enlightenment and into the unwitting humility of one who knows just how much they don't know. Simpler to say no wisdom at all, in that case. Simpler to say she had been conferred nothing except, apparently, according to her own tongue, unspeakable pain.

Was that her world, then? Why else would she have said that? Had hers become a world of *unspeakable pain?* She wouldn't have said so, except, well, she kind of had. But…she'd spoken it, so how could it be unspeakable? That was kind of the whole thing with unspeakability. Look: she felt happy, for the most part, as a baseline. She'd built herself a good life, a better family (in as much as that was possible without Tomjohn…and betrayal though it was, Jenmarie had to acknowledge that it *was* possible), a nice group of friends. She, uh, there was probably another thing with which she was pleased. And even if there weren't, she had the means of rearranging the things in her life until they did please her. So she was happy most times, and had the tools to address her unhappiness in the others. What room was there for unspeakable pain in such a life? Of course hers was not a life of unspeakable pain. Who was even bringing that up, unspeakable pain? Granted, of course, just to play devil's advocate, ok, if she were truly, ecstatically happy, if there weren't at least *some* pain swirling around the margins, she probably wouldn't even be considering her own death, wouldn't be thinking of it as "freedom" from the "cycle." Context clues, then, that was how one might perhaps receive the impression that there was some unaddressed pain of a not-so-speakable sort. Ok, and yes, come to think of it, there were crying jags every once in a while, but Jenmarie didn't really count those because whenever she had one, she would go back to the Tomb, to back before the jag had happened. *Et voilà,* no crying jags! So, alright, fine, that was kind of a cheat. There was pain, *obviously,* because she was alive and a living person, and all living people who were alive had some pain sometimes, because life was pain and everything was shit, unless and until you could go back in time and make things not be shit anymore, but life was still life which was pain and so yes then fine alright, sure, but she was speaking about it, the pain, so it wasn't unspeakable. See? She was talking about it. Well, thinking about it. And thinking was the talking of the brain, or something. Why did it even matter if it was speakable or not, anyway? What was so special about speaking it? Just saying, or thinking, or whatever, 'hey, there's some pain here,' and then leaving it at that, what was wrong with that? Huh? Anybody? What was the big fucking problem with that, then, well? Did that make the pain, what, less good? Or better? Or worse? Hard to know which was better (or worse) when one was talking about pain. But, see, *talking* about it. Speakable, that was the pain. Unless you wanted to take a super narrow and frankly restrictive and closed-minded and pretty lame and stupid definition of the word 'speak', then yeah, she supposed, she wasn't actually *speaking* her pain, but not because it was *un*speakable. Not because the pain *itself* was unspeakable, no, she didn't speak it because the pain would freak other people out because what did they know about High Tombs that you get in by hitting them with a crowbar and they send you back in time in your own body, what did they know about it, how could they begin to understand that pain as anything other than the ravings of a madlady who needed to be locked up in a looniest bin they could find? So, yeah, there was pain, and it was unspeakable, but only, you know, not because of the pain itself. But ok, fine, it was unspeakable, and it was pain, and Jenmarie was in it, so therefore consequently as a result, Jenmarie was in unspeakable pain. QED. Q the fucking E fuck D. Oh. Ha. It was fine though. She was fine. Oh. Ha. Oh. Oh. Oh Christ. Jesus fuck.

Ha. Oh.

So whence the pain, then? How could it have followed her through this charmed life she'd sculpted for herself out of the moving marble of the Tomb? She'd worked her ass off, suffered through all manner of adolescent tedium to attain what she now had. And the fact of the matter was, she could be just about goddamned certain, that were she to topple everything she'd built with one ill-considered trip through the Tomb, she would venture back to her most distant childhood memory – the one that hadn't been a real memory until she'd *made* it one – to discover that there *was* no cause of her pain. That it was something innate to her. That she *was* her pain.

This was a hypothesis, then. One she could only test in the instant of its confirmation. In the moment of death. For if she was her pain, the only way to be free from pain…was to be free from herself.

Gimme a Q! Gimme an E! Gimme a D!

There were other ways to sneak a sip of selflessness here or there, though, prior to the Great and Terminal Glug. She knew of these – had never forgotten them. Had learned to practice them even without…golly what was that guy called? Two letters…not T.J.…definitely wasn't a B there…oh, K.J.! He'd taught her, and Jenmarie had carried the lessons with her.

Breathe. Focus. Stop fighting. Don't become the thoughts, or the feelings. Be the space. Be awareness.

All well and good to say, that. Much harder to do. But Jenmarie did feel she could touch that tranquility, if not fully grasp it. This was a skill that had refined itself over time, not like a muscle built through the repetitive application of willpower, but as a diamond formed from coal under pressure. Which wasn't actually how diamonds were formed, she knew. But she didn't know how diamonds were formed, actually. She only knew how they *weren't* formed. That was probably the sort of thing one could point to and say "just goes to show," but Jenmarie didn't know what it would just go to show either. She didn't know anything, it seemed. She'd lived too long for knowledge.

Except, of course, for the one thing she had learned, the only thing she knew for certain anymore: she was too tired to go running after every thought, every feeling. Especially that unspeakable pain. She was too tired to let the hurt run her. Or to run from the hurt. She was far too tired, and so it was exhaustion that ultimately took her hand and introduced her to something resembling equanimity.

This was a gentle revelation she might have missed, were it not for perhaps the greatest, stupidest, most magnificent of happenstance's interventions into Jenmarie's life.

Here was how Jenmarie found herself in the dreaded Times Square: it was Barry's sixty-ninth birthday (nice), and he wanted to go visit New York City to celebrate. He'd never been, after all, and he felt the Big Apple was one of those places every American ought to visit before they die.

He called Jenmarie to inform her of this, along with the fact that her presence would be expected. Harmon and Melody had already booked their flight, so to speak. Melody was probably going to take the bus but *at any rate* they were committed, and so Jenmarie would be a very poor daughter indeed were she to refuse the invitation. Jenmarie, having been a very poor daughter in more than a few of her lives, felt the urge to talk Barry down... and let it pass. Ditto for the fear of once more setting foot in the Tomb's territory on terms other than her own. Oh, it was not lost on her that this was going to be the first time, in *centuries* perhaps, that she had gone to Manhattan without the intention of going in, Down, and back. That fact carried with it a veritable conga line of contradictory emotions, pride and fear and humiliation and hope, all swirling around the thought that perhaps there was a difference between being able to resist something and simply desiring it less. Yet each tremor of the spirit bopped its way through Jenmarie's mind before dissolving the way that all things did, in time. These things arising and passing away, Jenmarie smiled into her phone and accepted the invitation. Which was how she wound up in Manhattan late one summer – and being there with someone who had never been, it was inevitable that she would find herself surrounded by her family, frowning in the dead center of Times Square, glomming on to quite a few unpleasant emotions as starscream-bright advertisements competed to see which could make her feel worse about her body, her bank account, her husband. Her ex-husband.

Jenmarie blinked, shook her head slightly, and blinked again. She lingered on a street corner as the signal changed and her family crossed.

Through the scrum of tourists and ticket-hawkers and costumed creepazoids, Jenmarie saw him. Alone. Just walking. Looking perfectly pleased about both of those things. She couldn't imagine what he was doing here – except, of course, that he had always loved Times Square. She'd never known why. Had never begun to understand how Eddie Mark, that Eddie Mark halfway across Times Square there who knew absolutely nothing about Jenmarie, who didn't even know she existed, yet about whom she knew so very very much, except the aforementioned fact... she had never begun to understand, and well, that was it, and there he was. And here she was.

Jenmarie turned in the direction her family had walked. She didn't see them anywhere. They'd gone on without her. Fine. She would catch up.

She turned back towards Eddie. He was still there. Hadn't gone anywhere. Was, in point of fact, walking towards her now. Not *to* her. Just in her direction. The sidewalk only went in two directions, after all. It was supremely improbable that she should find herself here at the same time as him, here on this same stretch of sidewalk. But once they were here, once they were both on this sidewalk, it wasn't all that odd that one should move towards the other. Not odd in the least.

As he approached, Jenmarie greeted a line of thinking she couldn't believe hadn't put in an appearance before this moment: why had she, oh, ok, speak the word, *obsessed* over Eddie? Why had she allowed a failed relationship to define her, to haunt literal centuries of her existence? It was a question she'd been puzzling over, a pain she had long been fashioning into something appr-oaching speakability, and the best she could come up with was this: she had fixated upon Eddie because he had hurt her, in ways he had never even seemed to realize, to an extent she had no reason to believe he'd ever fully appreciated. Every time, in every timeline, Eddie would do something to hurt her, and she would let him, accept it, silently. Quietly. Hush. Shh. Listen. She would break, sometimes because he broke her, most times because she *let* him. Each time, though, he would never know. He wasn't the listening type. He wasn't one to hush. But that was all she wanted from him now. She wanted him to understand what he had done to her. Impossible, now that he hadn't done it. She'd undone it for him.

Except…that wasn't true, was it? Because Eddie was not her never-ex. He had meant something to her, been something. Even if it had been once upon a time, in a life long ago, the endless ex-panse between then and now was near to choking on all its varia-tions on a single theme. They were not new things, these lives, these variations. They were one thing. They were all one thing. One long life, in one million and one acts.

Which gave her hope that Eddie could know. Whether or not he would…he *could*. He could recognize himself, if only he listen-ed. Listened as she proved to him that she knew who he was, listened as she told him that his name was Eddie Gary Mark, that he had a scar on his left shoulder that he told people was from a fight he got in when he was little but was actually from a rash he'd scratched at too hard, that he secretly thought he looked good in bow ties but couldn't work up the courage to wear one because he thought there was no way to not look pretentious in one and he was terrified of looking pretentious because not-so-deep-down he worried that he was, that he always ordered his whiskey straight so he could swirl it in the cup and 'check the legs' because he'd learned about that on a whiskey tour in Scotland, but he couldn't remember what it meant for a whiskey to have long legs or short legs so he would just say what kind of legs it has, that he picked his nose when he thought nobody was looking but he was a really bad judge of when people were looking, that he liked to be tied up and slapped but *not* spoken to harshly, he was very sensitive about being called names or talked down to, that he thought Steven Spielberg was 'the most overrated hack in film history' but he'd only seen seven of his movies and he'd loved every single one, that he had a recurring nightmare about buying bus tickets to cities he'd never been to, usually in the southwest like Reno or Phoenix, and trying to text a friend in those cities about when to pick him up from the station, but he could never remember their number, that he thought it was unfair that he couldn't dress like "the people in *Black Panther*" without it being problematic, not because he wanted to but because he wanted to have *the option* to, that he always thought people who bragged about being able to drive manual transmission were assholes because he could only drive automatic but around what would have been four years ago in the very first timeline at least he'd learned how to drive manual and *couldn't fucking shut up about it*, that he'd started telling people he was allergic to beestings because he was always embarrassed by how afraid of bees he was and needed an excuse to shout at the kids who were making fun of him for it but then he started telling his doctors he was allergic to beestings and thus it became one of his listed allergies even though he wasn't actually allergic to beestings, not really, he was just afraid.

No, he might not know her, but he would recognize himself in her words, and so he might finally, for once, hear her as she told him…what? Oh, what did it matter, she could tell him any-thing. The Tomb was so close, after all, so close, that she could say whatever it was she wanted, *needed* to say. And if it wasn't right, she could come back and try again. So, then, what did she *need* to say? That the two of them had been romantically involved in countless alternate dimensions that she herself had created, just like she had created this one? Yes, she could tell him they'd even been married dozens, maybe hundreds of times. And every single time, he had been…fine. He'd been unbelievably sweet, right up until she'd really needed him. And she had needed him. Then and now, she got depressed and anxious and angry, for no reason. She tried not to, and she was getting better at recognizing these horrible little lurches into unpleasantness as they happen-ed. But they were just a part of her. The lurches. And you, Eddie, the Eddie of her imagination, the Eddie with a vacant smile on his face now stepping near enough for Jenmarie to have been confident of hitting him with a well-thrown baseball…you couldn't handle it, Eddie. Not once. But you get arrogant when you're feeling insecure, which is often. You put other people down and you cut people off and close up and don't have time for anybody who won't tell you you're right. Because, listen to me, that's just a part of *you*. But I hung in. Because I loved you, all the way, even those shitty parts of you. Which, trust me, there are a *lot* of. Maybe not as many as there are good parts, but, fuck man. Seriously. You never, ever, in any dimension, in any time-line, did the same for me. You weren't all the way, goddamnit. You *never* were. You just wanted all of the good times, and none of the…

Jenmarie noticed her anger. A red-hot tangle of rebar in the throat, a shimmering hollow in the chest. She noticed it as one might notice birdsong in the distance. As nothing more than a thing to be noticed. It didn't make the anger any more pleasant to experience…but she wasn't quite *experiencing* it anymore. She was studying it.

Until it melted away.

She watched as Eddie Gary Mark strolled past her, eyes angled gently upwards, offering not the slightest sideways glance in her direction. He melted into her peripheral vision, and then out of it entirely.

Jenmarie remained as and where she was for several seconds. Just staring straight ahead. Staring down the same stretch of sidewalk she'd been staring down for nearly thirty seconds now. She watched as people came and went, passing through the spaces Eddie had filled just moments ago. As though he'd never been there at all.

He had been, of course. It was ridiculous to pretend that he hadn't. Just as ridiculous to pretend he *was* there in some capacity, when he, well, wasn't. He'd come and he'd gone. The way all things do. In time.

Simple as that.

Jenmarie gave herself the option to cry. Just have a grand old sob here in Times Square. She wouldn't have been the first, she knew, nor the last. Yet no tears came. Instead, she felt a strange little smile bloom on her face. Just a bunch of teeth, she knew. Like all smiles. Just teeth.

She turned and followed her family across the street, just before the signal changed back. They hadn't noticed her falling behind, which saved her having to explain why she had. Which she might well have tried to, had they asked. She found that…interesting. Until the thought and her interest in it both melted away.

U
P

She managed a solid week
of imagining she'd fully sorted her life out by finally, at long last, allowing Eddie to walk out of it. A week during which self-loathing nibbled rather than consumed, a week during which she found herself quicker with a joke (and more confident in her delivery), a week during which her joints creaked and cracked a bit less than usual. A good week, in short. A very good week. And short. For it took only that short and good week for Jenmarie to find herself out at some *Cheers* knockoff bar for trivia with a few friends, confronted with the question "what is the name of the bar and grill mentioned in Thin Lizzy's 'The Boys Are Back In Town'?" The field was quickly narrowed to Gino's, Tino's, or Dino's. It was definitely a letter, and then *-ino's*. Most folks at the

table were leaning towards Dino's, which was the correct fucking answer, but Jenmarie thought it was Gino's. Not only did she think it was Gino's, she *insisted* it was, with the aforementioned confidence until now reserved for the jokes. So they hastily erased Dino's, which, to review, was the *correct* answer, and changed it to Gino's, which was *not* the correct answer. Because Jenmarie had sounded so confident about it.

She had another fifteen-odd minutes after that to enjoy the feeling of having a fully sorted-out life, at which point the round was over and the answers were read. In the course of which, the emcee said "Dino's."

Everybody at the table groaned and elbowed Jenmarie playfully, and returned their attention to the host to hear the remainder of the answers. Everybody except for Jenmarie herself, who accepted her friend's gibes and japes with good humor, before being slurped into a wormhole of self-doubt, self-recrimination, even a bit of self-loathing, self self self, at the bottom of which was the very same lever she'd pulled more times than could ever possibly be numbered.

For the first time in that good and short week, Jenmarie thought: this didn't need to have happened. She couldn't undo it in quite the way she'd fooled herself into believing was possible, she understood that now. It would always have happened to her. But that didn't mean it had to have happened. If that made sense. Which it didn't, of course.

While *her team getting the name of the bar and grill from Thin Lizzy's 'The Boys Are Back In Town' wrong at trivia because they'd had the right answer until she'd insisted they'd had the wrong answer so they should use* her *right answer which was the wrong answer* wouldn't have been the most frivolous pretense Jenmarie had found for using (i.e. abusing) the Tomb – not by a *long* shot – it did strike her as suddenly insufficient. Yes, this was quietly embarrassing. She felt like a fucking idiot, to be a bit more precise. But, well, hey. You know. That's life. Sometimes you feel like a fucking idiot. Then the feeling passes. Hey.

Despite the best efforts of The Boys and their choice of bar and grill, Jenmarie managed to resist the call of the Tomb on that particular night. Yet to hear the call was to answer it, in time. Jenmarie knew this from bitter experience. She may have let Eddie go, but the Tomb had yet to get over her in quite the same way.

It made such a compelling case for getting back together. Trying one more time. They'd tried giving each other space so how about time, more time, all the time in the world. One more. Time.

These were seductions Jenmarie knew enough to resist. Oh, but that was the wrong way to look at it. Calling them *seductions* gave the Tomb too much power. Too much agency. No, these were *cravings*. And Jenmarie knew all about those. Didn't have the strongest track record with them, if it came to that. Which it did. Because she couldn't muster up any confidence that things would work out differently now. It wasn't enough to scowl at herself in the mirror and say "alright asshole, no more trips to the High Tomb!" Because all it took was one mortifying social faux pas that could have been avoided, one night of dancing so incredible she wanted nothing more than to repeat it, one karaoke performance she could absolutely nail now that she'd biffed it, and the temptations of the Tomb became downright gravitational. Hers was not the sort of iron will that could resist such coquetry, and there were more than a few instances in which she succumbed to its promise of a better Next Time. How could she not? That wasn't just a hypothetical; it was a genuine question, and it wouldn't be until she discovered the answer that she would be free to move on with her life. If only that weren't the case! If only she were stronger, if only she had greater self-control, if only she were better able to make peace with the present, the here in which hippies insisted everybody be, *now!*

Could she seal up the Tomb somehow? She didn't see how – even if the building itself had a remarkable camouflage, one Jenmarie herself could wear by merely focusing upon it, she didn't have a great deal of faith in her ability to sustain that kind of focus for, say, the length of time it would take to brick up the door, Cask of Amontillado style. Short of that, though, how to keep herself from it? Well, time was her inexhaustible resource – she could, what, use all of that time to pioneer some new technique to selectively erase memories, wipe the High Tomb from her mind? Of course not. Get real. No, there was no way she could see by which using the Tomb could become the means of *not* using the Tomb; she quite obviously carried the knowledge of the Tomb with her into whatever new timeline she entered. Could she, then, perhaps, dream up a timeline in which the Tomb simply didn't exist? She'd dreamt Cherry Chirpworth into being. Why couldn't she fantasize the Tomb out of it?

Because, came the obvious answer, she hadn't dreamt up Cherry and made her so. She had *genuinely misremembered* the moment, and it was that mistaken recollection into which the Tomb had delivered her. Unless she could somehow convince herself that, despite her having used it more times than she could count, the High Tomb actually didn't exist, and then *use the High Tomb* to cobble together a new reality from that mistaken memory… no, not possible. No battery of wacky mind-altering substances could pull off that cognitive coup, a sad fact she knew because goddamnit she *tried*. She also tried seeing a hypnotist, but the poor guy couldn't quite wrap his head around what Jenmarie was asking him to do, and so first tried to convince her that no buildings in the world were over ten stories tall, then that marble was actually just a stubborn liquid, then, most perplexingly, that salt and sugar had gotten confused and were now each other. Jenmarie paid him for a full session but used only three quarters of one, and then used the High Tomb to go back to just before she'd entered the dope's office and parted with her hard-earned cash.

How in the ever-loving fuck was she supposed to get her head right as pertained to the Way Things Were, find the fortitude to suffer through life's little indignities, *despite not needing to?* That was dumb, right? But taking a year of subjective time to get through what the calendar called a month, just because she insisted on every little detail of her life being *perfect,* was no way to live – or, perhaps, it was *too many* ways to live. Such was her dilemma, then: she had a High Tomb that she used, but didn't *want* to use, but couldn't imagine having and *not* using, but didn't know how to get rid of.

It was a dilemma that would prove perfectly intractable. There were vanishingly few angles from which she could attack it, approaches that were exhausted within about a week of subjective time, and the High Tomb yielded not a whit to a one of them. It took only a few more days of fruitless brainstorming for Jenmarie herself to become similarly exhausted, so existentially wiped she could hardly summon the courage to face the sole remaining path that yawned open before her, a path that squiggled and squirreled its way through the omniverse, a path of such dreadful expanse that it was only that final, marginally greater fear that kept Jenmarie from drinking a jug of bleach and leaping off the nearest bridge high enough to get a good *splat* out of her. This was to be her life, then, a draft forever in revision, days passing over the course of weeks, weeks taking months, months taking years, years decades, decades centuries, centuries millennia, millennia…billennia? Was that a word? Fuck it, why not. Billennia trillennia quadrillennia etceterennia. This was Jenmarie Bell's life now, and would be until the world couldn't fit any more universes, until time did one too many lines and OD'd. Unless, of course, she should have an epiphany, discover some crafty, clever way to break free of the eternal recursion to which she was forever condemning herself, an ingenious way to escape the wet spaghetti path and live life along a drier noodle. Some trick to seal up the High Tomb, a stratagem to take back her present.

Boy, that'd have been pretty fucking swell, wouldn't it?

Instead of that, though, instead of a crafty clever ingenious epiphanous strategous trickerous treat to dry out the old temporal pasta, Jenmarie lived a High Tomb lifestyle, trying and failing to accustom herself to misfortune, becoming less and less able to sustain any kind of shame at her near-constant trips to Fourth and 57th. She was quite proud of herself for not allowing this particular, yes, addiction to derail her entire life as she might have in the, ha, past, which was only ever a bus ticket away. That was kind of the point, though: it was, and remained, a bus ticket away. Jenmarie *didn't* move to New York to be closer to the High Tomb, having the self-awareness to recognize that if she couldn't keep herself from entering its jellyfish foyer and slipping down its unlit depths, she could at least curb the frequency with which she did so by making it as mildly inconvenient as she could. She also refused to purchase a crowbar to have just hanging around the house – forcing a trip to the hardware store each time she intended to use the Tomb was just the sort of tiny imposition capable of convincing her that her latest mistake wasn't worth the hassle. She also set herself a few ground rules, chief among them being that she would no longer use the High Tomb to fundamentally manipulate or orchestrate her personal relationships. That was a simple enough rule to adhere to, as her relationships were all doing pretty darn well at present (whatever *that* meant). The llamas turned out to have more than a little of the Dalai in them, bringing a truly astonishing spiritual serenity to Jenmarie's parents, and giving them a productive hobby to boot. They were happy together. It was only seeing them happy together now that Jenmarie fully appreciated how unhappy they had been in that impossibly distant timeline, the "first" one, the one that was by now just a largely-forgotten dream. Harmon and Melody were each doing quite well too, all things considered. Still struggling with substances, but this time neither silently nor alone. Their parents provided a top-down stability from which demons could be hung like pork sides and scrutinized. Things weren't perfect, but nothing could *ever* be perfect. That wasn't how things worked. Jenmarie knew this better than perhaps anyone in the history of the human race. Case in point: Tomjohn still didn't exist and never would. Mavis, however, *did* exist, and met a guy named Stu out in San Francisco, eventually marrying him and starting a family just as she had in the original timeline. This, perhaps, raised some interesting questions about the teleology of divergent timelines. Or maybe it didn't. Jenmarie didn't really care anymore. The Tomb had long since lost its dreadful sense of mystery; it was just a big microwave to her now. How did a microwave work? She didn't know! But it did, and that was fine. So it had become for the High Tomb. Not for her, the scratching of the head, the stroking of the chin. She couldn't be free of the damn thing, no. But she could live with it, without letting it own her. She could learn to live with it until she died. Live the best life she possibly could. Until she died.

The life, then. What to say of the life? After all of the dramatics, all of the fireworks, all of the excitement and adventure of her discovering the High Tomb, the life was quiet, as all lives truly are. The small moments are those that make the most noise – the life-altering events, the ones upon which fortunes shift, are silent. Hush, then, and listen. Shh. Shut up.

Over eons, between dimensions, through timelines beyond number, in body after body, Jenmarie lived a single life. It was a life of small wonders and brief disappointments, a life that was like any other, albeit with a more open relationship to its own chronology. Only that wasn't right – it just had a different kind of chronology to it. Jenmarie's experience remained unbroken throughout, and what was that if not a life? The Jenmarie who went into full-time oncology and tended to her patients was the Jenmarie who would have a glass of wine with dinner every now and then but not much more was the Jenmarie who had formed an improbably deep connection with the grey-and-brown speck-led llama named Dotty that her parents seemed dead-set on sell-ing but whom Jenmarie would succeed in persuading them to keep despite the evident quality of her fiber which would have fetched a high price indeed was the Jenmarie who liked going thrifting by herself because if she went with a friend she had a tendency to not buy the things she truly liked because they were often rather silly vintage toss she was more than happy to wear but for some reason the *buying* of it in company was somehow humiliating was the Jenmarie who got a cat and regretted it because it wasn't a friendly cuddly cat but a big fat ginger lump that only appeared when it wanted food or to stink up the litter-box or to slice Jenmarie's ankles was the Jenmarie who was mor-tified to discover that no matter how many times she went back to the Tomb and no matter how far back Down she went her sister would always have a stroke at the age of thirty-seven that would paralyze the left side of her face was the Jenmarie who saved up her pennies and took up the offer Mavis had probably made facetiously for her to come live in San Francisco which seemed like a better and better idea the more Jenmarie thought about it because it would take her even further from the High Tomb and anyway if it didn't work out she could always just go back to before the move so what did she have to lose was the Jenmarie who couldn't afford San Francisco and so Tombed back to before the move was the Jenmarie who realized that this was the beauty of the Tomb or at least some of it was the Jenmarie who thought she might take up gardening because she liked how freshly turned soil smelled so she built herself a little windowsill garden out of two by fours and cardboard which she was pretty proud of having built but then none of the damn seeds sprouted no matter how much water she poured on them or classical music she played for them so she threw out the seeds and soil but kept the garden itself because it was pretty cool and would probably be useful for something at some point though she would never figure out what was the Jenmarie who went hiking north of the city just after it had rained which was definitely not her brightest idea and she'd slipped on a muddy patch and fallen from the path down a hill and she only sprained her ankle but as she was falling she wondered if this might not be how she finally died if the some*thing* that had shepherded her this far had finally forsaken her and how that would have sucked but at the same time it'd have been something like a relief and certainly vindicated her position on hiking's being terribly overrated but then the ankle was the day's only casualty and that was alright too was the Jenmarie who somehow aged into a tree nut allergy which was a nightmare because she loved almonds even though they were bad for the environment and for a time that made the

293

Tomb a more challenging lure to resist because all she would have to do was go back to before the allergy developed and she could eat all the almonds she wanted but she somehow managed to resist was the Jenmarie who cried for two days straight when her mother suffered a fatal aneurysm in her sleep which was weird to Jenmarie because her mother had died in other timelines and anyway Jenmarie hadn't quite realized how close she'd become to her mother but and so therefore she wept and wailed because she knew this time it had to be for keeps there was no way she could go back and stop her mom's brain from exploding but she could go back and call her mom up and ask her about her day and tell her how *her* day was going and tell her she loved her and do all the stuff moms always wished daughters would do and so she did was the Jenmarie who was pissed as all getout when self-driving cars took over because she'd always really liked driving it was soothing well not the stop-and-go freeway gridlock or really driving anywhere in the city or any city but when the roads opened up it could be so nice but that was gone but on the other hand so was the gridlock because the self-driving cars were a lot more coordinated than people were was the Jenmarie who thought she was just the smartest little cookie when she bought a Rosetta Stone for Mandarin Chinese thinking she would become fluent in a single "day" by studying some and repeating the day and studying further and repeating and studying and repeating and so on but turned out you couldn't just skip to a later module in the program you had to pass the previous modules so by repeating the day she was erasing her progress and preventing herself from moving on so she'd have to learn the language some other way but books seemed harder than a program so she just went back to before she'd dropped hundreds of fucking dollars on the stupid program was the Jenmarie whose doctor told her that her cholesterol was getting high so she might want to phase out stuff like saturated fats and work in some foods that might work to lower cholesterol like oily fish or soy or nuts and Jenmarie asked the doctor why would you say nuts to me you're the one who told me I was allergic to nuts and then the doctor said ah nuts and Jenmarie didn't laugh and the doctor looked like she wished *she* had a High Tomb was the Jenmarie who somehow got pregnant by a guy she'd been dating for just about a month and a half even though he'd used a condom and she was on birth control but the first stick said she was with child as did the second so she zapped back to the night in question and begged off because frankly the sex hadn't been that good anyway but for weeks afterward she was terrified that the blessed event would follow her through the Tomb like the scar on her chin and was quite certain she was on the brink of giving herself an hysterical pregnancy when she simply decided that no she wasn't pregnant and she turned out to be correct there were no babies in this belly no sir no ma'am was the Jenmarie who went a whole week without even *thinking* about the High Tomb once was the Jenmarie who looked in the mirror one day and suddenly accepted that the bags under her eyes were not due to a poor night's sleep or the light catching her at an unflattering angle no she was just getting old and those wrinkles were just her face now and she would have to be ok with that and you know what she was was the Jenmarie who just prior to being clobbered by menopause developed an inexplicable and frankly indefensible affinity for honeydew which she had always made a point of plucking from her fruit salads but now she was eating the strawberries and pineapples first and saving the honeydew for last because they were her favorite all of a sudden what was the deal with that was the Jenmarie who cried for just one day when her father died because he had been so sad since the passing of Carrie which hadn't fit his conception of the natural order so it was sad to see him go but he'd had one foot out the door for years now was the Jenmarie who got a bad haircut like *really* bad and amazingly enough didn't once consider undoing it with the High Tomb as she had other bad haircuts which really was amazing because this was a *bad* haircut like so super boxy and also it was a crap haircut like seriously you should have seen it was the Jenmarie who had gone on dates and more dates well into her fifties and decided that maybe Eddie had turned her off the idea of long-term pair bonding but then she met a fellow named Chris which was pretty boring but he was a good Chris with a soft smile and a nice butt even at fifty-three and at fifty-six he still had it and Chris and his nice butt proposed to Jenmarie and she said yes to both and nobody broke up with anybody over text and the ceremony was in Hawaii but two hurricanes converged on the island when most of the guests were planning on coming in but they couldn't get the venue at a later date so the wedding went ahead and it was pretty small and slapdash but it was also very sweet and Mavis made it which was really all Jenmarie cared about because she'd never make another friend as dear as Mavis was the Jenmarie who couldn't wrap her head around Harmon's suicide and no matter how many times she went back she could only delay it but never prevent it but that wasn't a surprise because she knew how corrosive certain thoughts could be she was only sorry that there was nothing she could do but all the same he'd had more years than he'd had when it had been a drunk driver cutting his life short and they'd been happy those years she hoped overall obviously not happy at the end but for the most part on the whole she hoped he'd been happy until he hadn't been was the Jenmarie who had expected to grow closer to her sister now that it was just the two of them against the world so to speak but try though she might she and Melody could never connect not because they didn't get along they just didn't quite click in some way Jenmarie couldn't define which meant she couldn't address it was the Jenmarie who got mad at Chris for mumbling but it turned out she was losing her hearing which she did slowly but surely until she was nearly deaf which killed her not literally but it might as well have because now she couldn't listen to music or hear Chris' voice and everything really was silence but she couldn't listen it didn't matter if she shushed or not and that nearly sent her back to the High Tomb because how could she live without music but she got a hearing aid and persevered because she was almost there was the Jenmarie who didn't know what the *there* she had almost reached was except that it was a dream of a vine and a tree and if she could only hang on and live as long as possible then she would reach it and then she would know she would know what would she know who knew maybe that was what it was she would know what she would *know* was the Jenmarie who thought she might have lived long enough now and went to New York and entered the High Tomb even though it was getting hard to swing the crowbar around and she definitely got funny looks when she bought it because old ladies don't buy crowbars and wow she was an old lady when had that happened anyway into the Tomb she went and she wasn't quite there the dreamlight was still above her head through the syrup in the future in the next in the not yet so she returned to before she'd bought the plane ticket and kept on living was the Jenmarie who would keep on living until she turned eighty-six was the Jenmarie who wouldn't make it to eighty-seven was the Jenmarie who would never get the chance to make it to the High Tomb again was the Jenmarie who would find out how the cycle was broken was the

Jenmarie who died silently in her sleep next to the man with whom she'd enjoyed nearly three decades of bliss which he would take about as well as a guy can take a thing like waking up next to his dead wife at the end of three decades of bliss but well yeah that sucks for him so good thing he took it about as well as a guy can and anyway for a wonder it really had been just about three decades of bliss for Jenmarie she'd hardly ever used the Tomb at all and when she had it had more often been to relive a happy thing rather than correct a sad thing because the sad things were necessary and the happy things weren't which was why they were so precious and she'd had so many of them and that made her lucky was the Jenmarie who dreamt of a brown tree and a grey vine and a grey tree and a green vine was the Jenmarie who wasn't going to be for much longer was the Jenmarie who smiled softly as she passed in her sleep as mentioned silently because lives shift in silence and death is a part of life so its not like it comes in with a big brass band what were you expecting it's death it's silence so shush so listen.

Shh.

D
O
W
N

The path bends and branches but never breaks. In this, the Jenmarie who smiled as she met her dream had been correct. Hers had been, for whatever else one might wish to say about it, a single life inviolate.

But this was not to say that hers was the only one. Come, descend. Down for the last time. Watch your step.

The Jenmarie who smiled was, once upon a time, the Jenmarie who wanted to relive a happy moment, specifically the first birthday of her grandniece, to which Melody had quite graciously invited both Jenmarie and Chris. It was not the celebration itself Jenmarie wished to relive – that had been a rather perfunctory affair, birthday parties for infants were to Jenmarie about as sensible as throwing a bar mitzvah for a beanbag chair – but the evening after, when she and Chris defied their aching limbs and crawled into the hammock strung up behind their bed and breakfast (a regular one, not an Air one) and just lay there shushed hushed *listening* to each other's heartbeats until they drifted off to sleep, awakening seven hours later to joints so stiff they had to shout, laughing all the while, for someone to come and help them out of the hammock with a push from below. *This* Jenmarie had so adored the simple ecstasy of the moment that the day after she and Chris returned to their home in Boston, she booked a ticket to New York, to pay a visit to the High Tomb. She nearly threw her back out swinging the crowbar, but connected with the not-so-door all the same, and so the Jenmarie who smiled entered the Tomb for the last time. But how could she have known, how could she ever have known, that she left behind a Jenmarie who had just as strong a claim to Jenmarie-hood as the Jenmarie who smiled? That there remained a Jenmarie who, as far as she was concerned, had come back from Boston and gone to New York and bought a crowbar and swung it at the door of the Tomb... and who could but mutely boggle as *nothing happened?* Whatever magic the Tomb had possessed must have evaporated at long last, she mused. Ah, well. She was far enough along in her life, and happy enough, that she felt perfectly able to get by without the Tomb anymore. It was, indeed, a relief to be rid of it. There would be other hammock moments in her life – and indeed, re-living a happy moment already passed could only diminish it. And so this Jenmarie – who was *not* the Jenmarie who smiled – went back to Massachusetts, back to Chris, and on to a life that was ultimately not all that different from that other Jenmarie's, one that would end with her smiling and dreaming and drifting away. Both Jenmaries would be the Jenmaries who smiled, then. But they were not the same Jenmarie. One woman, two lives.

But listen, look: there are other Jenmaries than these. Further down, to a deeper light. The Jenmarie who wanted to relive her evening in the hammock was, once upon a time, the Jenmarie who took Chris to the Coolidge Corner theater in Brookline for a screening of one of her very favorite films, *Airplane!*, playing on a one-of-a-kind restored 35mm print commissioned by one of those doltishly eccentric tech billionaires. Chris had, astonishingly enough, never seen the film before (to which Jenmarie had said "surely you can't be serious," to which Chris had replied "I am" because he *didn't know*), and so Jenmarie dragged him to the theater, all the while feeling that ageless tummyfluttering one gets when introducing a beloved human to a beloved work of art, and wondering, if they don't take to each other, which of the two will be downgraded to just 'beliked.' Fortunately Chris loved the film just as much as she did, laughing so hard he literally fell from his seat. They quoted it all the way home, and halfway back Jenmarie knew she was going to Tomb this experience. Seeing the film with Chris had allowed her to see it, vicariously, for the first time again, an experience so thrilling she would risk diluting its joyful intensity to recapture even a fraction of the same. So this Jenmarie went to the High Tomb and banged on it with a crowbar, at which point nothing seemed to happen, the crowbar just went *bonk* against the fake door. Whatever magic the Tomb had possessed must have evaporated at long last, she mused. Ah, well. She was far enough along in her life, and happy enough, that she felt perfectly able to get by without the Tomb anymore. It was, indeed, a relief to be rid of it. And even as she thought this, a different Jenmarie, the one who would eventually wish the relive the hammock moment, entered the Tomb. And so the Jenmarie who returned home and awkwardly explained her absence to Chris by shrugging and mumbling something about being so inspired by *Airplane!* that she wanted to experience the real thing via a tremendously frivolous Boston-to-Big-Apple ticket, continued to live her own life, becoming the Jenmarie who would field Chris' wariness at her strange departure for a few weeks until he seemed to suddenly make his peace with it, a shift (shh) Jenmarie would only later discover was due to Mavis' intervenion, for dear Mavis, having gotten an earful or three from Jenmarie about Chris' quiet suspicions, had decided the best thing for her own wellbeing as well as her friend's would be to call up Chris and insist that Jenmarie had been scouting out locations for a dramatic anniversary getaway and doing a piss-poor job at being sneaky about it, which committed this Jenmarie to a dramatic anniversary getaway but that was fine with her, she could hardly complain about being committed to a trip, though the trip would end up falling on the week of her grandniece's birthday which she would miss, along with the hammock moment, but that was fine because first of all there were other (metaphorical) hammock moments to be had in Cuba where she and Chris eventually went, but also because this Jenmarie didn't know what the other Jenmaries, the two who would experience the hammock before their final divergence, had that she didn't, or vice versa. What all three shared, of course, was the final smile, the embrace of fantasy. They were all the Jenmaries that smiled, but they were not the same Jenmarie.

And so it goes, down down down the High Tomb. For each visit to the Tomb, a new Jenmarie blooms while the old remains behind, believing the Tomb to have lost its magic (at long last). Through realities, in new universes, one million and one Jenmaries live one million and one lives, a Jenmarie jamboree to the umpteenth power. For those million and one lives, though, there is the same death: a tree and a vine and a vine and a tree. There end the similarities. For not all of the Jenmaries are blessed with a final smile.

Some Jenmaries are left to deal with the consequences of choices they believed could be erased. The one who was impregnated by a guy she'd been dating for just about a month and a half, for instance, is left to self-finance an abortion, a choice about which she is devastated, but ultimately unconflicted. And, perhaps due to having been abandoned by the Tomb to a world of inexorable permanence, or perhaps due something else entirely, this Jenmarie launches herself into a greater degree of political engagement than will be found in any other Jenmarie. Her agitation remains at the grassroots level; she never even considers running for any kind of office. She does, however, achieve a modicum of regional fame in New England for organizing and leading a protest into Maine to combat proposed anti-choice legislation. Though she never regrets the decision to terminate her pregnancy, the whole experience (compounded by her activism's demands on her time) leaves her more wary of 'getting back out there,' as the kids say. So she never meets Chris, and never gets remarried, and when Melody invites her to her grandniece's first birthday party she demurs, pretending to be ill but in truth not wanting to field the inevitable questions about a love life which hasn't been a concern of hers in quite a while. She'll pass alone in her home, still sleeping far to the right side of her queen mattress, where she's always slept, not smiling but not quite frowning either, greeting her dream with a healthy skepticism.

Deeper down but never darker, the Jenmaries pass in pairs, all oblivious to the others, the same and yet utterly distinct. The Jenmarie who achieved a modicum of regional fame in the Bay Area *wasn't* the Jenmarie who was left to grapple with monumental debt and declare personal bankruptcy three years later and go home and live with her parents and work on the farm which didn't turn out to be all that bad and in fact she'd take it over from them once they got too old to enjoy it *wasn't* the Jenmarie who got a lousy haircut and was so mad at the High Tomb for sticking her with the haircut that she swung the crowbar at its shifting marble and maybe she wasn't focusing on the building hard enough because a cop who was the very same cop that many universes below had given her a talking-to about hanging her posters atop POST NO BILLS notices yelled at her and she yelled back and next thing she knew she was getting slammed to the concrete and cuffed which she chalked up to the cop getting close enough to notice that she wasn't as white as she looked and what was she doing swinging a crowbar in this part of town any-way and well yeah anyway she escaped that terrifying encounter with nothing worse than a busted lip and got booked which in-cluded having her mugshot taken with her stupid fucking haircut which in her opinion was the biggest crime of all so which detective was in charge of bringing that barber to justice was her question *wasn't* the Jenmarie who had some splainin' to do re: her sudden decampment to New York from wherever she happened to be be it San Francisco or Cambridge or any of the other places various Jenmaries wound up which included Salt Lake City and Philadelphia and Chicago and Lake Geneva and Mora Minnesota and one even wound up in Independence Kentucky which it went without saying that Jenmarie didn't die with a smile on her face that was for sure but anyway there actually were quite a few Jenmaries who suffered the burden of an awkward explanation to account for their absences and some of these explanations were to bosses and some to lovers (one of whom remained, in just one life, K.J. Hanifan) and some to Mavises and some to nobody but herself but even amongst this subclass of Jenmaries there were variations beyond counting for instance the Jenmarie who plead for sympathy by citing a mental breakdown *wasn't* the Jenmarie who fabricated a family emergency *wasn't* the Jenmarie who leaned into it and claimed she'd had enough and was starting a new life and surprisingly enough committed to it because to be fair to have a High Tomb for centuries or maybe longer and suddenly *not* have one at least as far as she was concerned was of course going to prompt some mental recalibrations *wasn't* the Jenmarie who simply denied she'd vanished for two days whaddyamean I was just binge watching the latest TV show you've never heard of it was pretty good but I fell asleep what did you text me or something *wasn't* the Jenmarie who cut the crisis off at the knees by simply never returning to what had been her home family job life and *none* of these were the Jenmarie who limped her way through a community college because of her awful primary school performance because despite being smart enough for the Ivy League no university wanted to touch someone with such a consonant-heavy report card so her life was spent working a series of low-paying jobs wherein she tried to help customers whose chief concern was verbally abusing her the high point of which was an assistant manager position at a T.C. Clitterhouse which she lost when too many of the employees complained that she was giving them instructions that contravened those given by the *manager* manager which to be fair was true but also the *manager* manager could barely manage the tying of his shoelaces which was a salty way of saying he couldn't manage a store but maybe Jenmarie shouldn't have said that directly *to* him because then he went from asking for her resignation to just firing her which made finding another job a lot harder which explained why she couldn't but her parents didn't have the farm in this timeline so going back to live with them was so depressing she got deeper into drink and then drugs and this time she passed into a dream while zonked out on fentanyl *wasn't* the Jenmarie who was so set adrift by the loss of her High Tomb privileges that she failed to notice the changing of a crosswalk sign and stepped in front of a driver who didn't fail to notice the changing of *his* light but did fail to notice Jenmarie's failure to notice the changing of *hers* and so he hit her and broke her legs and walking was painful for the rest of her life so she had plenty of time for school but nobody wanted to encourage an oncologist who could hardly stand for long periods of time without supporting herself on nearby furniture even if everybody pretended like that wasn't a big deal it was an equal playing field and all that nonsense it was well it was nonsense nobody wanted a doctor more fucked up than they were so Jenmarie washed out and applied to MIT for science writing instead because if nobody wanted a fucked up doctor *everybody* loved a fucked up writer and she got in and got the degree and was a moderately successful popular science writer *wasn't* the Jenmarie who went for a walk on her parents' farm one day and asked her dad what was that flower she kept seeing everywhere and he said elderflower which rang a ha ha bell so she Googled it and found there was a popular liqueur called St. Germain made from elderflower so a little lightbulb went on and she collected a bunch and found a distillery in Kentucky trying to break out of the Bourbon box and sold them the elderflower with a provisional second order for 'as much as she could get them' the following year which turned out to be thirteen pounds thanks to the extra she'd planted all over her parents' property but as it happened American elderflower weren't as amenable to fermentation or distillation or whatever the hell they did to them to make the liqueur as the French ones so long story short none of the booze turned out halfway drinkable which in an instant turned the elderflower from a cash crop into a weed and in the process soured Jenmarie on the entire concept of entrepreneurship *wasn't* the Jenmarie who had walked away from Eddie's headless body in the car thinking she would just zap herself away from it only to discover that no she was stuck here stuck in a world in which she'd just wandered away from the grisly death of her ostensible sweetheart which made her a minor viral villain for a hot second and so rather derailed her pretensions toward the esteemed anonymity afforded highly competent doctors because now Googling her name got you countless accounts of and memes about the accident and in one case a shoddily done reenactment video well the whole thing was shoddy except for the gore effects which were practical and she had to admit both effective and accurate but alas her infamy was enough to make her a hard sell to future employers but not so widespread that she could leverage it into a slot on a Dancing with the D-listers show or something and over time it diminished and she legally changed her name to Cherry Chirpworth (no reason, it just felt right) and flew away to a private practice in central Pennsylvania but she never wholly escaped her past because the internet never forgives and never forgets *wasn't* the Jenmarie who left the bird who would be the original avian Cherry right where she was because it was bad to touch baby birds because everybody knew that then the bird would smell like you instead of the momma bird and momma birds hated it when their babies didn't smell like them so the momma wouldn't come back and get the baby which had never made sense to Jenmarie because if you cared about your baby in the first place why would you leave it just because it smelled different but whatever she wasn't a bird who was she to judge so she left Cherry there and the next day went back to check on her and discovered her missing which she hoped was a good thing but knew deep down wasn't because good things didn't happen to baby birds left alone *wasn't* the Jenmarie who was thirty-three and at her wit's end, taking the train to the nearest hardware store, some mom and pop outfit called Quality Equipment, and buying the biggest crowbar they had, crowbars were the best way to open things up and that was what she needed, she needed to open a thing up, and furthermore because fuck it, the Jenmarie who made no effort to disguise her approach to what she then called The Citadel but would come to call the High Tomb's fake doors, specifically the push-pull piece of shit on the left, and jammed the crowbar between the fake plastic setting of the fake glass and the fake frame itself, the Jenmarie who was stunned to discover that not only did nothing happen upon striking the strange building, but the mere act of striking it seemed to divest it of its mystery. It was now, and had always been, just a building. It had been a function of what, her anxiety her depression or what, that had rendered it somehow mystical. A delusion that had passed, a mirage that had evaporated, that was all her obsession with the Citadel had been. Yes, look at it now. The striations in the marble were still. She focused intently on them, as people suddenly stumbled into her and suggested, in a vartiety of exciting and anatomically improbable ways, that she relocate herself. If there had ever been something spooky or strange about this structure, she had bonked it away with a ten-dollar crowbar.

Which just left Jenmarie Bell. The only Jenmarie Bell in town, swaddled in the sort of ten-dollar solitude that had helped her to smile in the moments before so very many deaths, free from the dreadful knowledge that would have allowed the wrapping of her head around the impossible truth of the million and one Jenmaries that were all Jenmarie, and yet distinctly themselves. Perhaps,

were the astonishing divide between the Jenmarie who had approached the strange obelisk on Fourth and 57th and the Jenmarie
who walked away from it now put to her in fullness, presented
to her in this moment of exquisite gormlessness as being at once
fiction and reality, at once metaphor and fact, at once and at all
times beyond comprehension...perhaps she might have accepted this, had there been anyone capable of putting this to her, in
this moment.

But there wasn't. And there's no sense dwelling on the hypothetical. So move on.

F
O
R
W
A
R
D

Jenmarie Bell, this Jenmarie, the OG Jenmarie, returned to her crummy apartment, flopped down on her couch, and slept. She'd only stepped out for the afternoon, not done anything much more active than swing a crowbar, and yet she was as exhausted as she'd ever been in her entire life. She slept dreamlessly and awoke refreshed.

There was so much she wanted to do. And for the first time in the aforementioned life, she felt there was so much she *could* do. Rough though her lot had been, emotionally or otherwise, she was still young. Well, young-*ish*. But thirty-three was the new twenty-three, wasn't it? She wanted to be a great oncologist. Not *the greatest*, but great enough that people came from at least around the tri-state area to see her, er, *be* seen by her. She also, at the same time, wanted to drop out of school. Throw it all away and open a…llama farm? Where, how, *why?* She couldn't say, but the want was there all the same, precise in its preposterousness. Alas, she could only do one of those two things. And fallacious though it may have been, sunk-cost thinking kept her pointing towards oncology. Maybe she could convince her parents to invest in some livestock, though…

That was another thing; she wanted to call her family. Boy, talk about delusions. Since when had she ever *wanted* to call her family? What did she even want to talk about? Unclear. She tried to draft a script in her head and came up blank. Didn't much matter to her what was said, it seemed. Merely that something was said. She wanted to hear their voices. Why? Who could say. It was just another desire, unbidden and unintelligible, but persistent. Ok, ok, she would call Barry and Carrie. When? Well, what about now? Alright then. Now.

Jenmarie pulled out her phone and unlocked it. The camera popped up. Last application opened. She noticed that the latest photo on her camera roll was one of herself crying in a dark room. She didn't recall taking that. Why had she taken that? *Yikes.* She deleted that photo and, after a bit more scrolling, discovered a load of stitched-together panoramas of the New York City skyline. Again, no memory of what these were or why she had them. Delete, delete, del-

The screen faded to darkness. "Aw, man," Jenmarie mumbled to herself, recognizing this as the mark of an incoming phone call.

A call from one Tomjohn Bell. Who was her younger brother. For some reason she had to remind herself of that fact. It wasn't as ready at hand as it probably ought to have been. Tomjohn, calling her, as he sometimes did. Nothing unusual about that.

She answered the phone with "hey, kid."

"Hey," Tomjohn's voice replied. Jenmarie turned to glance out the window, towards the brick wall that constituted her view, as her younger brother continued: "got a minute?"

Jenmarie wrinkled her nose at the bricks, took a deep breath, and let it out. "I don't know," she replied, soft surprise in her voice and heart alike.

"…what does that mean?"

"I don't know," Jenmarie repeated a touch more confidently. "I'm kind of in a weird…feeling. I'm feeling weird. Can I call you back?"

"Are you…" Tomjohn's tone deepened slightly. "Do you need to go to the hospital?"

The word *again* was fully implied, and not lost on Jenmarie. Yet she once more surprised herself by responding without defensiveness. "No, no, it's not a bad weird."

"It's a *good* weird…?"

"I guess…" she blinked and pulled her attention back into her own apartment. "I don't know. I guess so, but I don't know." Another deep breath brought her a smile. "Can I just get my shit together and call you back?"

"So we're never going to speak again, is what you're telling me."

The smile widened. "I'll call you back."

"Alright, fine."

"Cool. Love you, Tomjohn. See ya."

"Woah," Tomjohn laughed, "you *what* now?! What, are you fuc-"

Jenmarie hung up on her baby brother's incredulity and once more smiled at the brick wall across the narrow alley outside her window. Considered calling her parents. Opted against it. Or, at least, opted to do it later. She had plenty of time. Not much time at all, in the grand scheme of things. But enough for that.

What else could she do with her life? What other paths stretched before her? She wanted to get more politically active and try her hand at gardening and hear a new song every day and see more of the country and fly first class at least once and appreciate the firmness of the ground beneath her feet and spend more time with her eyes up instead of down and read fifty books a year and relearn how to do a cartwheel and adopt a dog and crush it in the city (*it* being life, not the dog) and move out to the country and so many things she couldn't do not because she was incapable but because she was thirty-three years old, she was young*ish* but not so young that she could do *anything* anymore. Her late twenties had been the age of coming to discover her limitations, the ways in which she had failed to attain the platonic ideal of Young Woman. She couldn't run without getting shin splints, her dance-until-dawn days were already behind her (she was lucky if she made it past eleven), she had no concept of what music was popular anymore, she couldn't spend too much time looking at a computer screen without getting a headache. Her early thirties, then, had been a period of resentment and denial, cursing the impersonal universe for denying her a career as a long-distance runner, or the superpower of being a Morning Person, or a life as a hacker. It had been something slightly more than arrested development – it had been a regression.

When she had been younger, she'd often not-so-facetiously justified her ordering dessert, or slamming another beer, or eating an entire jar of peanut butter by herself on the couch (that was a *dark* time there), by insisting that she'd work it off when she was older. Likewise with getting out there and making new friends, or trying to find a new recipe to cycle into her repertoire (such as it was), or having a go at learning guitar like she'd always wanted to. That, she had always insisted, would all be the responsibility of a future version of herself.

Well, the time had come to accept that she *was* that future version. She was older. It wasn't that she was beyond making bold choices, striking out on unexpected new ventures or gathering all of her life's accomplishments on a little table and then flipping it over like an angry baseball coach about to give an inspirational monologue. She could do all of that and more. Well, she could do *some* of that. But…didn't that make it a little more special, that she wouldn't be able to do *all* of it? That she'd have to choose? Ten years ago she'd have said no way, she wanted to do it all. Which was almost certainly a big part of why she'd been so unhappy: there was, ha, *no way* she could *ever* have done it all.

Which, ok, no sense trying to dress it up. Whether or not it was somehow beautiful that life was finite and choices had consequences and nothing would ever be perfect or turn out just the way she wanted…the fact was that all of those things were true, and the only way to find any beauty at all was to spend less time thinking about the could-have-been, more time on the could-be, and still more on the *is*. What was ideal was secondary to what was, which wasn't ideal, but you get the idea.

So Jenmarie took a deep breath, upon which she focused, and let it out. In through the nose, out through the nose. One and the same. After her first breath, the once-spooky building on Fourth and 57th slipped from her mind so entirely that she would never return to it, not once (and so never discover that it had grown by one story). In, out. After the second, that feeling of needing a drink to take the edge off went with it. In, out. After the third she decided that tonight, she would go out and dance, for the first time in who knew how long. Not until dawn, no, but endurance wasn't the point. It had never been the point. Furthermore, there was no point. There didn't have to be. Dancing was dancing. The end.

That would be tonight, though. For now, for the moment, for this moment, Jenmarie grabbed a book and went outside, because it was a beautiful day that wouldn't come again, and before she set off on her wild one-way ride into a little pine box she felt like she ought to take an afternoon to get to know this strange new Jenmarie who wasn't the Jenmarie she'd known, but perhaps that said more about how well she'd known herself than it did *about* herself. Or maybe not. That was what she was hoping to figure out. In, Out. Upwards, Onwards.

The day was beautiful. And when it was over, she danced.

Made in the USA
Middletown, DE
11 May 2022

65508150R00189